"We rea

Neal said—

"We've talked too much already," Lisa replied. "It's time to fish or cut bait."

He needed to make this whole affair—whoops, poor choice of words. He needed to make this whole situation an intellectual thing. He needed to keep his treacherous body out of it.

He closed his eyes and imagined snowy mountain peaks, frozen lakes and a world of no women. He thought of icy streams and sleet and hail and wind chills that bottomed out the weatherman's charts.

"Enough of this nonsense," Lisa said. "You promised to father my child and I just want to know when the hell you're going to do it."

His eyes flew open. *Father a child?*

Dear Reader,

With Mother's Day right around the corner, Special Edition commemorates the warm bonds of family. This month, parenthood brings some unlikely couples together in the most wondrous ways!

This May, Sherryl Woods continues her popular AND BABY MAKES THREE: THE NEXT GENERATION series. THAT SPECIAL WOMAN! Jenny Adams becomes an *Unexpected Mommy* when revenge-seeking single father Chance Adams storms into town and sweeps Jenny off her feet with his seductive charm!

Myrna Temte delivers book three of the MONTANA MAVERICKS: RETURN TO WHITEHORN series. In *A Father's Vow,* a hard-headed Native American hero must confront his true feelings for the vivacious schoolteacher who is about to give birth to his child. And look for reader favorite Lindsay McKenna's next installment in her mesmerizing COWBOYS OF THE SOUTHWEST series when a vulnerable heroine simply seeks solace on the home front, but finds her soul mate in a sexy *Stallion Tamer!*

Listen for wedding bells in *Practically Married* by Christine Rimmer. This final book in the CONVENIENTLY YOURS series is an irresistibly romantic tale about an arranged marriage between a cynical rancher and a soft-spoken single mom. Next, Andrea Edwards launches her DOUBLE WEDDING duet with *The Paternity Question.* This series features twin brothers who switch places and find love—and lots of trouble!

Finally, Diana Whitney caps off the month with *Baby in His Cradle.* In the concluding story of the STORK EXPRESS series, a *very* pregnant heroine desperately seeks shelter from the storm and winds up on the doorstep of a brooding recluse's mountain retreat.

I hope you treasure this book, and each and every story to come!

Sincerely,

Tara Gavin
Senior Editor & Editorial Coordinator

Please address questions and book requests to:
Silhouette Reader Service
U.S.: 3010 Walden Ave., P.O. Box 1325, Buffalo, NY 14269
Canadian: P.O. Box 609, Fort Erie, Ont. L2A 5X3

ANDREA EDWARDS
THE PATERNITY QUESTION

Published by Silhouette Books
America's Publisher of Contemporary Romance

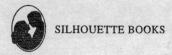

SILHOUETTE BOOKS

ISBN 0-373-24175-5

THE PATERNITY QUESTION

Printed in U.S.A.

Books by Andrea Edwards

ANDREA EDWARDS

is the pseudonym of Anne and Ed Kolaczyk, a husband-and-wife writing team who have been telling their stories for more than fifteen years. Anne is a former elementary school teacher, while Ed is a refugee from corporate America. After many years in the Chicago area, they now live in a small town in northern Indiana, where they are avid students of local history, family legends and ethnic myths. Recently they have both been bitten by the gardening bug, but only time will tell how serious the affliction is. Their four children are grown; the youngest attends college, while the eldest is a college professor. Remaining at home with Anne and Ed are two dogs, four cats and one bird—not the same ones that first walked through their stories but carrying on the same tradition of chaotic rule of the household nonetheless.

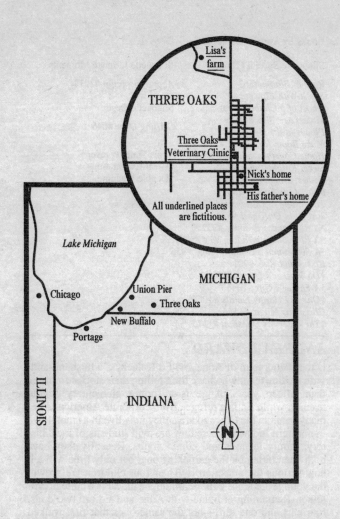

Lisa's farm

THREE OAKS

Three Oaks
Veterinary Clinic

Nick's home

His father's home

All underlined places
are fictitious.

Lake Michigan

MICHIGAN

Chicago

Union Pier

Three Oaks

New Buffalo

Portage

ILLINOIS

INDIANA

N

Prologue

"The whole rest of July?" Neal Sheridan exclaimed, his stomach plummeting to his shoes. "You want me to go busing around back-country roads for the rest of July?"

"Actually for the first two weeks of August, too," his business manager muttered.

"You *can't* be serious." Neal leaned his long, lanky frame forward. Like all the offices for on-the-air personalities at this New York TV station, his was small and cramped. That meant a six-foot-three guy like himself had to sit sideways if he wanted to get comfortable. "It's July second. You want me on the road in three days?"

"Hey, I just found out myself." John Hockaday's smile looked almost genuine—which Neal knew meant he was lying—as he went on. "Love came up with a wild new concept. You'll love it."

"How wild?" Love Pet Foods was a great sponsor but they had a tendency to go overboard at times. "Am I touring with a troupe of singing cows again?"

"Singing cows?" John laughed. "No, not this time."

Great. Not singing cows, but maybe Mr. Billy, the dancing goat from those Love Pygmy Goat Food ads. Neal suddenly felt very tired of being America's favorite vet and didn't want to know the details. "Look, I'm not really up for this."

"Now's not a good time to assert yourself."

"Damn it," Neal said. "I've been a good trooper for eight years. I've taught people how to care for their pets, not to mention having llamas throw up on me, dogs chew my pants and parrots pierce my ears."

"I'm not saying there'll be problems with your new contract," John said. "Just that this isn't a time for people to question your level of commitment."

"Why do we have to do a bus thing?" Neal asked with a sigh. "How many people are we going to hit on the small-town, back-roads route?"

"Numbers don't matter," John replied. "Bus tours play good on the tube. That's why presidential candidates do them."

"I'm not running for office," Neal snapped.

"Yeah, you are," John replied. "You just don't have a fixed term."

Neal bit back a reply. His business manager was right. People voted for or against him every day. Instead of casting ballots, they bought pet food. Buying Love's product was a vote for Neal Sheridan. Buying someone else's was a vote against him. Measuring his worth was very easy.

"I had some personal things planned for later in the month," Neal said.

"Buy her some bauble, tell her you'll always remember her and send her on her way like you always do." John stood up. "See you the day after tomorrow in St. Louis."

Once the door was closed, Neal let his head drop on his arms. Contrary to John's opinion, Neal's personal plans weren't with a woman, but his twin brother, Nick. Since

Nick's wife had died two years ago, Neal had wanted to get Nick away in July. It hadn't worked out last year and didn't look like it would this year, either.

"Shoot," Neal muttered as he reached for the phone and dialed his brother's veterinary clinic.

"Three Oaks Clinic. Lisa speaking."

Lisa? His brother must have hired someone new. "Hi, Lisa," Neal said. "This is—"

"Neal, right?" she interrupted, her voice ripe with all the disgust of someone finding a cockroach in her soup. "You sound just like Nick."

Neal tried to coax a smile from her. "How do you know I'm not him, then?"

"Because I can see him sitting in his office."

"That could be Neal, you know."

"Nick has a beard. I saw you on television last night with that Humane Society demonstration in New York and you didn't have one. You couldn't have grown one since yesterday." She made it sound like a failing on his part.

Neal gave up. "You got me there. Is Nick available?"

"I'll get him."

Nick came on the line. "Hey, bro, I was just thinking about you. What's happening?"

"Bad news," Neal replied.

"Don't tell me. You've dated all the English-speaking women in the world and now you're wondering whether to wait for more to come of age or learn a new language."

"Cute, Nick. Almost clever."

"Thank you."

Neal took a deep breath. "Actually, I have to cancel out on our outing."

"That is bad news." Nick's tone lost all its joking. "I was looking forward to it."

"So was I. But I have to go on a marketing tour. My sponsor is busing me all over Illinois, Iowa and Missouri."

"Sounds like fun."

"Yeah, right."

"Hey, I mean it," Nick said. "It may not be Paris or New York, but you're going to all those new places. Places you've never seen before with their own history and uniqueness. It sounds like fun."

"Only because you've never done it."

"It's got to be better than Three Oaks in July."

"Three Oaks may harbor some ghosts, but at least it's home."

They both fell silent. Nick really needed to get away, Neal thought. He was never going to get over Donna, not if he was constantly around reminders of her. Why'd they have to spring this stupid tour on him now? Why couldn't they send someone else? Surely there had to be other people who'd be happy to—

A wild idea began to take root. It would never work. Why not? It could. It might. Who would it hurt?

"You know," Neal said slowly.

"If you really think," Nick began.

"The tour—"

"The town—"

They both stopped.

"What about my patients?" Nick asked.

"I am a licensed vet, you know, and so is your partner." Neal paused. "But you hate public speaking."

"Not like I used to," Nick admitted. "But what if they decide to establish that State Animal Welfare Committee this month? You know my name's on their list."

"And it's been on their list for three years now. Nothing's going to happen in the next six weeks." Neal hesitated. "I don't know who my traveling partners are supposed to be. Could be singing cows, for all I know."

"I work with a local rescue group, and we have a big fund-raiser coming up. Think you can handle that?"

"What kind of question is that?" Neal asked. "I've handled more fund-raisers in a week than you have in your whole life."

Damn it, anyway, Neal thought. Nick was a workaholic. Ever since Donna died, he'd buried himself in his work. If Neal couldn't get him to break away now, he'd probably never have a life. Neal waited, giving the idea time to burrow into Nick's hidebound head. His brother liked to think he was making the decisions.

"You know," Nick said slowly. "We'd be doing the area a favor. We could use some rain."

For some reason, it always seemed to turn into monsoon season when Neal played he was Nick. "And there must be hundreds of animals awaiting rescue across the Midwest."

"I've stopped having to rescue everything in sight," Nick said.

"So what do you think? You game?"

There was another silence as the idea grew less preposterous. Maybe it was the stale conditioned air in the building, but Neal was beginning to think they could pull it off. Nick could have his six weeks of being fussed over, and as for Neal, well, he'd have six weeks of tension-free living. No problems, no worries. Hell, in Three Oaks, they didn't even lock their doors.

"Let's do it," Nick said.

Chapter One

Lisa Hughes stepped off her back porch into the long shadows of early morning, a cup of coffee in her hand. The caffeine had better kick in fast. She felt like she was slogging along on a deep mud track. Her dogs raced toward the barn, showing off their energy, but she refused to compete with them.

"Looks like another scorcher," Pucky said. The old horse trainer wiped his weathered face as he joined her on the path. "Don't think I slept a wink last night. It was too hot to breathe."

Lisa had found it hard to sleep last night, too, but it hadn't been the heat keeping her awake. She'd been counting the days backward, over and over again, checking the calendar in her mind as she watched the clock inch toward morning.

"No rain again today." Pucky was looking at the unrelieved blue of the sky.

Lisa was about to agree when she frowned. "I don't know,"

she said slowly as she stared at the western horizon. "It looks almost like storm clouds coming."

Pucky shook his head. "That's just the night being slow to leave," he said.

"Yeah, you're probably right."

"Ain't I always?"

Lisa smiled and sipped at her coffee. Pucky Dolan was like a second father to her. He had worked with her father for more than forty years, training Hollywood horses for movie roles, keeping an eye on Lisa after her mother died when she'd been four and finally helping with the horse farm after her dad bought it when Lisa had been thirteen. Since her father's death three years ago, Pucky had helped her run the place.

But there were some things she didn't discuss even with him.

"So today's the big day, eh?" he asked.

Lisa started, spilling some coffee onto the path. He didn't know. He wasn't there when she'd taken her temperature that morning.

"Ariel's been a mite impatient," Pucky went on.

Oh. Lisa breathed again. He was talking about her new mare. "Yeah," Lisa agreed. "Well, so's Johnny. Good thing Nick gave her a clean bill of health yesterday."

They stopped at an exercise pen, and Lisa leaned her arms against the top railing, its rough surface scratching her skin with comfortable familiarity. Ariel was in the grassy enclosure, running with high spirits in a large circle along the fence. Her smooth muscles rippled, her nostrils were flared, and a sheen of light sweat covered her sorrel coat. The white star on her forehead was bright and glistening. She was such a beauty. Her foals would be gorgeous.

"Couldn't think of a better way for a man to start his day," Pucky said, leaning against the fence next to her. "Breathin' country air, watchin' the sun come up and eyeballin' two of the prettiest fillies this side of heaven."

"Don't go giving me any of that Irish honey cake," Lisa said. "I've heard all about men like you."

"Lookin' at you is like seein' your mother thirty years ago."

Lisa looked away, a familiar burning at the corners of her eyes as she watched the horse. When she'd been in high school, Lisa had wanted to be a tall, long-legged beauty like her friend Colleen. She'd hated her dark auburn hair, petite build and pale coloring, even though it made her almost the mirror image of her mother. Time had erased the dissatisfaction she had with her appearance, but not the guilt that her blond dreams had been left behind. Or the wish that she had even a memory of her mother.

"I've got Daddy's blue eyes," she said.

Pucky snickered. "And his black Irish moods."

Her reply was to punch him in the shoulder, but rock hard that it was, Lisa doubted he even felt it. They both turned their attention to the mare, still dashing about, still pushing at the fence, nickering and moaning deep in her throat.

"That's one anxious lady," Pucky said.

"She's wanting a baby awful bad," Lisa agreed.

Pucky turned slowly to stare at her. "A baby?" he said. "What you got in that coffee?"

Lisa refused to budge. "You men all think the same," she said. "Ariel's getting older, and I think she could be feeling more than the need to mate. She could be needing to have a foal. It's an instinct, too, you know, just as strong as mating."

Pucky shook his head. "You been watching too many late-night movies by yourself," he said. "Next you're gonna say she and Johnny are getting married."

Lisa snorted and turned to the horse. "Marriage has nothing to do with instinct," she said. "It's a silly convention that some of us aren't suited for."

Pucky didn't say anything for a long moment. She could

feel his eyes on her, but she refused to turn his way. It was the way she felt, and he ought to know it by now.

"Me and your dad were too strict with you, but training stables and movie sets were no place to raise a little girl," he said softly, leaning on the fence next to her. "We thought it'd be different once we moved here. Maybe we should've made you go to your prom."

She flashed a frown his way. "If I remember my prom rightly, there was no 'making' involved. I didn't have a date."

"Nick would've taken you."

"Donna might have objected."

"He could've found you a date."

Yeah, right. Maybe if he'd been willing to pay somebody, and even then his offer would have had to have been pretty high. She hadn't exactly been popular in high school. But neither her dad nor Pucky had seemed to realize how badly she'd fit in. They kept telling her to invite her friends over or join some after-school clubs. Or her personal favorite—smile more often.

Maybe some of those would have helped, but she'd been so angry about moving here and leaving Los Angeles that she hadn't been willing to give the place a fair shot. She had never belonged because she hadn't let herself belong. Not until after college, when she'd had the chance to leave and found this was home.

"I didn't want to go to the prom," she pointed out. "I wasn't into hair and makeup and fancy dresses."

"We shoulda made you take those ballet lessons."

Lisa sighed. Pucky was worse than her dogs with a bone. "Stop blaming yourself. Not everyone has to be married to be happy, and I am happy."

"Why does it seem like something's missing from your life, then?"

Because something was. But it wasn't a husband, it was a child. A child of her own. She was thirty-four years old. She'd had a few romances in college and afterward but wasn't about to trust her happiness to some guy. She could have a child, though. Now was the time to tell Pucky her feelings, to start getting him used to the idea that one of these days there'd be a young one around.

"Actually," she started. "I've been—"

Just then the mare crashed into the far fence closest to where the stallion was stabled. Her screams for a mate echoed across the early morning barnyard, a tortured bellow that set Lisa's dogs racing over.

Lisa pulled away from the fence. Now wasn't the time for a discussion of any sort. "I guess we'd better let her have her way," she said.

There was nothing to tell Pucky, anyway. It didn't matter that she was ovulating today. There was no child on her horizon. Not unless Nick changed his mind about fathering it.

As the waitress put down two platters of pancakes, Neal looked across the table at his brother. The hustle and bustle of the breakfast crowd at the restaurant faded as a familiar eeriness came over him.

"It's funny seeing you without your beard," he told Nick. "Like looking at myself. I'd forgotten how strange that was."

Nick rubbed his hand over his jawline. "My chin's not all that pale either. I must have had the world's scraggliest beard. And I'd forgotten how naked it felt. It's got to be ten years since I've been beardless."

"Doesn't seem that long, does it?"

"Seems forever," Nick said with a quiet laugh.

But then, as Neal watched, the past came to claim Nick, for some reason. And while it might be a pleasant memory, it didn't seem to be doing Nick any good. Time to call him back.

"I'd better give you my hotel key before I forget," Neal said. "My clothes are all there. I just brought my personal stuff."

Nick took the key with a frown, like he was tempted to revert to his normal cautious self and change his mind about the switch. Well, Neal wasn't allowing it. His brother needed this time away.

Neal went on briskly. "John Hockaday, my personal manager, will meet you at the hotel tonight at nine. Or should I say he'll meet Neal at the hotel?" Neal added with a grin. "He'll be going along on the bus, and so will the sponsor's tour manager. Between the two of them, your days will be planned down to the second."

"Sounds easy enough." Nick put the key in his pocket.

Neal went back to eating, keeping an eye on his brother as he watched indecision play across his face. They'd done this countless times when they were younger—exchanging places in this very restaurant off the tollway in Portage, even—and Nick always had worried about everything. What if they got caught. What if one of them got hurt? What if somebody needed the real one? What if, what if, what if…

The waitress came by with more coffee, but after she'd refilled their cups, she didn't move. She stood there staring at Nick. "You know, you look just like that animal doctor that's on TV all the time," she finally said.

It was the moment of truth, and Neal held his breath. Either he would or he wouldn't. Either Nick would choose to let go of his painful past or he wouldn't.

But then Nick smiled. "That's me. Neal Sheridan."

The woman put down the coffeepot and shook his hand. "Oh, wow," she said, her voice gushing with excitement. But when she let go of him and turned to pick up the pot again, she frowned at Neal. "You look like him, too." Her voice was confused.

Neal tried not to laugh. "I'm his stand-in." He took a quick bite of his toast.

Her face cleared. "Really? Cool," she said. "Wait till I tell the girls."

Neal watched Nick as the woman walked away. His brother's face was thoughtful but not shadowed.

"This is gonna be fun," Nick said, and dug into his breakfast with new enthusiasm. "I think I might like being famous."

"Hope so," Neal said, then took a swallow of coffee before putting the cup down. "How about your practice? Any cases I need to be aware of?"

Nick shook his head as he ate. "I left a stack of files on my desk for you to review. Nothing's in a critical stage. The Millers' cat is being treated for a urinary tract infection. The Kerrigans' dog is due to whelp in two weeks. Routine stuff. If there's anything you aren't sure of, you can refer it to Jim. He only works part-time, but he's pretty flexible about his hours."

"What about your office staff?" Neal asked. "You hired somebody new."

Nick frowned. "No, I haven't."

"Yes, you did. A Lisa. She answered the phone when I called."

"Oh, that was just a friend of mine. Lisa Hughes. She's head of the local Hoofed Animal Rescue Society. I give them space at the office to keep their records, get mail and messages. That kind of thing. Lisa helps out on phones when we get busy."

"Oh." Neal ate for a moment as he stared out at the highway. Westbound traffic to Chicago was getting heavy, everyone rushing to join the rat race. It felt so good to be going in the other direction. He let his memories of Three Oaks wash over him, then frowned. Nick had gone to high school with a Lisa Hughes.

Certain memories came back with a vengeance. She'd been a skinny, tomboy kid with a serious attitude. No, "serious attitude" didn't begin to describe the girl's personality. Snarly was a lot closer. In fact, during one of his and Nick's switches in their sophomore year, Neal remembered being on the receiving end of a right cross to his mouth. Delivered by Lovely Lisa when he'd made some wisecrack. She'd had no sense of humor back then. He hoped she'd developed one by now. Or that Nick rarely saw her.

"You done?" Nick asked.

"All set," Neal replied with a nod.

They walked out to the parking lot together. The air was already heavy with humidity. Nick's pickup was parked next to Neal's rental car, and it took less than a moment to get their suitcases and exchange car keys. Nick looked like those second thoughts were fighting for control again.

"If you have any problems," Neal said, "let Hockaday take care of them for you."

"Sara pretty much runs the clinic and my calendar. Today's my day off from appointments—Jim handles them—but I go in to take care of paperwork."

"Dad and Grams around?"

Nick nodded. "Where's Mom? She still in Paris?"

"Until September," Neal said and put his suitcase behind the pickup's front seat.

"Good thing. She was always hard to fool."

"Yeah."

Neal just looked at him, letting the silence grow until Nick tossed his duffel bag into the back seat of Neal's car. "Hey, you've never said if you have a current girlfriend," Nick said. "Or is that a stupid question for the king of hearts?"

"Nope, feel free to woo all the ladies from St. Louis to Des Moines."

Nick started as if he'd been struck. "I just want to get away for a while. Relax a bit, that's all."

Maybe this was the heart of Nick's problem, Neal thought. "Donna wouldn't expect you to become a monk."

"And who said I am?" Nick snapped.

"If you're going to be me, you've got to be me," Neal

pointed out, then grinned. "Unless you want to concede my victory right here and now."

"No way," Nick said. "Your run of luck has ended. You are going to be detected as soon as you hit town, while I'm going to pass as Neal Sheridan for the full six weeks."

"Yeah, right." Neal got into the pickup, then leaned out the open window. "Hey, bro, one more thing."

Nick paused, halfway in the car. "What?"

"Remember. Love is nothing but a pet food."

"Oh, my God." Sara Wentzel, Nick's middle-aged office manager, put her hands to her mouth and stared at Neal with horror-filled eyes. "What in the world have you done to your face?"

"I shaved," Neal said. "Haven't you ever seen a clean-shaven man?"

"Not you."

"Well, I thought it was time for a change. Women are always changing their hairstyles. Why can't I?"

"You haven't changed anything about yourself in the twenty-five years I've known you."

"Well, then, maybe it's time." He strode into Nick's office.

"Thief! Thief!"

Neal stopped short inside the doorway, his heart racing suddenly as if he'd been found out. Two hours into the masquerade and he'd been caught?

But the shrieking was coming from a parrot in a huge cage in the corner of the office. Was it just loud and obnoxious or extremely perceptive? Glancing over his shoulder, he saw that Sara hadn't jumped up to investigate the bird's calls. Must just be obnoxious.

He forced himself to breathe again and went over to Nick's desk. It was a mess. He searched it, then went out to the reception area. "Is my calendar out here?"

"It's on your computer."

"Oh." Damn.

Sara sighed loudly. "One of these days you're going to have to learn how to use that machine," she scolded, and held out a sheet of paper. "Everyone else will be riding a jet and you'll still be using a horse and buggy."

"Slow but sure. That's me." He took the printed report from her and turned to the office.

"Where's Boomer?" Sara asked.

Double damn. He should have figured that his brother would bring his dog to work with him.

"Ah, he was a little under the weather this morning."

"Then why did you leave him at home?" Sara snapped.

Because when Neal had dropped off his suitcase at Nick's house, the old springer spaniel had been following him around, growling. Bringing the dog into the clinic was the last thing Neal wanted to do. Not if he wanted to pull this masquerade off.

"The kennel crew's almost done cleaning the guck," Sara said. "I'll send one of them out to your place for Boomer."

"Fine." Neal marched into the office and dropped into his brother's chair with a sigh. Damn, this was going to be a lot harder than it had been the last time he and Nick had switched. Then it had been a matter of tricking a few teachers or people who didn't know either of them all that well. Now he had to take over Nick's routine, and do it smoothly.

But he was up to it. He could handle anything. He always had. That's why he was leading in their switcheroo derby. He'd never been found out—well, only that once, sophomore year—and wouldn't be again. It was more of a challenge than it had been when they'd been kids, but he was still the best.

Taking a deep breath, he snatched up Nick's schedule for today. A few telephone calls he was supposed to return and a meeting of the Hoofed Animal Rescue Society at Lisa's house at nine-thirty this morning. Damn. And he'd hoped to avoid her.

He glanced at his watch. It was a little past nine, so he wasn't late yet. Except that he had no idea where Lisa lived, and he could hardly ask Sara for directions.

Or maybe he could.

He walked to the door of the office. "I'm taking your advice to heart," he told the office manger. "I want to learn how to use the computer."

"My," Sara exclaimed. "Catch me before I faint."

Neal smiled and stepped aside as she entered the room. "Let's start with something simple," he said, over the parrot's mutterings. "Like accessing our client data base."

"Okay."

"How about if—" he hummed and made a face, as if he was trying to think of something "—we look up Lisa Hughes's address."

"What do you need to look up her address for? You're out there every other day. If you can't find her place blindfolded, you're in deep doo doo."

"I know I know where her place is at," he replied. "I'm just using it as an example."

Sighing, Sara went to the computer and flicked it on. She entered in Nick's password—the name of Nick's first dog— and waited while the machine churned a bit.

"Now, you open the client data base file," she said. "Then choose the search function."

She stepped aside and allowed him to bring up a box that instructed him to type in Lisa's name, which he did. Smiling slightly, he leaned forward.

But his smile quickly disappeared as he gazed at the address flashing on the screen.

Lisa Hughes
Royal Arabian Farms
Box 38, R.R. #3
Three Oaks, MI 49128

Damn it. That was just a mail delivery designation. What happened to good old street names? This was no help at all, unless he could get a route map from the post office. He threw himself in his chair.

"That's great, Sara. Thanks for your help."

"Let's do another one," she said.

"If I can do one, I can do a thousand. Besides, I have to get going. I've got a meeting at Lisa's in a few minutes."

And if he didn't find out where it was, she was going to have ample reason to punch him again. In the corner, the parrot cackled loudly.

"Something must have happened," Ben Davis said, tipping his head so he could look at his watch through his bifocals. "A fella could always set his clock by that boy."

"I'm sure something came up." Myrna Newsome looked toward Lisa. "What did Sara say when you called?"

Lisa had already told them once what Sara had said, but she patiently told them again. "Sara said he'd left and should be here any minute."

"That was ten, fifteen minutes ago," Ben said. "Bet he's pulled over by the spot Donna had her accident and remembering."

"Not yet," Myrna said. "There's still two weeks before the anniversary. Somebody probably just asked him for a favor. You know Nick. He can't say no to anybody."

Except to me, Lisa thought, and wandered to the front window. Through the thick evergreen hedge along the front of her property, she could see flashes of the road. But those flashes remained the dull gray color of the pavement. No cars were approaching.

"I'm gonna go call Sara again," Ben said and got to his feet. "Maybe Nick called in."

Lisa nodded absently, still facing the window. Who was she fooling? Nick wasn't here because he was avoiding her. She should never have asked him to be the father of her child. But they'd been friends forever. She didn't think there'd be any problem. It wasn't like she wanted anything from him but his sperm. It wasn't like she wanted to take Donna's place.

But she would never forget the look on his face the other day when she'd asked him. Oh, he'd been kind and gentle, as always. He'd been understanding and supportive. But he'd said no. No way. Not him. Never.

"Is it raining?" Myrna asked.

Lisa started and took a real look outside. "No, not yet."

But it must have clouded over in the past hour or so, and it looked about ready to pour. She hadn't noticed. Somehow the dreary world outside seemed to be a part of her mood. Was there any chance Nick would have changed his mind?

She glanced at the sundress she'd worn. Another example of her idiocy. What had she thought—that if he saw her in a dress for once, he'd be overcome with desire and want to make mad, passionate love to her? It would take more than a dress to make her into a femme fatale. More than the touch of lipstick and the dab of perfume she'd put on. Instead of feeling sexy, she felt foolish. Like she was trying to act like Donna.

Maybe there was time to change. But Chipper and Rusty barking from the front porch pulled her from her thoughts. Nope. Nick's truck was turning into the drive.

"He's here," Lisa called out as the skies opened.

Myrna joined her at the window, watching as Nick parked his truck in the sudden downpour. "He's going to drown before he reaches the door," she said.

"I'll take an umbrella out." Lisa hurried into the hall, slipping off her sandals as she grabbed an umbrella from the front closet.

Nick was already getting out of his truck when she stepped onto the porch, so she quickly splashed out to meet him. The water puddling on the drive was warm and soothing on her bare feet. The two dogs bounded along through the rain with her, rushing to growl at Nick like they always did.

"Hi," she called out. "Chipper! Rusty! Stop it! Enough is enough."

Nick turned, then stopped as if in shock. "Hello," he said softly.

"You shaved your beard!" she cried.

He rubbed his chin slowly, as if just coming awake. "Yeah. The girls were all complaining my kisses were scratchy."

Lisa stared for a long moment. What girls? There'd been no girls in Nick's life since Donna had died. Unless he meant her. Maybe he was rethinking his refusal!

"Uh, you gonna share that umbrella or just gloat that you've got it?"

"Oh." Lisa hurried the last few steps to his side. "Sorry. Your new look threw me."

"Can't believe how handsome I am, huh?" He shut the door of his truck and moved under the umbrella.

She suddenly realized that Chipper and Rusty weren't growling and were wagging their tails.

"Would you look at that?" Lisa said. "After only four years of growling! Didn't I tell you they'd accept you one day?"

Nick laughed. "They must like my new look."

"They must." Lisa smiled at him. He was in a good mood, a more playful mood than usual. It had to mean something. It just had to.

"I was daydreaming on my way here," he was saying, splashing through the puddles at her side. "Missed the turnoff completely."

"That's okay. We forgive you." She paused as they climbed onto the porch, taking her time to shake the rain from the umbrella and set it to the side to dry. The dogs shook themselves, still fawning over Nick.

"Go lay down." Lisa ordered them to their favorite spots

on the porch, then turned to Nick. It was now or never. She needed to screw up her courage and ask him if he had changed his mind. "You know that little favor I asked you for? I was kind of worried that—"

"Worried about what?" Nick asked. "Since when have I ever let one of my friends down?"

Gracious. For one whole minute her world stood still. Her heart stopped and laughter rang through her soul. He was going to father her child. He was going to help her get pregnant.

Lisa felt strange. Light-headed, even. She tried to smile, tried to say something, but nothing seemed to be working right. She felt like she was going to burst into tears, then she realized that she had forgotten to breathe.

She took a deep, deep breath. "I really appreciate it," she said. What did one say in this situation? She didn't think Miss Manners had ever covered it. "You have time after the meeting this morning?"

"Sure," he said. "Just give me the specifics and I'm your man."

She hugged him—hard—and kissed his wonderfully smooth cheek. "You sure are."

He looked almost surprised at her reaction. Maybe she was overdoing it. Or maybe he was afraid that she was reading more into his agreement than she should. She'd have to reassure him that it wouldn't change their friendship a bit. That she wasn't expecting anything from him once she got pregnant. But now wasn't the time, not with Myrna and Ben waiting.

"We'd better get inside," she said. She felt so giddy, like dancing across the lawn in the rain. But that wouldn't do. He'd think she was crazy. He'd think she wasn't fit to take care of a child.

"Right."

She led him into the house, tamping down the grin that wanted to spread across her face. She had a meeting to run.

Once that was over, she'd think about the rest. After wiping her wet feet on the rag rug at the door, she picked up her sandals.

"What happened to your face?" Ben asked Nick as they walked into the room.

Nick grinned as he shook Ben's hand. "I started shaving this morning and was halfway done before I realized I had the wrong face."

"Are you sure you're not Neal?" Ben asked. "I heard that when Neal's here, it rains to beat all hell."

The others laughed while Lisa shuddered. Neal here—talk about real nightmares. She shook the thought off.

"It rains lots of times here," she said quickly as she sat down to put her sandals on. "Besides, if this was Neal, I wouldn't have let him in the door."

Nick seemed to stiffen. Lisa had forgotten how protective he was of his brother.

"I didn't think you knew Neal," Nick said to her.

"I met him a few times," Lisa said.

"That's not really knowing him."

"Hey, to meet Neal is to know Neal." Lisa grinned apologetically and reached over to squeeze his hand. "No, I'm sorry. You're right. I don't know him. Let's just say I know him as well as I want to."

"Didn't you slug him once in high school?" Myrna asked.

Lisa felt her face pale. "You knew about that?" She and Myrna had gone to school together—at least in the same building at the same time—but Myrna had been Homecoming Queen, a leader of the popular kids, while Lisa hadn't even been able to get a lab partner. How would Myrna have known about her fight with Neal?

But Myrna waved it away. "Oh, you know how fast news travels around here. Though we all wanted to know what he'd done to deserve it."

"Nothing," Lisa said quickly. She had no desire to dredge

up that day, or the humiliation she'd felt when she'd tried to confess to Nick that she had a crush on him, only to find Neal cracking jokes at her expense. "Just a difference of opinion."

Nick cleared his throat roughly. "If I remember Neal's recounting of it, he tried to make a joke and it backfired."

"Probably a dumb joke," Myrna said.

Nick frowned. "I always thought Neal had a good sense of humor."

"You know, I always felt sorry for the boy," Ben said, sinking heavily into a chair. "All that joking around and flirting. He was just trying so hard to belong. He must never have felt like he did."

"Yeah, you're right," Lisa said, and pulled her papers toward her. "He was kind of pitiful."

"That's crazy," Nick snapped.

They all stared at him. Even the rain seemed to pause.

"Well, look at him," he went on more mildly. "He's got a great life. No need for anyone's pity." He sat down, pulling a pen from his pocket as his face seemed to be fighting off a frown. "Now, aren't we supposed to be having a meeting?"

Neal tried to concentrate on the meeting's agenda—reports on an upcoming dinner-dance fund-raiser and plans for passing out brochures at the Fourth of July parade tomorrow—but his mind wouldn't concentrate. It wasn't that the rescue group wasn't a good cause. It was just...

Women didn't feel sorry for Neal Michael Sheridan. And certainly not ones as beautiful as Lisa Hughes. Maybe he could win some points with this favor she wanted from him. He'd do it so damn well and so damn cheerfully that—

"Well, that's about it," Lisa was saying.

Neal looked up. Myrna and Ben were on their feet. The meeting was over. He rose, also.

"You going to pick up the posters?" Myrna was looking

at him. "Want to drop off the program booklets when you do?"

"Uh…" The posters must be for the dinner dance they were planning, but where was he supposed to pick them up?

"Nah, I'll do it," Lisa said. "I've got to finalize the menu with Tabor Hill."

"Then what should I be doing?" he asked.

"Keep your checkbook out," Ben said with a laugh as they all moved toward the door. "I'll pass this list of music along to the deejay and make the rounds of the local merchants again. Remind them the dinner's only two weeks away." He nodded to them all, then went outside.

Myrna stopped at the door. "Maybe I'll follow you into town," she said to Neal. "Then you can give me that dewormer for my fosters."

The three of them stepped onto the porch. "Uh, I'm not going right back in," he said slowly.

"Oh, no?" Myrna said.

"He's going to check out one of my mares first," Lisa said.

Is that all she wanted? Neal found himself slightly disappointed. But what else would she want of her friendly neighborhood vet?

"Well, see you all later then," Myrna said. With a wave, she went down the steps and to her car.

It had almost stopped raining, and the damp earthy smell was fresh and alive. Neal took a deep breath, letting his sensitivity ease away. Damn, but he felt good here. There was something about the place that made him feel different. Energetic. Eager to take on new challenges. He wouldn't let the silly stuff that had been said inside bother him. That was the old Neal, the teenage Neal. These people didn't know the adult Neal. They'd be singing a different tune if they did. Everybody changed as they grew up.

He turned to Lisa. Talk about changing. He couldn't get over how beautiful she'd become. A body round in all the right places. Sculpted legs. And blue eyes deep enough to store the *Titanic* in. Man. How could Nick be just friends with her? How could he stay just friends with her while he was being Nick?

Once Myrna's car was headed down the lane, Lisa turned toward him. "Where do you want to do it?" she asked.

Where? He stared at her, wondering if it was her eyes that were mesmerizing him or that faint scent of perfume. Maybe it was a trick question. "How about the barn?" he said slowly. Where else would he examine her mare?

"Okay." But her tone was surprised. Hesitant.

He sensed a sudden nervousness about her. "Hey, if this isn't a good time, I can come back," he said.

"No, now is fine," she insisted. "It's the right time."

Her smile brought all his questions crashing onto the cliffs of her breasts. Damn. He couldn't think straight all of a sudden.

She took his hand and pulled him down the steps. Since he had no desire to see even the hint of her sway, he hurried to keep a half a step ahead of her. The rain may have slowed to a drizzle but the path was still full of puddles. Sort of like things had gotten around here in the last few minutes.

"I gave Pucky the rest of the morning off," Lisa said as she opened the barn door. "He won't be back until after lunch."

Neal had no idea who Pucky was, but he nodded and said, "That's fine."

Other than stumbling a bit when old Ben had asked him if he was really Neal because of the rain, he was handling this twin brother masquerade real well. Hell, with his talent he should have been a double agent.

Lisa grabbed a blanket off a rack near the door, then led him to an empty stall at the far end of the barn. She snapped the blanket out, letting it fall open onto the clean hay.

Neal looked around. There was no mare in sight, just a

couple of barn cats. "Is this going to take long?" he asked. "I've some calls I'm still supposed to make this morning."

Lisa walked to the blanket and turned to face him. "That depends on you."

She kicked off her sandals, then unbuttoned the row of little white buttons down the front of her dress. Ever so slowly she let it slip to the ground. Then she stood there in all her flawless womanly radiance.

Naked.

Chapter Two

Lisa stood before him like Venus rising out of the sea. Lithe, athletic and curved everywhere a woman was supposed to curve. Her skin glowed as if she'd been kissed by the sun.

Neal would have figured he'd died and gone to heaven if it weren't for his suddenly rasping breath and the painful-beyond-description heat in his loins.

"Nick?" she said hesitantly. She looked uncertain, unsure of herself, but took a step closer. "Is something wrong?"

Her voice was low and husky, making him think of evenings spent before a roaring fire, sipping brandy and making love. But the only smoke he smelled was from his own burning flesh. He was within an eyelash of ripping off his clothes and taking her. And if it weren't for the screams of his conscience, he would have.

She was his brother's woman. Whatever—whyever—Nick had denied it, she had to be. And there were limits to where Neal had let this masquerade take him. He tried to back away, but she'd gotten him turned around, and his step put him up against one of the barn's thick supporting pillars. He was trapped. He had to get her to put her clothes on.

"Golly, Nick." Her voice was a breath dancing on the air, feeding his hungers like gasoline fed a flame. "I never thought of you as the bashful type."

"Me, bashful?" Neal half laughed, half cried. No woman on earth had ever accused him of being bashful. "Aren't you afraid you're going to catch cold?"

She laughed at him. "Are you trying to run away from me?" She took a step closer, a frown throwing shadows across her beauty as she touched his chest with the gentlest of caresses.

Neal responded with something between a sob and a groan. Her hand seemed to burn, its faint pressure surely leaving scars on his skin. "It's just—" He swallowed hard and tried to replace that thready voice with something more manly. "It's just that there must be a million bugs in here," he managed to say. "You're too beautiful to get all bit up."

A warm glow covered her face. She bit her lip and looked away. "You know you don't have to make compliments." But her voice held a throb of pleasure, and her eyes were teary when she looked at him.

She acted like she'd never been complimented before. What kind of a jerk was Nick that he never told his woman how beautiful she was? But then what kind of a jerk would run away from this gorgeous creature?

She slid her hand up to touch his cheek. "I'm feeling kind of silly," she said. "Being the only one without clothes."

Neal closed his eyes as her touch seared him. His body felt ready to explode. He gasped for a breath, then another. "Maybe you ought to—"

Her hand stopped. "I didn't know you had a scar here," she said. There was something new in her voice— puzzlement?—as she lightly rubbed the scar on his jaw that he'd gotten playing hockey in college.

Damnation. He felt a faint trembling of worry even as the

hot scent of her nearness drove him as close to the edge as he could get and still not fall. She could not find out he wasn't Nick. That would be the absolute worst thing that could happen. She already hated him for having humiliated her in the past, and that time had been nothing compared to how she'd feel now. Whatever else happened, he could not let her find out he was masquerading as Nick.

He took her hand from his cheek. "That's why I wore the beard, to cover the scar," he said, and pressed her hand lightly to his lips.

Bad move. Real bad move. The fire inside him flared up even hotter, the pain even more intense. Damn, he had to get her dress on her and get the hell out of here. Get away by himself so he could settle down and think.

"Come on, Nick," she said and took her hand from his to start unbuttoning his shirt. "Which do you want? Top or bottom?"

He stared from her to the blanket and back again. He was going to have to start concentrating here. "That doesn't look like a bunk bed to me," he replied.

Lisa stared at him for a long moment, then burst into laughter. "You're so funny," she said and planted an earth-shattering kiss on his cheek. "But we really do need to get down to business. Pucky might get back soon, and he doesn't handle surprises well."

"Maybe we ought to wait, then," Neal said. "Let me get your dress and—"

But she had his shirt unbuttoned and was pulling it from his jeans. Then she encircled his waist with her arms. Her breasts pressed up against his bare chest. He had thought he couldn't throb any harder or feel any hotter, but he'd been wrong.

Oh, man. He hurt so much he was ready to cry. Maybe he should make love to her. Just so that she wouldn't be suspicious and find out he was really Neal. It would be for her own good. It would be a selfless act. It would be what a real gentleman would do.

It would also be immoral, unethical and despicable.

He should let himself ignite so that the wind could blow away his ashes. He should find some hungry wolves and let them feed on his body. He should throw himself into a bottomless pit. Anything that would put him out of his misery. And then he'd come back to haunt Nick for putting him in this position.

"Oh, Nick." Lisa moved against him, setting every inch of him ablaze. "I can't tell you how this makes me feel."

He closed his eyes. He couldn't tell her how he was feeling, either. There were no words. And if there were, he had no strength to say them. All he could do was stand real, real still. Just hold his breath and think of...of the states in alphabetical order. That was it. Alabama. Uh, Alaska. Um, damn. Arkansas?

Then he felt her tugging at the waist of his jeans, and his eyes flew open. Her hand slipped down to rub at the hard bulge in the fabric.

"Well, not every part of you is bashful," she said.

"Lisa," he groaned, trying to warn her away. But her touch felt so good, even through the layers of material, that—

"Whoops," Lisa said.

It wasn't even a split second. Not even time for the blink of an eye. One moment he was standing at the ready, and the next there wasn't a shred of wind in his sails. He was dead in the water.

Her cheeks turned pink. "I'm sorry," she said.

He tried to smile. Tried to shrug it off. He didn't think he played the part too well. He hadn't gone off early in ages. It had been so long ago, he couldn't even remember when. Maybe never. It had to be all the traveling had worn him out. Or the pressure of slipping into Nick's life. Hell, it could be the barn. He was probably allergic to hay.

"I guess that's it," Lisa said softly, a tentative smile on her face.

Hey! he wanted to cry, but kept his mouth shut. Talk about being between a rock and a hard place. This was worse, much worse. He was stuck between macho pride and decency. Between wanting to slink away and wanting to show Lisa that his rifle was a repeater, that there was no need to wait for a reload. Between wanting so desperately to make love to her that he was willing to sell his soul to the devil and knowing that she was his brother's lady.

The only thing left was to go to his brother's place, get stinking drunk and hide under the bed until Nick came home.

"I think I'd better go home," he said.

She nodded.

But unable to follow his own advice, he took a few steps to where Lisa's dress lay on the blanket and picked it up. Being ever so careful not to touch her skin, he slipped it on her shoulders and buttoned the top button.

Her eyes looked so wistful, so sad and disappointed, that he could scarcely bear it. He leaned in to brush her lips lightly with his, then turned and practically ran from the barn.

Lisa pulled another nail from the pocket of her cutoff jeans and whacked it into the two-by-four. This gate wasn't going anywhere soon. She pounded the nail all the way in, then wiped her forehead with the back of her hand. It was cooler in the barn than outside, but it wasn't chilly enough to cool her embarrassment. She refused to let her glance stray anywhere near that last stall.

She had made a total fool of herself that morning. She wasn't sure where she had gone wrong, but gone wrong she had. Otherwise, something would have happened. Nick had been aroused, that had been obvious, so why hadn't he done anything?

Lisa shook her head. Guys were a lot more trouble than horses. You wanted a stallion to mate, you put a mare in heat with him and it was as good as done. There was no need to play a bunch of head games. Games that she was not good at.

The sound of a phone ringing was a welcome interruption, but she wasn't sure she wanted to answer it. What if it was Nick? She should just let the machine take a message. But her curiosity got the better of her, and she stripped off her work gloves, then picked up the cordless phone from the shelf where she'd left it.

"Lisa?" a feminine voice asked.

"Colleen!" Lisa tossed her gloves onto the shelf. "You are just the person I need to talk to. You've got to tell me how to seduce a guy."

She and Colleen Cassidy had met when she'd been nine and Dad had been training the horses for a western movie Colleen had had a part in. The two girls had hit it off, both kids in a world that didn't seem to recognize childhood. They'd stayed friends even after Lisa had moved to Michigan and Colleen had made the move into low-budget adult roles. A movie role Colleen had a few years ago had been turned into a TV series, but Colleen still found time to call. Needing to talk to a "real person," as she put it.

"I what?" Colleen asked. "What in the world are you talking about?"

Lisa gazed out at her world. Off to her left, down the far path, Pucky was in the exercise ring, working with a colt. Off to her right, the dogs were worrying a squirrel that was running along the pasture fence, chattering insults at them. And straight ahead of her, under the high canopy of oaks, the house sat looking cool, safe and welcoming.

And empty.

Lisa took a deep breath as she sank onto an old wooden bench, but she couldn't say the words aloud. She hadn't told anyone—not even Nick—how much she wanted a baby, but it was all she could think about—having someone to love and take care of, someone to share her life with, someone to leave the farm to. The need was so deep, so very private that she couldn't tell anyone—not even a close friend like Colleen.

"Look, Colleen, I just want this guy to bed me. I need your expert advice."

"Are you trying to snag him?"

"No," Lisa cried.

She wasn't trying to catch Nick. She wanted a baby, that was all. But what had that trembly shaky feeling been that had come over her this morning at Nick's touch? It must have been excitement over the chance of getting pregnant. She had touched Nick a lot in the past. All right, not exactly like *that,* but she had touched him and never, ever felt the slightest bit wobbly afterward.

"I like him, but I don't love him," she said. "He's a friend. A decent, caring friend."

"Decent and caring?" Colleen repeated. "Such a creature doesn't exist."

"He does, too," Lisa insisted. "He's dependable and honest and—"

"And what—married? Don't tell me you fell for the *my wife doesn't understand me* line?"

She'd forgotten how cynical Colleen was. "He's widowed, if you have to know, but that has nothing to do with this."

"I see. It was his *I'm so lonely* line."

"I didn't fall for anything," Lisa insisted hotly. "If you must know, I want to have a baby. I've wanted one for ages and I want him to be the father."

Stunned silence followed her announcement. Colleen probably thought she was insane, and maybe she was, but it didn't change her desire.

"So are you going to help me?" Lisa asked.

"I can't," Colleen said dryly. "You'll never seduce a decent guy. He'd be too concerned about the ramifications of making love to do anything. You should use a sperm bank."

Lisa leaned back against the worn planking of the side of the barn. "There aren't any ramifications," she argued. "I don't expect him to hang around or pay child support or anything. I chose him for his bloodlines. He's from good stock. Hardy stock."

"You've been breeding horses too long. You make it sound like the same thing."

"Isn't it? Come on, Colleen. You're my only hope."

She could hear Colleen sigh as she gave in. "Okay, okay. First of all, you need to act sexy. Wear flimsy, sexy dresses. Sway when you walk. Lick your lips real slowly. That turns men on. And your hair. It's still kind of long, isn't it? Pin it up, then shake it loose when he's watching."

Sway, lick, shake. Lisa closed her eyes. She could never pull this off. "Haven't you forgotten batting my eyelashes at him?"

"Hey, you want to make it with this guy or don't you?"

"I'm not arguing."

"Good." Colleen was silent for a moment. "What you really need is a book. One of those *How To Drive Your Guy Wild with Desire in Seven Days or Less* things."

"Oh, Lordy." Lisa turned to lay on the old bench, covering her face with her hand. "Nick'll laugh me out of the room."

"Nick? This is about your vet friend Nick?" Colleen asked. "I need to know all about his brother. What's he like?"

"Neal? Scum of the earth." Just thinking about him was enough to darken the sunshine. "No integrity. Insensitive. Not a shred of decency in his body."

Colleen laughed. "Sounds like the guy you should be after. He's got the bloodlines and probably wouldn't worry about ramifications."

"Are you crazy?" Lisa cried and got to her feet. Colleen didn't know what she was saying. "I'd sooner die childless than go to bed with Neal Sheridan. I'd adopt a nest of baby tarantulas before I let that obnoxious jerk near me. Just thinking about it is enough to give me nightmares for the rest of my life."

"Can he really see into a woman's soul by looking in her eyes?" Colleen didn't sound like she was taking this seriously.

"I wouldn't put it past him," Lisa said. "You can't trust him an inch."

"I'm spending the next six weeks touring the Midwest with him."

"Oh, you poor thing. You need all the luck in the world."

The idea of spending that much time with that jerk was enough to give Lisa the chills. Thank goodness, Neal Sheridan was a million miles away. She needed to think about the man she was with that morning—the sweetest, nicest man alive. The man who was going to father her child.

"You like me a lot," Neal said, holding the piece of hamburger just out of the dog's reach. "And you aren't going to growl at me anymore."

Boomer was all wagging tail and eager agreement, the picture of a devoted dog, but Neal didn't believe it for a minute. He looked at Nick's Siamese cat, sitting on the chair watching them. Pansy was deaf, so she couldn't hear the pleading in Neal's voice, but her disgusted look said she understood that he was groveling to a dog. And she most definitely did not approve. Neal sighed and gave the dog the meat.

He was batting a thousand. A dog that liked him as long as he fed him hamburgers and a cat that thought they were both the lowest life forms on earth. Not to mention Lisa, who liked Nick a whole bunch but wouldn't wipe the floor with Neal. Obviously, he had to work at this harder. He crumpled the hamburger wrappings. Boomer woofed, a dark, threatening undertone in the sound.

"Hey, you had the whole hamburger," Neal protested. "I had zilch, fella. Not even the French fries. You should like me at least until morning."

Boomer obviously didn't believe the larders were empty and sniffed at the papers. His tail slowed to a soft, suspicious wag.

His eyes accused Neal of holding out. The cat turned her back on them both and began to bathe herself.

"I thought everybody in small towns was friendly," Neal said.

"Hello?" a voice called from the back of the house. "Anybody home?"

Neal hurried into the mudroom off the kitchen. His grandmother was standing at the screen door, a frown of major proportions on her face.

"Hi, Gram." He unlocked the door for her, leaning forward to peck her on the cheek as she came in. Boomer had changed from growling to wagging his tail. "How are you?"

"What's your door locked for?" she asked, bending over to greet Boomer. "And why'd you shave off your beard? I liked it."

Damn, he'd forgotten and locked the door like he was home. He'd better start leaving it unlocked. "I must have hit the lock when I came in," he said and rubbed his chin. "As for my face, I was tired of the beard."

She walked past him into the kitchen. "I left a message on your answering machine this morning. You didn't call me back."

"I just got in," he said and followed her into the kitchen.

"Hmph." She just gave him a look that said she knew he'd been sitting on the back porch bribing the dog into playing along for the past hour. "You know, when your grandfather shaved his beard, his skin was all white and scratched up."

Neal rubbed his cheek with his hand. Damn. Gram always had been the sharpest of them all. "I guess I'm lucky, then."

She gave him another hard look as she sat at the kitchen table. "Always were."

What did that mean? He started to sit in the chair across from her, only to find that Boomer was laying beneath it so it couldn't be moved. He frowned at the dog, who bared his teeth slightly in response.

"Fine, I'll sit over here," Neal said and took another chair. He glared briefly at the dog before turning to his grandmother.

She was watching him. "What's the matter with Boomer?"

"We had a disagreement. He wanted to use the truck over the Fourth and I said Pansy asked for it first."

Gram stared at him, making no response. He felt a bit of his unease returning. Didn't Nick ever crack a joke? Neal cleared his throat to break the spell she seemed to have fallen under. "Uh, so how are you?"

She seemed to shake herself slightly, then sat back. "Do you have time to stop in at Lola Albright's tomorrow?" she asked. "Leo's got the sniffles and Lola's all worried."

"I could go over there now," Neal offered. "It's not that late."

But Gram shook her head. "You know how Michael is."

Well, no, he didn't. But he let it go as Boomer flew out from under the chair and into the mudroom, panting and squealing in excitement.

"Are you expecting company?" Gram asked as she got up from the table.

Neal just shrugged as he got to his feet, too. The only thing he was expecting was that things were going to get even more confused.

"Hello?" Lisa called.

There was the sound of the door opening and then she came into the kitchen. She was wearing a pale blue sundress that molded itself to her fabulous curves. Her dark hair was pinned up with faint little curls falling down to caress her skin, and her smile was enough to make his sanity disappear forever. Neal's mouth went so dry he thought his tongue would crack.

"Well, hello, Lisa," his grandmother was saying. "What a lovely dress. I didn't know you owned anything besides jeans."

Lisa laughed as she came into the room carrying a pizza box and a wine bottle. "I have a few other things, but no one sees them much. It just got so muggy with all the rain today, a dress seemed cooler.''

Neal's grandmother smiled at him. "The way it was pouring there, I thought Neal had to be around.''

Neal felt his breath catch—due to his grandmother's words, not Lisa's nearness. "Neal's in Chicago,'' Neal said quickly.

"What's he doing there?'' Gram asked.

Neal shrugged. "Something for his sponsor.''

"Thank goodness,'' Lisa said as she put the packages on the kitchen table. "Instead of rain, he'd probably bring floods.''

That stung. "He doesn't always bring trouble with him,'' Neal told her.

"He does when he comes here,'' Lisa said.

"Oh, now that's not true,'' Gram said as she patted Lisa's shoulder. "The rain isn't trouble. It's cleansing. Washes the old dust away.''

"So do tears, and come to think of it, he probably brings them, too,'' Lisa said.

What was all this? "Neal doesn't make women cry,'' he pointed out sharply.

To his surprise, Lisa laughed. The sound rang through the room like sunlight hitting a glass and breaking into a million rainbows.

"That doesn't say much for old Love 'Em and Leave 'Em, does it?'' she said.

"Hey! I'll have you know—'' Neal bit his lip to keep the protests to himself. He tried again, calmer this time. "One of these days Neal is going to surprise you.''

"One of these days, Neal is going to surprise himself.'' Gram flashed him a brief smile. "Now, Lisa, what are you doing here? I hope there isn't a problem with one of your horses.''

"Oh, no. I just came over for dinner.'' She nodded toward the pizza box and wine bottle on the table. "It's a game night tradition for Nick and me. We share a pizza and root for the Cubs.''

"It is?"

Gram raised her left eyebrow and looked at Neal. He tried desperately for a smile, but the best he could manage was a grimace and a shrug. He had to keep Lisa busy, that was all. There'd be no repeat of this morning's disaster if they both stayed busy.

"Well, don't let an old woman's yacking get your food cold." His grandmother stepped toward the door, then stopped and turned to Neal. "I really came over to borrow two of your lawn chairs. Marjorie and I are going to the park to watch the fireworks tomorrow night."

"Sure. I'll get them."

With a nod to Lisa, he followed his grandmother outside, letting the wooden screen door shut behind him with a cozy thud. The evening's coolness was just nudging the heat from the air. He walked across the backyard to the garage, taking deep breaths of the soft summer air. A game night tradition? And what went along with the wine, pizza and TV? He could already feel that fire simmering in his loins.

"So how long has this been going on?" Gram demanded. "And why are you keeping it such a secret?"

"There's nothing to keep secret," Neal protested as he found the folding lawn chairs in Nick's garage and got two of them. "We're just friends."

"There's no such thing as just friends between a young man and a young woman."

Well, there would be this time. But Neal said nothing as he put the chairs in her trunk. He closed the trunk for her and went around to get her door.

But she waved him toward the house. "Get back inside, will you? I swear, you could use some lessons from your brother on how to take care of a lady."

"Gram…"

But she kept making those impatient motions at him, obviously not going to leave until he went inside. Taking a deep breath that set his stomach jittering even worse, he turned and climbed the stairs.

Soft music was coming through the screen door. Unless Boomer was into ballads, Lisa had put it on. Lordy, what time did the ball game start? Maybe they could take a jog around the neighborhood beforehand.

He pulled open the door and stepped inside. Lisa wasn't in the kitchen, so he went down the hall to the living room. Putting candles out on the coffee table, she was bent over, giving just the merest hint of her cleavage. A jog would not be enough. He needed full-scale sprints to Michigan City and back.

Over the scent of the pizza, he could smell perfume and the musky fragrance of a beautiful woman's desire. She straightened and smiled at him, then she licked her lips ever so slowly. Oh, my word, but he was hurting again.

"I'll just get things ready," she said. "Then we can start."

Start? Start what? "Uh, I was thinking of rearranging the furniture in here," he said quickly. "Maybe you could give me some tips."

She stared at him, then looked around the room. "What are you talking about? The television's got to stay by the cable outlet. The stereo cabinet wouldn't fit anywhere but that wall, and if you move your sofa, you won't see the TV from it."

"Oh, yeah. I guess you're right."

So much for that brainstorm of keeping busy. But there had to be a way to keep her from knowing the effect she had on him. That was what had gone wrong the last time. She had seen his erection and it had given her power. He had to appear immune to her.

"I have to take care of something," he said, and headed toward the stairs. "It'll just take a minute."

"Sure," Lisa said. "I'll be here."

Neal watched her float toward his kitchen with the wine bottle in hand. The gentle sway of her hips almost sent him hurrying after her. Choking a gasp of pain, he hurried to

Nick's bedroom, where he closed the door and locked it. Then he sank onto the bed and buried his head in his hands. He'd put Nick on a dull bus trip, traveling the back roads of the Midwest, while his brother had put him in hell.

But he was not going to break. He was a man. A man who knew how to control himself. Neal got to his feet.

All he needed was a good strong jockstrap. Something that would keep his body from reacting to Lisa's nearness. Or at least keep his reaction hidden from her. He began to search Nick's room, pulling things out and throwing them on the floor as he searched madly for an athletic supporter.

Nothing in the dresser drawers. Nothing in the closet. Nothing in the hamper in the bathroom. Nothing anywhere. This was ridiculous. "How can he jog?" he muttered.

He sank onto the bed and pulled open the nightstand drawer. The usual nightstand stuff—a few pieces of jewelry, an old pair of glasses, some adhesive bandages and a roll of white athletic tape.

"Any old port in a storm." Neal picked up the tape. "This'll work."

Quickly shucking his jeans, he crisscrossed long strips of tape over the front of his briefs. That and his determination would keep things under control. He pulled his jeans up, then started downstairs to wrestle with the temptations of Lisa Hughes. He didn't know what his brother had had in mind, but no one, not even his own twin, could put something over on Neal Sheridan.

"I was starting to get worried about you," Lisa said as he returned to the living room.

She smiled at him, then reached up to pull a barrette from her hair. The soft curls fell to her shoulders, whispering to him to come closer. To run his fingers through her hair and crush those curls as he pulled her lips to his. The pressure shot up in his loins. The damn tape was slipping and he had to gasp for breath.

"Uh, I don't feel too well," he stuttered.

She frowned, obviously concerned as she swayed to his side. "What's wrong?"

She felt his cheek, her hand so wonderfully cool against the fire of his skin. The throbbing—was it in his heart or else-where?—echoed in his ears, and he could scarcely think.

"You do feel flushed," she said.

"Probably just a bug," he said and backed up a step toward the stairs. He had to put some space between them. He felt himself straining against the tape.

"I didn't think there was anything going around," she said.

"Who knows? Maybe I've been harboring it for weeks." He tried to make his voice sound weakish.

"Are you nauseated?" she asked.

Maybe he'd come across too weakish. "Of course not," he said. Real men didn't get nauseated.

"Achy?"

"No."

"Sore throat?"

He hesitated, realizing that he was running out of symptoms. Maybe he'd better risk looking less manly and more sick. "Yeah. Hurts to talk," he said.

She frowned at him. Probably thinking how contagious he was. And how she should leave before she caught something. Maybe even worrying she already had. This just might work.

"Well, there's only one thing to do." She took his hand in hers. "We need to get you to bed."

Chapter Three

Lisa fanned herself with the stack of Hoofed Animal Rescue Society brochures. She wished the parade would move a little faster. It was never going to be their turn to start. She was rapidly getting tired of this church parking lot, not to mention the high school cheerleading squad, which was going to march behind them.

"How's Buster doing?" she asked Myrna. Buster, a gentle Appaloosa gelding, had been their group's first rescue, and one of Myrna's children had ridden him in the town's Fourth of July parade for five years now. This year her ten-year-old son, Mickey, got the call.

"He's fine," Myrna said, sounding surprised by the question. "How should he be?"

Lisa shrugged. "I don't know. It seems like we've been waiting for years, though." But then Fourth of July parades always had so many kids' groups marching in them.

She went over to check with the 4-H volunteers who were marching with her. The two girls carrying the large horizontal flag were all set. The boys leading the rescue goats were fine. And the group passing out the leaflets to the crowds along the parade route had plenty.

All of which left Lisa to stew on what an abject failure she was. Destined to remain childless forever. Nick wouldn't even let her near his bed when he was feeling sick.

Bill Wurty waved for Mickey and Buster to start out, and Lisa sighed heartily. At last. Except she was working the crowd on the east side of the street, and the first people she saw were Betsy Martin and her three little kids. Lisa moved past one of the teen volunteers and saw Julie Dwyer, who was eight and a half months pregnant.

The streets seemed lined with pregnant women, babies and little kids. There was no escape. Everywhere she looked, she saw reminders of what she didn't have. Maybe never would have.

This wasn't anything new, Lisa told herself as she kept smiling and passing out the leaflets. She'd been extra conscious of pregnant women and babies for a while now. She should be used to the emptiness inside, to the feeling that something was lacking in her life. It was just that she'd come so close this month. But next month would be better. After all, it wasn't Nick's fault he'd gotten sick—

Lisa's feet stopped and her eyes narrowed. Up ahead, looking remarkably healthy, stood Nick. His grandmother was with him. Lisa walked slowly over, swallowing hard.

"Good morning, Mrs. Sheridan," she said to his grandmother before turning to him. "Nick. You look like you're feeling better this morning."

"Uh, yeah," he said. "Must have been one of those twelve-hour bugs."

"Feeling better?" His grandmother frowned at him. "When were you sick? You were fine when I left last night."

"It came on suddenly," Lisa told the woman.

"It must have," she agreed, still frowning.

"These things do," Nick said. "If I hadn't been sick, would I have passed up a great pizza and a bottle of wine?"

"Not to mention Lisa's company," his grandmother added.

His eyes got a strange look in them. "Right," he agreed quickly. "Especially Lisa's company."

Except that he hadn't mentioned her company. Not until his grandmother did. That little fact hadn't escaped Lisa's attention. Or the fact that the cheerleaders were passing behind her. She'd always thought they were too perky for words, but today she listened to their cheers.

Go. Fight. Win. Hey, why not?

Go. "Well, I'm glad to see you're feeling better," Lisa said brightly. "That's the important thing. And if you really missed the pizza, I've still got most of it in my refrigerator."

"Oh, yeah?" His voice tried for enthusiasm, but his eyes fell short.

"And I didn't drank the wine."

"Great." This time enthusiasm missed his voice by a country mile.

"What is the matter with you?" his grandmother asked him. "If you were younger, I'd take you home and give you a dose of castor oil."

Fight. Lisa laughed. "It's all right. He's probably still not up to snuff. Some of these bugs can hang on a while." She paused. "Especially once you get past a certain age."

The flash in his eyes told her he'd taken the bait. "I'll have you know I feel fine," he said sharply. "I'm in perfect health."

"Oh?" She dropped her voice to a low, teasing tone. "The Cubs are playing again." She paused. "Tonight."

"Tonight?" He paused, obviously caught off guard. "That would be great, except that my dad always has us all—"

"Oh, didn't I tell you?" His grandmother put her hand on his arm. "Your father's not having his Fourth of July picnic this year. Called me this morning. Said he's sick of barbecuing for the whole family."

Nick turned to his grandmother. "He what?"

It was hard to believe. The whole town knew the only thing Joe Sheridan liked better than barbecuing was his weekly poker games, but Lisa wasn't going to question Gram's words.

"Seven o'clock then, your place?" she said to Nick.

He looked lost. "Fine." He sounded lost.

Win. "Great." She ignored the guilt tugging at her heart. He'd said he'd father her child. It wasn't her fault he was being such a pill about it. "See you tonight."

Lisa stepped back. The cheerleaders had passed, and she was in the middle of a Cub Scout troop. Not the place for discussions.

"I'd better catch up with my gang," she said and turned, hurrying ahead.

But the look on Nick's face seemed to follow her. He was not looking forward to the evening.

It had to be her. There was no getting around it. She was an utter failure at arousing a man's interest. No matter that she looked presentable and wasn't asking for a grand passion—just sex. She thought guys were always willing to have sex. Well, maybe they were, just not with her.

Darn. She was going to have to get one of those sex how-to books, like Colleen had told her to. Why was something so natural turning out so hard?

Damn, men were a pain in the butt, Lisa thought as she slowed her truck for a turn. She'd learned that years ago, living on the back lots of movie sets. Dad and Pucky had tried to isolate her, but she'd still stumbled upon enough women, actresses to makeup girls, crying their eyes out over some guy. And she'd overheard enough guys boasting and bragging about their latest conquest to know that men and women had very different definitions of relationships.

Men had all kinds of mood swings, and you didn't know from one minute to the next what the heck they wanted. They'd say one thing and do another. They'd promise you the moon, then give you a used flashlight battery. And no matter what they did or didn't do, it was always the woman who cried. Any female who took them seriously was destined for a load of heartbreak, which was why she didn't. Never had and never would.

She pulled her truck into the parking lot of the discount department store, second thoughts crowding in on her. Why were all these cars here? People were supposed to be out shooting off illegal firecrackers. Not here shopping.

She sat in the truck for a long moment. What would a book tell her, anyway? Mating was a basic act, like eating or drinking. And what if someone she knew saw her buying the book?

"The heck with it all," she muttered. No guts, no glory. Taking a firm grip on her fears, she forced herself out of her truck and across the lot.

The basics were pretty much the same with any mammal, but Colleen insisted that men didn't know that and each figured he was unique. So if a woman wanted to make it with a guy, she had to play to his fantasies.

It seemed like a pile of foolishness to Lisa. She didn't want to fulfill a man's every dream—she wanted a baby. That was all. Bed her once or twice or three times, if that's what it took, and then that was it. She didn't want to pretend to be anything but herself. But it was looking like she might not have a choice on the matter.

The store was fairly crowded. People should have better things to do on a holiday afternoon than walk around in air-conditioning. They should be at family picnics, playing horseshoes and croquet while Dad barbecued and Mom made potato salad.

A knot twisted in her stomach. All right, so her baby would never have a picnic like that. But she could barbecue as well as anybody and buy potato salad as good as, if not better than, homemade.

Lisa hurried toward the book section in one corner of the store, anxiously searching the faces around her, hoping she wouldn't see anyone she knew. Not that it mattered if she did. It wasn't like she was breaking the law.

The relationship books were easy enough to find. That was because there were so many of them—and an awful lot of them seemed to focus on sexual instruction. How could sex be so complicated? How did people who couldn't read have babies?

She reached for the first book and flipped through it, then another and another. Horsefeathers, she wasn't looking at all these books. They all looked the same, and standing here from now until kingdom come would surely mean someone she knew would come along and see her.

Ah, this title looked good. *One Hundred and One Ways To Turn Your Man On.* It was like picking strawberries—the bigger the selection, the better her chance of finding something good. She took the book, held it so the title faced her chest and went toward the checkout counters.

As it happened, her path took her by the books on horses, and she decided to look at a few. Just a glance. Something interesting to wake her up for the trip home. A photo collection of Arabians was the first thing she picked up, and she was soon lost in admiring the beauty of the splendid animals.

"Lisa?"

Her heart stopped and she looked up, feeling like a deer caught in the beams of a searchlight. "Myrna."

"What a surprise to see you here," Myrna said. "I didn't imagine anybody I knew would be shopping on a gorgeous day like this."

"I had to get a book," Lisa mumbled, returning the photo book to the shelves.

"Oh. What did you get?" Myrna reached toward the book Lisa was clutching to her chest. "Is it something on Arabians or just horses in general?"

"No," Lisa snapped.

Myrna blinked, looking surprised.

"It's for Pucky. I got him a book," Lisa said.

"What did you get him?"

"It's a secret."

Myrna was blinking again.

Lisa felt like a fool. "I mean, it's a surprise."

"Well, I won't tell him."

"I know." Lisa tried for nonchalant, but all she got was sweaty palms. "But you know how things just slip out. Especially in a small town like ours."

Myrna stared at her with a look that people reserved for the mentally deranged.

"Oh, my gosh. Look what time it is." Lisa made a production of looking at her watch. "Boy, I gotta go. See ya."

She walked toward the checkout counter, but was out of breath by the time she got there. She put the book on the counter as the clerk turned around. Oh, no!

"Hi, Miss Hughes," the boy said, picking up the book. "How are you?"

"I'm fine, Roy."

Lisa felt herself slump, like a balloon slowly losing air. Roy Dieter was the regional president of the Southwest Michigan 4-H Club. He'd helped out on a number of rescues her group was involved in. In fact, he reported the suspected neglect that had resulted in the group taking over the two goats that had marched in the parade. She considered crawling out the door.

"Oh, wow." Roy was staring at the book cover, his eyes open wide. "Are there really a hundred and one different ways to—" he almost giggled "—you know."

This day was turning into a total disaster. She had to take charge of the situation. Right now. "Put it on my credit card, please," she said, holding out her plastic card.

But Roy was perusing the pages, not listening to her. "Holy cow!"

"Roy," Lisa snapped. "The price is on the cover."

"Oh, yeah." He glanced at the price, but his attention quickly returned to the text. "I can't believe there are that many different—"

She couldn't take it any more. Reaching across the counter, she pulled the book from his hands and ran it over the scanner. The cash register beeped, and the price came up on the screen.

"Now take my credit card and let me get out of here," she said.

It seemed like an eternity while the young man stared at her. Then he smiled. "Sure. No problem. I can understand that you might be in a hurry. Like, you got other things to do, right?"

She would have loved to wipe the smirk off his face. But she couldn't afford to get arrested for assault. Not until it was too late to get pregnant this month.

"I really appreciate you coming to take a look at little baby Leo," Mrs. Albright said. She was a tiny, birdlike lady who had to be at least ninety.

"It's no problem," Neal said.

Baby Leo, on the other hand, was a twenty-pound, battle-scarred orange tabby who'd be chewing tobacco and spitting if he'd been human. Neal was certain the cat could curse in twelve languages.

"Sure you can give him the medicine?" he asked.

"Oh, he's a sweetie. I can give him anything."

Neal glanced at the sweetie who glared at him, then put away the stethoscope. "Well, give him a half tablet twice a day for ten days. If he's not better, give me a call."

"Oh, he'll be fine. I just know it. He wouldn't want his mommy to worry."

Neal grunted. What Leo wanted and didn't want wasn't likely to affect the upper respiratory infection he had.

"Now, you come sit on the porch and have some lemonade and cookies," the old woman said. "I made your favorite."

"That's not really necessary," Neal began, but Mrs. Albright waved his words away.

"I thought we got this all settled when you came to see

Leo last winter," she said. "You have to let me pay somehow."

He had inadvertently stepped on her pride. "Well, just a small glass," he said. "Then I need to be on my way."

She led him to her porch, with its dollhouse-like furniture. If he sat in one of those chairs, it would surely break.

"Sit, sit," she insisted as she carried out a tray with two glasses of lemonade and a plate of cookies.

"Only once you are," he said, and took the tray from her hands, putting it on the table. "Now, you relax."

She sighed as she sank into a chair. "If only I could," she said.

Neal sat gingerly, not sure what to say. He wasn't good at these situations. He didn't like them. That was why he was in television. But then he wasn't in television now. He was Nick.

"Gram said something about Michael," Neal said, not having any idea what he was talking about. "He giving you a hard time again?"

She nodded and handed Neal a glass of lemonade. "He means well. I know he's worried about my dizzy spells, but he doesn't understand."

Michael wasn't the only one. Dizzy spells didn't sound good.

"What would happen to Leo if I went into a retirement home?" she asked.

"But dizzy spells could be dangerous."

"I've tried to find him a home, but it's not easy." She pushed the plate of cookies toward him. "He's kind of set in his ways."

He took one. "You need to think about yourself."

"Michael says I should just take him to the humane society, but I know what would happen to him there."

"He might get adopted," Neal said. "Most people want kittens, but some people adopt older cats."

Mrs. Albright gave him a look, then picked up her lemonade. "I may be a crazy old lady, like Michael thinks I am, but

I made a commitment to Leo when I got him. I promised to take care of him as long as he lived, not until he became inconvenient.''

"Things change."

"Some things don't." She put her glass down, and Neal could see her hand was trembling. "When Leo has a home, I'll go with Michael to look at those retirement places."

This was insane. What was he supposed to say? What would Nick say? "I'll take him." Neal was astonished at the words that had come out of his mouth. Then it opened once more. "When you're ready to go into a nursing home, he can come live with me."

Mrs. Albright looked just as surprised. "Are you sure?"

Neal shrugged, then thought that might look like he'd been pressured into it. He bit into a cookie decisively. "Why not? If he doesn't get along with Pansy and Boomer, he can be an office cat."

The woman looked about to burst into tears, which only made Neal feel like a fraud. Well, he could take Leo home with him, too. Sure, he traveled somewhat, but he made enough money to hire a cat sitter. That's what he'd do. Leo would come live in New York with him. He'd been wanting a pet anyway. Why not Leo?

"I knew when you were twelve what a good person you were, and you haven't changed," she said, definitely weepy. "You were always so much more responsible than that brother of yours."

Neal stiffened slightly. "Neal's a good person, too."

She sniffed. "Well, he was a real rascal when he was a boy. I remember one time you boys were working the Little League pancake breakfast and he came with his arm in a sling just to avoid the messy jobs."

How did people remember these things? "Maybe he really'd been hurt," Neal protested, though he remembered the incident all too clearly—and knew her assessment had been right. "He did work the ticket desk the whole time. And you know he never even played baseball here in town."

"I never thought of it that way," she admitted, then smiled. "What a good brother you are, always defending him. I'll wrap up these cookies for you, shall I? I'm never going to eat them all."

"That would be great," Neal said as he got to his feet. A sling just might work again, come to think of it.

"I'm going now," Lisa told Pucky. "Don't wait up for me. I may be late."

"Whew! In that outfit, I would say everybody's gonna be late."

Lisa refused to look his way and got the cold pizza out of the refrigerator. "What's the big deal about my outfit?" she said, then grabbed the bottle of wine she'd bought for last night. "It was hot, so I decided to dress comfortably."

Actually, *comfort* wasn't the best word to describe her shorts and halter top. *Poured into them* might be better. Or *second skin.* But she was just following suggestion number one in *One Hundred and One Ways To Turn Your Man On*— don't be afraid to let a little skin show, but not all. Covered is sexier than uncovered.

According to the book, that was where she'd gone wrong in the barn. It didn't make much sense to her, but obviously she wasn't the expert. If she was she'd be pregnant by now. The fact that she wasn't was proof she needed the book.

Her dogs were dozing on the porch when she came outside, but they woke up and escorted her out to her truck. "I don't want you guys waiting up, either," Lisa said as she slid into her seat. "Like I told Pucky, I may be late."

Real late, she thought as she sped down her lane. Tonight was going to be the night, even if she had to use all one hundred and one ways. She patted her purse as she tooled down the narrow two-lane road, feeling the hard edges of the book she'd tucked inside. In all those suggestions, there had to be one that would work. When she pulled into Nick's driveway, she paused to take several deep breaths before gathering her things and stepping out of the truck.

"Hello?" she called as she let herself in the back door.

Boomer and Pansy came running to greet her, followed a few seconds later by Nick. He had a stunned look on his face when he saw her.

And his left arm in a sling.

"What happened?" she asked and put the pizza and wine on the kitchen table.

"I tripped on the basement stairs," he said, sounding embarrassed to admit it. "I think I sprained my wrist."

"Good thing we're just going to watch baseball, not play it." It wouldn't affect her plans for the evening, would it? Surely they could have sex without further hurting his wrist.

"Yeah, good thing." He seemed to swallow hard and looked away.

She put her purse on the table, noticing a slight tremble in her hands, then picked up the wine. After a glass or two of wine, she'd be more relaxed. More able to follow all her book's suggestions.

"Why don't you put the pizza in the oven to warm up?" she said. "And since I've got two good hands, I'll pour the wine."

"Okay."

She glanced his way as she went to get the corkscrew. He was watching her, his face a tinge rosier, but he looked away quickly when she caught him. Good old cool Nick wasn't quite so cool when faced with a sexy outfit, it appeared. She hid a smile as she opened the wine. Maybe the author knew what she was talking about.

She poured two glasses of wine. "Want to relax in the living room while we wait for the pizza to warm up?"

"Sure." He reached for one of the glasses, but she shook her head.

"I'll get them," she said. "You just go on ahead."

He shrugged and went toward the living room. After a quick glance at his back, Lisa gulped about half of one glass, then refilled it. She could feel some of her tension ebb away. On to suggestion number two. She went into the living room.

"The game doesn't start for another half hour," Nick said, checking the television guide.

Lisa put the glasses on the coffee table, then sat on the sofa with what she hoped was an inviting smile. "So we find something else to do for a while."

He cleared his throat as he came over to the sofa. "True, there's always the pregame show." He winced as he sat.

She let her smile fade. "You okay?"

He shrugged. "Just a little stiff and sore," he said. "I must have pulled some muscles when I tripped."

This was almost too easy! "You poor baby."

She got to her feet and came around to the back of the sofa as Nick eyed her uncertainly.

"You just relax," she said.

She'd seen this done a million times in the movies, but had no idea just how one went about giving a massage. Well, she'd rubbed down enough horses and groomed enough dogs and cats. How different could it be?

She laid her hands on his shoulders and was stunned by the jolt of awareness that shot through her. She could feel the heat of his skin, the iron of his muscles through the thin fabric of his shirt. This was Nick, her old buddy. Her best friend. The last person in the world she had romantic feelings toward. Had she had too much wine?

Yet her mind's eye kept visualizing Nick without his shirt, her hands sliding over his bare shoulders. She wanted to touch him, to feel his skin beneath her fingers. Her breath began to quicken, and she forced her hands to move. She'd definitely had too much wine.

As her hands kneaded his shoulders her cheeks got hotter. She was never more conscious of her own womanliness. Of her breasts crammed into this halter top. A fire seemed to light within her, a small, smoldering heat that cried out for more.

Unfortunately, her massage didn't seem to be doing Nick any good. She could feel him grow more tense beneath her touch. Twitchy. Yet at the same time, he seemed to move into her caress. Suddenly, he pulled away from her and got to his feet.

"Boy, that feels much better," he said with a laugh that seemed unsteady. He rolled his shoulders one at a time. "It's great. Perfect."

"Good."

But then he took his wineglass and sat away from her in the recliner. "Boy, how about the Cubbies this year, huh?"

She sat on the sofa, reaching for her wine and taking a good, solid gulp. "What about them?" she asked. "They're losing, just like always."

"But they're coming closer this year," he said. "Losing by less."

"Close doesn't count." Not in baseball. And certainly not in getting pregnant. "Except in horseshoes and hand grenades."

What was the matter with him? What was the matter with her?

"I think I'll go check on the pizza," she said.

She took her wineglass with her and filled it before taking an obligatory look into the oven. Then, after a quick glance down the hallway to make sure Nick wasn't coming in, she pulled her book out of her purse. She quickly flipped past suggestions one and two—both failures—and went on to number three.

Get him out of his clothes, even if you have to spill something on him.

Spill something. That should be no problem, given her level of nervousness. She grabbed the bottle of wine and headed to the living room.

"Pizza's not quite warm enough," she said and sat on the arm of his chair. "Want a refill?"

"Sure." He held out his glass, his voice eager, but his eyes looked almost haunted.

She poured some in his glass then forced her arm to twitch slightly so that some splashed onto his shirt.

"Oh, I'm so sorry," she cried, certain that he must know it was deliberate. "I am such a klutz."

"It's all right." He wiped at the spot—the tiny minuscule spot—with his free hand. "No harm done. I can barely see it."

Horsefeathers, she couldn't even spill stuff right. It seemed like she'd poured gallons on him. "Let me clean it off," she said and got to her feet. "You don't want it to stain."

"I don't think zinfandel stains."

She put her glass down and took his. "Come on, it'll only take a minute to rinse the stain off and it'll make me feel so much better."

She tried to unbutton the buttons, but he pushed her hands away.

"It's okay, honest. It's an old shirt."

She stood there staring at him, feeling like an incompetent idiot. Why had he promised to father her child if he couldn't do it? And if he couldn't, why didn't he just say so? Did he enjoy seeing her make a fool of herself?

"Hey, if it's means that much, go ahead," he said softly. He slipped his arm from the sling, then unbuttoned the shirt and gave it to her.

She held the shirt to her, barely conscious that she had it as she gazed at his bare chest. What would it be like to run her hands over him, to feel that broad chest pressed against hers?

"I'll go get another one," he was saying.

"What?" she stammered. "Oh, no. This'll just take a minute."

She practically raced into the kitchen with the shirt, trying all the while to calm her pulse, to steady her definitely unsteady hands. What was going on? Was she suffering from an overdose of hormones this month? She'd never had this reaction to Nick before. Never.

She found the infinitesimal spot and rinsed it off, then dumped the shirt on the table. Okay, this was it. This was her big chance. She had to have a surefire, foolproof, absolutely guaranteed suggestion to try this time. It was now or never.

She picked up the book and flipped through it, opening somehow to a chapter called "Can't Miss Techniques." It was an omen. This was her night.

She read Can't Miss Suggestion Number One, frowned. Shook her head, then shrugged. Who was she to question their suggestions? She still hadn't gotten to first base.

She shoved the book into her purse, rummaged through Nick's cabinets for a few minutes, then pulled out a rolling pin.

Chapter Four

Neal stared at Lisa standing in the living room doorway. His breath was coming hard and fast. He was never going to last through six weeks of this.

Her shorts clung to her hips like skin, and her halter top came as close to nothing as something could and still not get her arrested in downtown Three Oaks. Her blue eyes were so deep and mysterious, her lustrous dark hair hanging loose. And…

And she was carrying a huge rolling pin.

With an odd look on her face, she came toward him. The rolling pin seemed to grow bigger with each step.

"I've got an idea," she said slowly.

Nervousness got the better of desire as he remembered her determination they make love over the past two days. He sprang out of his chair, forgetting his left wrist was supposed to be sprained.

"What's that for?" he asked. "You doing some baking?"

She stopped and stared at him, but he couldn't read her

expression. Not while that rolling pin was swinging ominously from her hand.

"I know a few little tricks I thought we could try," she said softly.

Her voice was low, with just a tiny quiver in it that could be apprehension or excitement. Whichever, it was damned sexy. It called him closer, spoke to that hunger that was starting to eat him alive. It was almost enough to make him ignore the rolling pin.

But a rolling pin? He'd thought small towns were conservative places. Safe places. Doors unlocked and kids playing outside after dark. Now he had to add rolling pins to that list, and it skewed the results.

"Maybe we should save the tricks for Halloween," he said. Nick would be back by then.

She didn't laugh. "What about the treats?" Her words floated on the air. "We don't have to wait for them, do we?"

His gaze slid slowly over her. Over those luscious breasts just barely confined in that halter top. Over that trim waist his hands wanted to measure. Over those long legs that spoke of strength and softness all at once.

Oh, Lordy, Lordy, but he didn't want to wait for anything, least of all Nick to return. He wanted to taste those lips and touch that skin and lose himself in Lisa's womanliness. But he couldn't. He had to find some breathing space.

"Ah, I'm on a diet," he said, dragging the words from the painful dredges of his soul. It was like spilling the last drop of water onto the desert floor and watching it fade away. "I have to stay away from treats."

All the softness, all the sweet seductiveness faded from her eyes. Her lips tightened into a thin, angry line. A storm was brewing. She brought the rolling pin up to bounce it lightly in her free hand.

"Maybe I should just bean you good and hard with this," she said. "Maybe then you'd stop all playing your stupid games."

"Me?" he protested. He wasn't the one playing games. Well, maybe he was playing just a little one with the masquerade, but that was different. He tried to laugh as he reached toward her. "Come on, Lisa—"

"Oh, go to hell," she snapped, throwing his hand off. "Do not pass go. Just go straight to hell."

"We need to talk, don't you think?"

She looked ready to argue, her eyes dark and turbulent, but she didn't come any closer to him. With a sudden dejected sigh, she dropped onto the sofa, the rolling pin hanging loosely from her hand. She looked so broken and dispirited that he felt his heart ache with her.

"Why did you say you'd do it if you weren't going to?" she asked slowly.

A spurt of anger flashed through him. What had that bum of a brother gone and done? The hell with breathing space. Neal sat next to Lisa—the side away from the rolling pin— and took her hand in his. Everybody kept telling him what a great guy Nick was, but great guys didn't hurt defenseless women and then leave a mess for others to clean up.

"Maybe we need to talk about it some more," he said gently, trying to get her to give him a clue what this was all about.

"We discussed it and discussed it until I was blue in the face," she said, pulling her hand from his. Her voice was back to harsh and unforgiving. "There isn't anything left to say."

"Maybe I just need to hear it all again."

"I'm done talking," she said. The rolling pin came up to her lap.

"You're not giving me much of a chance to rethink this, are you?" he asked. Damn it. If she'd just give him a clue what Nick had—

"You agreed yesterday."

"Well…" Neal felt a sudden gnawing in the pit of his stomach. Was this something to do with the mysterious favor she'd wanted of him? "You're right. I did."

"Damn straight you did."

But what the hell did he agree to? Neal took a deep breath. "Sometimes," he said, "in situations like this, misunderstandings can develop."

He paused, giving Lisa a chance to jump in, but she glared at him.

"In complex situations—" like when your brother cuts out and leaves you holding the most wobbly house of cards ever "—like this—"

"What in the world are you babbling about?"

Neal wished he knew.

"When you came to my place yesterday I went out to meet you with an umbrella. You do remember that, don't you?"

Did he remember? Did he remember the lithe body encased in a sundress that hugged every curve in her body? Did he remember her dark hair hanging in damp ringlets around her face? Did he remember her bright blues eyes and anxious smile?

Neal didn't have to say anything. His body was screaming its answer. The memory had gone on, like a tape left playing even when it was past the replay you wanted. He saw her lead him into the barn again. Saw her smooth and perfect body. Breathed in the heavy scent of her longing.

And felt again the agony of his desire.

He got to his feet and walked to the front window, wishing Nick was here. It was too difficult to kill somebody at a distance, and so much less satisfying.

"We really need to talk more," he said—no, groaned.

"We've talked too much already," she replied. "It's time to fish or cut bait."

He needed to make this whole affair—whoops, poor choice of words. He needed to make this whole situation an intellectual thing. He needed to keep his treacherous body out of it.

He closed his eyes and imagined snowy mountain peaks, frozen lakes and a world of no women. He thought of icy streams and sleet and hail and wind chills that bottomed out the weatherman's charts.

He wasn't going to open his eyes until his body was under control. Until his mind was calling the shots, not other parts of him. He thought of cold so deep that frost collected on eyebrows, of air so frigid it hurt to breathe, of body parts numbed by the freezing hand of an endless winter.

"Enough of this nonsense," Lisa said. "You promised to father my child, and I just want to know when the hell you're going to do it."

His eyes flew open.

"This is idiotic," Lisa snapped. "As idiotic as your sprained wrist."

Neal stopped to let Boomer sniff at a bush but kept his eyes on the dog, not quite brave enough to look at Lisa yet. He knew the muggy, hot weather was due to some stalled storm system out west, but there was another storm system closer by, serving up its own heat. He needed to work on building his resistance.

"Hi, Nick, Lisa," someone called from a passing car.

Neal waved and smiled brightly as the stranger passed before turning to Lisa. "Boomer needed to go out, and a walk will tire him out more than just a romp in the backyard."

"What does he need to be tired out for? You have something planned for this evening that you don't want interrupted?"

Thankfully Boomer was done with his inspection, and they moved on at the brisk pace the dog set. It gave them time to wave at neighbors, call out a hello now and then, but not stop to talk.

After Lisa's bombshell of an announcement, Neal had needed a few minutes to recover. To start breathing again, jump-start his brain into processing information, turn off other parts of him all too willing to comply with her wishes. And definitely get out of the house where he was too likely to agree to anything.

Just what was Lisa and Nick's relationship? Were they friends, lovers, would-be lovers? Was she in love with him? How did he feel about her? This whole mess was enough to drive a sane man over the edge.

So when Boomer had shown a halfhearted interest in going outside, Neal had jumped at the chance to take him for a walk. He'd turned off the oven and taken the pizza out, warned Pansy not to eat it while they were gone and gotten Boomer's leash. Three blocks from Nick's house, Neal was starting to regain use of his brain.

"Hi, Tammy," Lisa called to someone across the street.

"Hi, Lisa. Hi, Nick," the woman called back. "Great rain yesterday, wasn't it?"

"Sure was," Lisa said, then spoke to Nick. "Look, all I need to know is if you're able to help me out or not."

Neal stopped at an intersection while some kids on bikes raced past. "It's not that I'm not able," he told her under his breath. "I'm just not sure I should."

"Oh, get off your high horse. You agreed."

"Yes, well, we need to talk about that." He cleared his throat roughly. "Actually, I thought I was agreeing to something else."

She frowned at him. "Like what?"

"Well, I don't know," he said. "But you didn't mention what you were talking about."

"So it's my fault now?" She snorted. "Always blame the woman. So typical."

Neal sighed. "I'm not trying to assign blame," he said. "I'm just trying to explain that I misunderstood."

"You sure did."

She was watching some little kids across the street. In their bathing suits, they had squirt guns and were chasing each other around with wild squeals. The children looked cool, Neal thought, envying them their carefreeness. It must be nice not to have any worries, any responsibilities. Then he glanced at Lisa's face and knew she was feeling something else.

He could see the longing on her face, and more—some other need was written there that he could not define and probably would never share. Her eyes no longer held anger, but pain. Pain and emptiness so intense he felt them cut into him. They turned a corner and only the sounds of the children's laughter haunted them.

"Being a single parent would be hard," he said softly.

She kept her eyes straight ahead. "I know."

"Why don't you just wait until you meet the right guy and—"

Her harsh laughter interrupted him. "The right guy?" Her eyes were flashing again, not with anger but impatience. "Come off it, Nick. I'm never getting married."

"Thirty-four is a little young to give up on marriage," he said.

"I gave up on it years ago, and you know it."

He didn't understand her attitude at all. "Then maybe you should try looking around again. You're young, beautiful and interesting. There must be lots of men out there who would jump at the chance to get to know you."

"Yeah, sure. As long as it doesn't involve responsibility and commitment."

His heart ached with surprising sympathy. "Maybe if you acted like you were interested in a guy, he might get interested in you."

"Been there. Done that."

No, she hadn't. Not really. Neal didn't need to have known her for the last fifteen or so years to know that she had done no such thing. There was something about the way she held herself that said she didn't let anyone close. That she kept a big part of herself private, never letting anyone near.

Except for Nick.

Suddenly he saw the light. The truth came and shouted in his face. The been there, done that was with Nick. She had been in love with Nick when they were in high school and still was. In all probability, knowing his brother, Nick was unaware of it. She'd been dreaming that she could win his love with this little father-my-child plea. Nick might even be in love with her and still fighting his memories of Donna.

"Nick! I thought you weren't coming. Hi, Lisa."

Neal looked up to see his father grinning at him over his fence, along with a dozen or so other relatives. Neal glanced around in surprise. Their walk had taken them right by his father's house. This was the last thing he needed—or maybe the first. At least this would give him time to think through this latest discovery.

He sniffed the air and made a face. The smoke said something was being barbecued to a crisp. "Good thing you were a better doctor than cook," he said to his father. "Otherwise you wouldn't have practiced forty years."

"You coming in or just going to stand there criticizing?" his father asked.

"Uh, I've got Boomer with me."

"When haven't you got Boomer along?" His father turned to Lisa. "Get this boy in here, will you? We've got more than enough hamburgers for all three of you."

Lisa looked torn between telling his father that the last thing in the world she wanted to do was spend more time with his son, and being polite. Polite won, and she led him through the gate.

"Hi, Nick," a cousin called out.

"Looking good there, old man," another said.

"Howdy, Lisa."

"Wanna play soccer, Nicky?" a young voice asked.

"First things first," his father said, waving the greetings away. "Beer and soda's over there in the tub of ice. First round of burgers are already spoken for, but I'll get more on in a few minutes."

"Okay," Neal said.

His father was going to his barbecue, so Neal led Lisa and

Boomer toward the big metal tub on the patio. It was filled with ice, with cans of pop and beer tucked in among the cubes. Neal gave an ice cube to Boomer, who started chewing it vigorously.

"What'll you have?" he asked Lisa. "Beer or pop?"

"I shouldn't be here," she said, looking around. "This is all family."

He put a can of pop in her hand and took one for himself. "Don't be silly. Nobody cares if you're family or not."

"Everybody'll talk."

"About what? There's plenty to eat."

"About us, dummy," she hissed at him. "They'll make us into a couple. Are you always this dense?"

She was playing this well, hiding her feelings under a cover of normality, but he wasn't fooled. "They'll think we're friends, which we are. What's wrong with that?"

She rolled her eyes. "Have you just moved here or what?" She glanced at Boomer. "I'm going to find him a real bowl for some water. Come on, Boomer."

Neal watched her and the dog go into the kitchen, drawn by the slight sway of her hips but something more, too. He knew how she felt, the sense of not really belonging. Hadn't he felt that way every time he'd come here? He'd never been up on the latest stories or jokes, not even among his family.

He'd always felt like an outsider and guarded his words carefully, anxious not to give his status away, not to give anyone a reason to laugh at him. Not that they had. The family had always been great, welcoming him warmly no matter his mood. It was just that everything had to be explained for his benefit. He never seemed to be around when the real things were happening.

"I thought you two were skipping this."

Neal turned. His grandmother was at his side. "I thought Dad had canceled it and you were going to watch the fireworks with Marjorie."

"He changed his mind at the last minute, and the fireworks

don't start until after dark.'' She smiled at him slyly. "I guess that's true of a lot of fireworks, isn't it?"

This was not a discussion he wanted to get into. He glanced at the sky. "Looks like you'll have good weather for the fireworks tonight," he said. "If there's any rain in the forecast, it doesn't look like it'll come until late."

She didn't bother checking out the sky. "Can't ever tell, can you?" she said. "These storms have just been popping up at the oddest times."

"That's summer in Michigan."

"Want to open me a beer?" she asked, then waited until he'd popped the top of one for her. "You'll never guess who called a little while back. Neal."

Neal? "Oh?" His hand shook only slightly as he handed her the open can. "How is he?"

"Okay, I guess. Seems he got a slight concussion with a run-in with a steer. Was afraid we'd see something about it on the news and worry."

Neal frowned. "But you said he's okay?"

"Sounded fine. Said something about having some lady taking care of him, but that's Neal for you. Always has a lady around. He says this pet food tour is great."

"Huh."

"Strange, isn't it?" she said. "I wouldn't have thought this tour was something that would appeal to our big-city boy."

"I guess you never can tell," Neal said, wiping the condensation from his can on his shorts.

"Hmm." His grandmother handed him a paper napkin. "I see where the governor's finally going to name that State Animal Welfare Committee."

"He's what?" Neal froze.

Nick had been waiting years for that committee to be named, and it had to go through now, the one time he was not available. What was involved? Nick had never mentioned the specifics.

"Saw it on the midday news. The governor's taking rec-

ommendations from local officials and should have a list of
names of possible nominees in a week or so. Then I guess the
press will be hanging around, looking in your windows.''

He found it suddenly hard to breathe. ''Oh, I doubt that,''
he said with a forced laugh. ''Any of us on that committee
are pretty small fish. Not worth investigating.''

''Not unless you're part of that recall movement and want
to discredit the governor. Then you might be looking hard for
a nice juicy scandal.''

''Nick?'' Lisa was at his side. ''Your dad wants to know
how you want your hamburgers done.''

He looked into those fathomless blue eyes with their de-
mands of him and felt the governor's enemies breathing down
his back trying to jeopardize Nick's dream of bettering the life
of millions of wild and domestic animals.

''Well-done,'' Neal said. Charred to a crisp like his goose.

Lightning flashed and lit up Lisa's bedroom. She hadn't
thought she'd been sleeping, but it was almost three o'clock.
Somewhere after midnight she must have dozed off. Thunder
rolled along the night air, shaking the house and drowning out
the sound of the pouring rain. Another storm. She got out of
bed and went downstairs in the dark.

It was over now, her time to get pregnant this month. She
knew there'd be other chances, but letting this one slip away
hurt. She had thought she was so close. Damn that Nick.

Lisa stepped onto the porch. The storm had brought cooler
air. The breeze blew through the knit shorty pajamas she wore,
cooling her fevered skin. It felt wonderful.

Maybe it had been her fault. Maybe she shouldn't have
approached Nick with this right around the anniversary of
Donna's death. Maybe once the summer was over, he'd feel
differently. Or maybe not.

She noticed a slight movement at one end of the porch and
walked down there. The dogs usually slept here, but they were

gone, off to the barn, probably. In their place sat Clyde, a little orange kitten born to a barn cat last spring.

"Hi, little fellow," she said and stooped next to the dogs' beds. Clyde walked around her legs, rubbing against them as he purred almost louder than the thunder. "What are you doing up here? You looking to be a house cat?"

She picked the kitten up and carried him inside. He snuggled into her arms as she went from window to window, checking to see if it was raining in. It felt good not to be alone tonight. She carried him to her bedroom.

"You're not going to hog all the covers now, are you?" she asked him.

Clyde settled at her side, still purring as she slowly petted him. She could feel the aggravation drain from her system.

"I don't know where Nick's mind has been," she told the kitten. "From the way he's acted the past few days, you'd think I'd been talking to a post for the last month."

Clyde continued purring. Cat talk for "Don't stop petting now."

Lisa didn't. "We've discussed him siring my child nine ways until Sunday and then he's got the gall to say he misunderstood me."

A loud clap of thunder startled Clyde, causing him to sit up, but Lisa lay against her pillow, listening to the water pelt the pane. With rain like they'd been getting, folks were going to be saying Neal was around.

Lisa snorted and rolled over on her side. Hellfire. From the way Nick had been acting he might as well be Neal. Someone who lived in New York and was totally—

Another clap of thunder sent Clyde scurrying under the bed. Lisa sat straight up. Oh, my Lord. It had to be. That was the only thing that made sense.

The smoothly shaven, evenly tanned face, on a man who'd worn a beard for the last ten years. Her dogs suddenly liking him. The scar on his chin. The way he played dumb about her wanting a child.

Hell, Nick hadn't been playing dumb. He had just been Neal.

That horse thief. Those two horse thieves, for obviously the two of them were in this together.

She thought of how she'd stripped in the barn for him. How she'd tried to act sexy and even bought that stupid book. How she was going to kill him.

She jumped from the bed and raced downstairs, grabbing her truck keys on the way. Barely noticing the pouring rain, she ran across the yard and hopped into her truck, then raced into town.

That scoundrel. That complete and total snake.

There was no traffic, and she swung into his drive a short time later. The house was all dark, but that didn't matter. He was here, she could sense it like a dog senses a varmint. She marched through the unlocked door into the kitchen, giving a quick pet to Pansy and a surprised Boomer on the way to the bedroom.

Even though the room was dark, she could see Neal on the bed. She heard his heavy breathing and knew he was asleep. How could he sleep after what he had done? The vermin.

She glanced around. In the corner of his bathroom was a small bucket of water for the animals. Perfect. Wasn't that how you cleaned away vermin—washed it away?

She picked up the bucket and tiptoed to the side of the bed.

"Oh, Neal," she purred.

"Hmm?"

"Neal?" she said a touch louder.

"Yeah?"

"You bastard," she shouted and dumped the bucket of water on his head.

Chapter Five

Neal was awake. Wide-awake. He was also soaking wet, along with the pillow, the bed, the headboard, everything. What the hell was going on?

A flash of lightning lit the room, then he was in darkness with the rumble of approaching thunder and the pounding of rain against the house. Was the roof leaking? No, Lisa had been here. Or had that been a dream?

The sound of the door slamming downstairs got him scrambling out of bed and to the window. He was in time to see Lisa's truck pull out of the drive.

Damn. She had been here. Why? And why had she dumped water all over him? He kicked the dog's water bucket on his way across the room. Well, that explained where the water had come from, but not why.

He picked the bucket up, turned on the lights and went into the bathroom. Pansy jumped on the sink to watch him fill it.

"So what happened?" he asked her.

She stuck her paw out to bat at the running water. Neal wiped himself dry as he tried to remember.

They'd stayed at his dad's until after dark and watched the fireworks from his backyard, or at least the ones that had been above the trees. Lisa had seemed to have a good time. Then they'd come back here, and she'd gotten in her truck and gone home. He'd gone to bed—alone.

And woken up drenched—with Lisa leaving the house.

"Why'd she come over?" he asked the cat. "Did I do something? Did I say something?"

He didn't know which proved his idiocy better—asking a deaf cat to explain his life or needing the explanation in the first place. He turned off the water and put the filled bucket in the corner as Boomer shuffled in.

"How'd she get in, anyway?" he asked the dog, then grimaced. The good old unlocked doors. He was going to have to start locking them. And if it made people suspicious, that was tough.

"Well, you could have barked or something, you know," he told Boomer. "I thought you were a watchdog."

Boomer wagged his tail.

"Right, I know," Neal snapped. "That's what you were doing—watching."

He walked into the bedroom and stared at his water-soaked bed. The animals followed him. Not to help, though, just to practice their great, skillful watching.

"How could I have done something?" he muttered. "I was asleep. I couldn't say anything, either. I don't talk in my sleep."

A vague memory was shifting in and out of focus. He sat on the edge of the bed. Someone had called his name, and he'd answered. No big—

He closed his eyes. Damn. He could hear her voice whispering his name. Neal. Double damn. She knew.

What would she do now? A sick feeling settled in the pit of his stomach. He'd convinced Nick to do this, promised him that no harm would come of it. No harm to his patients, to his life. To his reputation.

Triple damn. Neal tossed the towel onto the floor and pulled on a pair of shorts, then slipped his feet into some shoes as he grabbed his wallet and car keys from the dresser. He had to talk to her, had to explain why they'd done this. Pansy was sniffing with disdain at the wet pillow while Boomer was wagging his tail, ready to join whatever game Neal was playing.

"No, you have to stay here," Neal told the dog. "Make sure nothing else happens."

Pansy looked up at that. Obviously something in the air told her that he'd just put a dog in charge, and she wasn't pleased. Oh, well, just another female mad at him. She could join the crowd.

He hurried to Nick's truck, getting even more soaked by the time he got in, and backed out of the drive. There was no one else on the roads. And judging from the dark houses he was speeding past, no one was even up.

He turned onto a country road. Away from the lights of town, it was blacker than hell.

His wheels crunched on gravel. "Damn it."

He'd wandered off the road. Slowing down to a tenth of a mile an hour, he eased himself onto the blacktop and opened his side window. Maybe he'd see better without the glass in the way. The rain poured in on him, not that it mattered. He could hardly get any wetter.

The road was black. The trees were black. The sky was black. He was totally surrounded by black and, with the rain coming down like it was, his headlights didn't penetrate two feet in front of the truck. Now he knew how Jonah felt in the whale's belly. Although Neal was sure he was in another part of the giant mammal's digestive system.

This had been one stupid, stinking day. He had to stop Lisa from telling.

"Ah, finally." The split rail fence across the front of Lisa's farm came into view. He took a right into the farmyard, then slowed to a crawl, watching carefully in front of him. Sure enough, within moments, the two black and white farm collies came dashing out to meet him. He brought his truck to a stop.

"You didn't have to come out in this rain, guys," he shouted as they all raced for the porch. "It's just me."

On the porch, they accepted his greetings, then followed him to the door. He looked for a doorbell, then frowned as thunder roared around him. Would she even hear a bell?

He pulled open the screen door, then turned the knob on the inside door. It was unlocked, of course. He pushed the door open just as an exceptionally bright flash of lightning lit up the world. For a split second he had a clear view of the foyer and the stairs right ahead of him, then the inside of the house was dark again. He hurried forward until his hand touched the banister, then he felt around with his foot for the first step. It would be crazy to stand in the doorway, shouting for her, when he could find his own way up. He'd call for her once she was in hearing range.

There was another flash of lightning when he reached the top of the stairs, and he saw several open doors along the hallway. The closest was on his left and he looked in, catching his breath as he did.

A night-light cast a pale beam through a doorway in the far wall. Enough to illuminate a slender form stretched out on the bed, covered only by a sheet. He forgot all about calling for her. His feet took him slowly forward as his body wondered if Lisa might be naked under that sheet.

He quickly rebuffed the idea. He was here to get some things straightened out between the two of them. Not for any other reason.

He stopped at the side of her bed, his heart beating a thousand times a second. A soft meow greeted him. A cat was leaning against the sweet curve of Lisa's buttocks. He wouldn't mind trading places with it, he thought. What had that cat done to deserve the best seat in the house?

Rather than groan, as his bad pun deserved, he found himself close to groaning at the hunger rushing through him. How was it that this woman had such power over him?

Maybe a touch, a slight brushing of his fingers on her cheek. It would be enough. It would carry him through the long weeks ahead. He bent closer and closer. It would—

Something hard collided with his head. The world exploded in a kaleidoscope of color and pain. "Damn," he bellowed, putting his hands to his head as he sank to the floor.

"Stay right there, buddy, or you're dead meat."

"Oh, hell," he moaned.

A light went on, but it didn't help a bit. The brightness made his eyes hurt.

"Nick?" She paused. "No, wait. You're Neal."

"Oh, damn it, my head hurts." His eyes adjusted to the light, and he was able to see the pistol in her right hand. "It's no wonder you can't get pregnant if that's how you greet the men who come into your bedroom."

"It's how I greet the men who sneak in."

"I wasn't sneaking," he said, his voice more thready than he would have liked. She hadn't been naked under the sheet, but the skimpy little knitted top and shorts didn't do calming things to his blood pressure. "Maybe you should try locking your doors if you don't want guests."

"Normal callers come in the daytime."

"You didn't. Oh, swell." He looked at his fingers. "Look what you did. I'm bleeding."

"Oh, come on." Sliding off the bed, she indicated the doorway with her gun. "Get in the bathroom and let me clean you up."

"I wish you wouldn't wave that gun around like that," he replied, pushing himself up from the floor. "It makes me nervous."

"It should." But she put the gun in the drawer of her nightstand.

"Thank you," Neal said. "For a while there I was afraid you were going to take me out in the field and shoot me."

"Not in this rain." She quickly made her way to her bathroom. "The ground being as wet as it is, it'd be pure hell to dig a hole to bury you in."

Neal followed, holding one hand to the cut on his head. She could flash him a quick smile over her shoulder. A little wink. He wouldn't mind. Anything to let him know that she had a sense of humor to match that beautiful body of hers.

But that was expecting too much. Hell would freeze over before she showed him an inkling of forgiveness. He should get a message to Nick, tell him the whole thing was off and just go home.

But he had promised his brother that he would take care of things. That nobody, but nobody, would bother him for the entire six weeks he was away. And a promise was a promise. Even to his low-down brother.

Lisa flipped the switch, flooding her bathroom with about three million watts of light. Neal blinked painfully.

"You need to use the facilities?" she asked, indicating the commode.

He gave her a confused stare.

"I heard that some people, when they've really been scared, have that reaction."

"Scared?" He couldn't believe this woman. First she thought he was a one-shot wonder and now she thought he was so scared he was about to have an accident. What kind of men did they grow here in Three Oaks? "What the hell makes you think I'm scared?"

"Your hands are shaking and you're whining a lot."

"For your information, I'm not whining." He gave her one of his thousand-watt glares. "And if I'm a little shaky it's because I haven't had my morning coffee yet."

He sat on the edge of the bathtub. The kitten that had been beside Lisa jumped into his lap, purring as it cuddled against him. She could take some friendly lessons from the little guy.

"Look up." She put a hand under his chin and lifted his head, then dabbed at the cut with a gauze pad.

Damn, but she had the most beautiful eyes in the whole world. That deep blue with her dark hair and fair skin made for a deadly combination. As if she could read his thoughts, her cleaning got more brisk.

"Ow." He tried to jerk his head back, but her small hand was damn strong. "Why are you scrubbing it like that?"

"We want to get all those nasty germs out."

She was smiling, but he couldn't call it pleasant, not even in his befuddled state. Her hands were surprisingly gentle, though, when she put a bandage on his cut.

"You didn't seem surprised when I came in," Neal said once she'd thrown the waste into a basket beneath the sink. "Did you hear me come up the stairs?"

"Nope." She wiped her hands. "Clyde played watch cat and woke me up."

"A watch cat?"

"And a darn good one, too."

Neal sighed, picking up the kitten so he could look him in the eye as he got to his feet. "Thanks, Clyde," he said. "So much for us guys sticking together."

Clyde yawned at him. Neal put him on the floor and followed Lisa into the bedroom. The storm seemed to be weakening. The lightning was less frequent and the thunder more distant. Lisa went through the bedroom, flipping on a hall light as she started down the stairs. No bed rest and nursing for his head wound.

"Why did you come sneaking around here, anyway?" she asked.

It had been stupid. Neal knew that now, but it was water under the bridge. "We need to talk."

"Talk?" She looked at him, rolling her eyes. "Is that all you big city guys can do?"

He wanted to tell her no, there were a lot of things he was capable of, but now wasn't the time for that discussion—or demonstration.

"No wonder New York has so many unhappy women," she said.

"We need to talk about Nick."

She turned at the bottom of the stairs, facing him as he came down the last few steps. "What should we talk about? What a big coward he is?"

Neal wished he and Nick had discussed this little situation so he would have had half a chance to handle it. Now all he could do was guess at things. "He's not a coward, Lisa."

"He ran away. And that's what cowards do." She made a palms-up gesture. "Ergo."

Then she turned away. But not before Neal caught a glimpse of the pain in her eyes. As far as she was concerned, the man she loved had rejected her. Nick had left an impostor to deal with her.

"You two are a little old to be playing your stupid games," she said. "They weren't funny when you were kids and they're even less so now."

"We weren't trying to be funny."

"Right."

"And it's really important that you don't say anything about this."

"I imagine." Her tone sounded extremely bitter. She pulled open the door. "It would certainly kill your fun if I exposed you two."

He didn't take her hint and leave. He wouldn't until this was settled.

"Now's not a good time to upset the applecart," he said. "That animal welfare committee is being named. I'm not sure Nick would get named to it if this came out. And that could severely hurt all the animal rescue groups in the state, not to mention yours."

He watched the blood drain from her face and was thankful her gun was upstairs. Although, given the fire in her eyes, that might not be far enough.

"You really are scum," she said.

He wanted to tell her it had all been for Nick's own good, but she was beyond listening. He shrugged.

"Get out," she said. "Get the hell out and don't ever come back."

"Lisa, please."

She turned away from him.

"Lisa, there's a lot at stake here. Personal as well as—"

"I said get out," she replied, not looking at him.

He didn't know what to say. His feet remained rooted to the floor.

"I'll think about it," she finally said, weariness filling every word. "Now get out."

His grandmother always said half a loaf was better than none. As far as he could see, he was getting a tenth of a loaf, but that was still better than none. He turned and left.

"What are you doing?" Lisa glared at Pucky cleaning out the horse stall, picking up the waste with a long-handled pitchfork and dumping it into a wheelbarrow. "Aren't Angie and Kurt supposed to be doing that?"

Her foreman leaned on his pitchfork and grinned as he wiped his brow with a large red and white handkerchief, but Lisa wasn't swept into Pucky's pleasant attitude.

When Neal had left early this morning, he'd taken the rain with him, and any chance she had of sleep. By the time the sun had come up, she'd had three cups of coffee but no food. After a quick shower, she slipped into jeans and boots and stomped to the barn, looking for somebody or something to cross her path. It wasn't Pucky's lucky day.

"Dr. Nick was out here pretty early this morning."

Lisa clenched her teeth. She'd been hoping that Pucky hadn't noticed Nick's truck but knew that was too much to ask. The old man was a light sleeper, and even though the dogs hadn't barked, he would have noticed them stirring. Or heard Nick's truck drive up the gravel lane.

"He was making a house call," she murmured.

"I thought as much." His grin grew even wider. "Seeing as how he didn't come out to the barn."

A red-hot glow filled her cheeks. "Where are Angie and Kurt?' she asked.

"They won't be here today," he replied. "The high school 4-H group is going on a picnic to the Warren Dunes."

Lisa made a face. "I keep telling you we should hire somebody full-time," she said.

"No need to. We ain't left short too often. Besides, it does me good to muck out the stables once in a while. It keeps me in shape."

"Not with your arthritis," Lisa replied. "You'll be laid up a week from this. Just like before."

They exchanged glares. "You're getting bossier than your father ever was," he said.

"Give me the pitchfork."

Sighing, he pushed the handle toward her and then, once she'd taken it, stomped off toward the door, where he paused. "Was Dr. Nick's visit too short? Or was it his leaving that made you so grumpy?"

Lisa had a good notion to send a load of manure after him, but he was gone before she could react. He moved fast for an arthritic old man.

The length of Nick's—oops, Neal's—visit this morning had nothing to do with her mood. It was the man that aggravated her so. A nagging little voice reminded her of the way her breath had quickened around him. How his touch had set her on fire with all sorts of longings.

It was all crazy. She was not attracted to Neal. No matter what name he used, no matter who she thought he was. There was nothing even remotely attractive about him.

Except for those shoulders. And his smile. And the way his voice seemed to slide down her spine.

What was the matter with her? He had laughed at her in high school. He had made her feel like a fool again now. There was nothing she liked about him at all.

That decided, Lisa worked through the morning, slamming the horse waste into the wheelbarrow and vigorously dumping it in a pile behind the barn. She checked Juniper's, Augie's and Starlight's shoes and took them out to the far pasture, put Nipsy through his paces on the jumping track and brought Ariel a treat of carrots. By noon, Lisa was exhausted but no closer to a resolution of her problems.

She'd like nothing better than to see Neal's butt in a sling and she wouldn't mind seeing Nick squirm a bit for going along with Neal's treachery. But she didn't want to jeopardize the rescue work they'd been doing. And none of that would get her closer to the child she wanted.

"Why can't men be more like dogs or horses?" she asked her two dogs.

She walked to the north side of the barn, relishing the shade and cooling breeze. She sat on the old bench and stretched her legs out. This evening, she'd give Colleen's answering service a call and ask her friend to call her back as soon as possible. It probably wouldn't matter much to Colleen which brother she was with.

"Nick and Neal have been switching places for years," she told the dogs. "And they usually got away with it. Heck, they even fooled their own parents."

Chipper sniffed the breezes while Rusty nibbled on his back leg.

"Them boys are alike as two peas in a pod," Lisa said. "Even more."

Physically they were identical. She used to think their personalities were different, but after this escapade, she suspected the differences were awfully slight.

"Both of them are two-bit sidewinders," she muttered.

Both dogs looked sharply at her. She glared back. "It's not like you guys are great character witnesses, you know. You were always growling at Nick, and he's at least got a shred of decency in his heart."

Rusty and Chipper turned their backs on her.

"Well, he does," she protested. "You shake hands with Neal and you'd better count your fingers when you're done."

As well as find an oxygen tank to help you breathe, Lisa thought, and slumped against the barn wall. Maybe that was the worst part of this whole ordeal—she could have taken being attracted to Nick in surprising ways. But to Neal? No, never!

"Now I'll have to find me another stud," she muttered. "And it's not going to be easy to find someone with the good, solid bloodlines Nick has."

Suddenly, she slapped herself on the head. "What a dummy I am! They have the exact same genes." She grinned widely and got to her feet. "And I don't have to beg anymore. I've got negotiating leverage, thanks to their little tricks."

Lisa picked up the dinner-dance posters from the printer the next afternoon, then went to the clinic. It was quiet. There were no animals in the waiting room, though the doors to all three examining rooms were closed. Good.

"What are you doing here?" Sara asked, looking up from her paperwork. "I didn't think you'd be in today."

"I brought in the posters." Lisa held one up.

"Nice," Sara said. "I can hardly wait. Tim and I haven't had an evening out in ages."

"Should be a great meal," Lisa agreed as she pinned a poster onto the bulletin board in the waiting room. She stepped back as if to admire it from a distance, then took a deep breath. "Oh, and I need to talk to Nick when he has a chance."

The phone started ringing as she spoke. "He should be out soon," Sara said as she picked up the phone. "You can wait in his office if you want."

Sara was busy on the phone, giving Lisa no chance to respond. It was just as well. Chatting was a strain. She was all knotted up inside and needed to get this whole thing settled with Neal. She took her pile of posters and went into the office.

"Thief! Thief!"

"Oh, hush, Baron," Lisa told the parrot in the corner. "I'm no thief." She felt a quiver in her stomach. Well, she wasn't. And once she had her child, she wouldn't bother Neal ever again. "Can't you think of something else to say?"

"Fire! Fire!" the bird cried.

"There's no fire here," she told the parrot and sank into Nick's desk chair. "None at all." She crossed her arms over her chest and glared at the feathered pest. "All right, there were a few sparks, but only because of hormones." She was not—and never in this lifetime would be—attracted to that scum of the earth Neal Sheridan.

"Excuse me, dearie," a quiet voice said.

"Thief!" Baron cried.

Lisa spun to face the doorway. "Mrs. Albright," she said. "I'm sorry. Were you there long?" *Please say no*, Lisa prayed. *Please say you didn't overhear all my nonsense.*

"No, no, Sara just sent me over. She said I could leave these on Dr. Nick's desk." The old woman was carrying a plate of brownies.

Lisa got to her feet. "They look wonderful," she said, feeling like a traitor.

She should tell the woman it wasn't Nick who'd be eating her brownies, but that impostor brother of his. But Nick wasn't an innocent bystander in this masquerade. He didn't deserve the brownies, either. Lisa kept her mouth shut.

"I can't stay," the woman was saying as she set the plate on the corner of the desk. "Michael is out in the car. We're going to see Shady Hills and then Ravenswood."

"He's finally talked you into a nursing home?" Lisa asked. The whole town knew how her son had been trying to get her into a managed care home for several years now.

Mrs. Albright nodded. "Oh, he's right. I've known I ought to move for a while, but I was worried about Leo. But now, because of Dr. Nick, I can."

"Because of Nick?" Lisa repeated.

Mrs. Albright beamed at Lisa. "He promised to take Leo for me and give him a good home."

If that wasn't just like Nick. "That's wonderful," Lisa said slowly. She felt some of her anger toward him easing. The masquerade probably wasn't his idea. Neal must have talked him into it for his own diabolical reasons, and Nick had been too good-hearted to say no.

"Yes," the old woman said. "Just yesterday, when he brought me some medicine for Leo's cold, he offered."

Lisa stopped. "Nick offered to take Leo just yesterday?"

It couldn't have been yesterday, that would have been Neal. And Neal would never go out of his way for someone else. Besides, that old battle-scarred reprobate of cat wouldn't fit into his life-style.

"Oh, yes, he was so sweet," Mrs. Albright went on. "He said dizzy spells could be dangerous and I had to think about myself. And that he'd take Leo when I was ready to go into the nursing home. I wasn't to worry about him anymore."

"That's really nice," Lisa said carefully. Why would Neal do that? He must have had some ulterior motive, something he figured he could gain from all this. Though knowing Leo, it was hard to imagine what.

"Well, I have to go," Mrs. Albright said. "Michael is so busy. I can't keep him waiting."

Lisa sat there long after the old woman had left, wondering what Neal was up to. She knew she couldn't be wrong about him. He was not a caring and thoughtful person. There had to be something about this whole deal that she was missing.

"Hello."

"Fire! Fire!" Baron screamed.

Neal was at his door—tall, broad-shouldered and utterly gorgeous. No, she hated him. He couldn't be any of those things. She got up from his desk as if she could escape her thoughts that way.

"Coochie-coo," Baron cried. "Coochie-coo."

"I came to talk," she told Neal.

His eyes glanced over her from top to bottom—probably checking for weapons—but she felt her cheeks redden from the inspection and that knot of tension tightened even more. Damn, but it was annoying, that residue left from her hormonal onslaught of the last few days.

Neal came into the room. "All right. I'm sure we can—"

"Fire! Fire!"

"Shut up, Baron," Lisa said. She needed to get this over with and then get out of here. She looked Neal in the eye. "I came to talk. You're going to listen." She walked to the door and closed it.

Neal sat against the edge of his desk, arms crossed as he watched her. His eyes were the softest shade of brown and she would have almost sworn they looked concerned. No, it was probably worry over what she was going to do.

"Nick and I already discussed the reasons I want a child," she said, looking not at his face but at the clinic emblem embroidered on the jacket he wore. "I'm not going to go through all that again."

He stood there so quietly that Lisa had to look up. His gaze was warm and sympathetic. She felt like kicking him in the shins. She knew it was all for show.

Lifting her chin slightly, she went on. "The fact of the matter is I've researched your brother thoroughly and I know he would sire a good baby."

Neal's eyebrows went up. He was surprised, but she wasn't going to give him a chance to start a discussion.

"But Nick isn't here, and you are," she went on. "And since your lineage is identical, you'll do as well Nick."

He stood away from the desk and took a step closer to her. A step too close. "I what?" he said.

She refused to let her feet move her backward. Not even an inch. "You're going to father my child," she said, taking a deep breath. "Or I'm telling everyone about the scam you and Nick are pulling."

Chapter Six

Neal felt Lisa's essence in the air all afternoon, along with the weight of her ultimatum. Given that he still had no idea what was really going on between her and Nick, there was no way in hell he would agree to father her child. So what was he going to do?

But no answers magically appeared between treating Mrs. Romanski's Pumpkin for ear mites and recommending a flea bath for the Waverlys' Rocky. He was able to put the problem from his mind for a time while he stitched up Blossom's foot and warned Missy Delaney not to let her puppy play where there was broken glass, but it was back full force by the time he got home.

"Oh, man." He slumped onto the sofa, stretching out on its length. "What am I gonna do?"

Pansy climbed onto his stomach, carefully walked up his chest and laid down, looking into his face.

"I tell you, little girl," Neal said, scratching the cat's head.

"This man-woman thing can really get complex. Especially with my brother involved."

Relationships were so tangled and twisted. Everyone's past wound around everyone else's, like a giant ball of scrap pieces of string. Pull the end of one little string and who knew what else in the ball would be affected.

"The only thing I do know is that switching roles isn't a good idea anymore," he told the cat. "Not now that Nick and I are grown-up. I know. It's a little late to decide that. So what am I going to do about this mess I'm in?"

Pansy rolled over on her side so he could scratch her stomach.

"Lisa loves Nick," Neal told her. "She told me she did back in high school and I bet she never stopped. The only reason she's trying to force me to father her child is because she thinks Nick's abandoned her."

Boomer came over, poking his nose at Neal's hand. Neal switched to scratching Pansy with his left hand so he could scratch Boomer with his right. Except that the dog had other plans—he'd brought a tennis ball for Neal to throw.

"What do you guys expect—that I can work magic?" he asked, but he tossed the tennis ball into the entryway for Boomer to chase.

A little magic would sure come in handy, but he wasn't holding his breath. Boomer came back with the ball.

"The real problem," Neal told him as he took the ball from the dog's mouth, "is whether or not Nick loves Lisa. But then, how could he not? Who wouldn't love her?"

He paused to swallow the growing lump in his throat. What man wouldn't love her, indeed? A beautiful body. Blue eyes that could be as still as a woodland lake one moment, then agitated the next. Rich, dark hair with a touch of auburn. The healthy glow of her fair complexion.

But that was only the surface. What really drew a man was the person all that physical beauty rested on. The direct way she looked you in the eye. How she told you the truth, no matter what. The way the air around her was clear and bright, and how everything looked more alive in her laughter. How you could spend a lifetime in her sunshine and never be bored. A sudden yearning took hold of him, a strange hunger for things out of reach. Oh, Lordy.

He moved Pansy to the sofa back as he sat up. "Oh, Lordy is right," he said with a shaky laugh and let the tennis ball fall to the floor. "This is all about Nick. Nick and Lisa. Not me. My job is to figure out why Nick ran away."

Since neither of Nick's pets was willing to clue him in, Neal wandered to the bookshelves at the far end of the room. On a bottom shelf was a stack of photo albums. Neal pulled some out at random and took them to the sofa. The first one he opened was from Nick's high school and college years.

There was a younger Nick at dances, before hockey games, painting the garage. In a good many of the photos with Nick was Donna. Sweet, quiet, always perfectly dressed Donna.

Neal picked up another album. It was from Nick and Donna's honeymoon in Hawaii. Picture after picture of a young couple deeply in love and delighted with each other.

The last album was a scrapbook of newspaper clippings going back to a mention of Nick's first blue ribbon at a county fair for a belt he'd made. He must have been about eight years old. Somewhere in his high school years there was a group photo of some of the town's county fair winners. Nick, with a dog he'd obedience trained, was among the half-dozen teenagers pictured. So was Donna, wearing a dress she'd made, and Lisa with a ribbon for a colt she'd raised.

Neal stared at the photo. It had so captured each of them. Nick was smiling at the camera, open, honest and relaxed. Donna was turned toward Nick, smiling nervously. Lisa was on one end, standing slightly apart from the others with a scowl on her face.

Neal closed the book and leaned back with a sigh. He'd always liked Donna well enough. She wasn't his type, but there was no denying that she had really cared for Nick. There was also no denying that she and Lisa were worlds apart.

Donna had been all ruffles, white gloves and lace. Lisa was denim and work boots. Donna did volunteer work in the elementary school library. Lisa rescued horses in need. Donna never raised her voice, never got angry. Lisa believed in slugging someone, talking out differences later.

Neal didn't see a thing wrong with the differences, but Neal wasn't Nick. Could Nick be afraid of his feelings because Lisa was so different from Donna? Or more likely, was he unaware of his feelings, never considering that he could love two such vastly different women?

Neal frowned. Regardless of what idiotic reasons Nick had for leaving, Neal was going to get him and Lisa together. They were made for each other. Neal could see that even if Nick couldn't. So he had to devise a plan to wake his dumb brother up. To make him see what a treasure he had for the taking.

And to do that, Neal needed to know just what Nick thought he felt about Lisa. There was no asking Nick, even if he could track him down, so Neal would have to depend on other people to get at the truth. Or as much of the truth as he could get without being totally truthful himself.

"This is gonna be tricky, Boomer," Neal said. "I have to find out what's going on between me and Lisa when I'm not really me."

Boomer had been snoozing and opened one eye.

"If you catch my drift."

It was hard to say if the dog did or didn't. He closed his eye and, after a huge sigh, went back to sleep.

Neal let him sleep, not needing a canine sounding board anymore. He got to his feet and put the albums away.

He would have to be clever, but that was no problem. He was the king of clever. He'd have these people spilling Nick's life's secrets without half trying. Then he'd know how to get his brother and Lisa together.

And when it was accomplished, he could go home. To what? a little voice asked. To his own life, Neal answered.

Neal honed his plan overnight. He would start with Sara. She was friendly, loved to talk and was around Nick and Lisa a lot. She would know anything there was to know about Nick and Lisa's relationship.

"Morning," he said brightly when he came into the clinic. "Looks like it's going to be a beautiful day." He waited until she was done writing something on the calendar. "We have a lot scheduled for today?"

"Enough."

"It was fairly slow yesterday." He paused while Sara pulled a folder from the file cabinet, then added, "I was glad Lisa stopped in."

"She came to drop off the dinner-dance posters." Sara put the folder on a pile on her desk, then flipped through several computer screens.

"We still had a nice visit," Neal said a little louder.

"Mmm." She found the screen she wanted and began to type something in.

Neal made a face. Some people were obviously harder to pump for information than others. "Of course, we always have nice visits." But then some people could just get more clever with their pumping. "Although that may be just my opinion."

"Here's your schedule for today." Sara pulled a piece of paper from the printer, then bent to look between the mini-blinds. "Looks like Mrs. Amanti's here already."

Fighting a growing frustration, Neal muttered, "Thanks," before turning on his heel and striding toward Nick's office.

All right, he'd forget about Sara. Trying to pump one of Nick's employees was a bad idea, anyway. She might feel she shouldn't say anything personal. What Neal really needed was someone close to Nick, like their father or grandmother.

As it turned out, though, Neal had no chance to pursue that line of thought. Along with a full schedule of appointments, he had three emergency walk-ins, a dog that had been hit by a car, a cat needing stitches after a run-in with a raccoon and a ferret who'd been stung by a bee.

He had no time to call his father until the clinic closed at five o'clock. But once Sara had gone home and the building was quiet, Neal picked up the phone.

"Hey, Dad," Neal said when his father finally answered. "How about if I buy you some coffee?"

There was a long moment of silence before his father finally said. "I just bought some."

It was Neal's turn to be silent.

"Although it doesn't spoil," his father said. "So I suppose I could take a can or two off your hands. Depends on what kind of a deal you give me."

Didn't Nick and his father go out? Neal knew his father didn't drink alcoholic beverages much, but surely he and Nick went out for coffee occasionally. Or in this weather, iced tea.

"It's a joke, son. I'm pulling your leg."

"Oh." Neal forced a laugh, feeling less and less like the king of clever by the minute. His father never pulled those little jokes on him when he called. He hadn't expected his father's relationship with Nick to be that different from his relationship with him. Which was idiotic, when he thought about it. Nick lived five walking minutes from Dad, Neal a two-hour plane ride and a two-hour drive away.

"Right," Neal said briskly. "I knew you were joking."

"Sure you did."

Time to regain his footing. "So where do you want to meet?" Neal asked, hoping his father wouldn't say, "The usual place."

He didn't. "I'm playing cards with some friends in Galien tonight," he said instead. "Like I do every Tuesday night."

Damn. Every way Neal turned, he ran into a wall. And reminders of how little he knew about the everyday details of people's lives.

"You got a problem, I can give you five minutes," his father said.

Oh, hell. He should do this some other time. "I just wanted to talk about Lisa," Neal said.

"What about her?"

"Ah…" Now that he had the opportunity, the words didn't want to come out. Couldn't he work without a script? "I was just wondering what you thought of her."

"What I thought of her?"

Damn. Hadn't Nick ever talked to their father about Lisa?

"She's a fine young woman," his father said. "You know that. I've told you that before."

So they had talked about Lisa. But how deep had the discussions been? "I know you—"

"Hey, Mike's here," his father said. "Talk to you later."

Neal stared at the receiver in his hand and listened to the dial tone. What happened to parents always being there for their kids? He was glad his father had a full, active life—he really was—but he needed to get this thing with Nick and Lisa straightened out. Although…

He dialed another number. His grandmother was actually a better source than either parent. She knew what everybody was doing.

"Yes." His grandmother's sharp tone cut down the lines.

"Hi, Gram. It's me." He cleared his throat. "Nick."

"What do you want, boy?"

"Nothing much. I just had a taste for some good old home cooking."

"Whose?"

Oh, man. He was really blowing this. Even Dad, a guy who never said a negative word about anybody, admitted Gram couldn't cook. The family joke was that if she sprayed processed cheese on your canned spaghetti, she'd provided a home-cooked meal.

"The Coffee Cup's," Neal answered quickly, naming a little restaurant in downtown Three Oaks. "That's what I meant."

"You in trouble, boy? Got some confessing that needs doing?"

Neal's heart skipped a beat. Damn. She knew.

"Spit it out, boy. I ain't got all day. I'm going down to Gary tonight and lose some of your dead grandfather's hard-earned money on one of them gambling boats."

This was swell. First his father and now his grandmother were going out gambling and carousing. He'd thought that small towns were into family values.

"That's okay, Gram. We can—"

"Oh, quit whining. You talk, I'll listen."

"Well, I—"

"But make it quick."

"I just wanted to ask you about Lisa," he said, trying to think quickly. "I...I wanted to get her a present and wondered if you had any suggestions."

"Me? You know her a lot better than I do."

"Yeah, but I'm a guy. I thought you might have some idea of what might be appropriate, based on our relationship."

"Based on your relationship?" she repeated. "And which relationship is that? Your old one or your current one?"

So Nick's relationship with Lisa had changed over the years. Just as he'd thought. "The current one, of course," he said. "I don't want to go backward."

"Then make sure your gift says that," she told him. "Let her know you've stopped running."

Neal sighed silently, tasting the bitterness of disappointment. So he'd been right. Nick was running from his feelings. This is what he had suspected, what he wanted to have confirmed. There was no reason for him to be disappointed.

"Well, I gotta go," his grandmother said. "I'm picking up Rita Bartell in ten minutes."

"Bye, Gram. Have a good time."

"I will." She paused. "You want some home cooking, boy? Lisa has a right nice home."

For the second time that evening, the dial tone sang its farewells into his ear. Neal laid the receiver in the cradle and got to his feet slowly. It had been a long day. He was feeling the strain, that was all.

He wasn't a relationship person, anyway, so it didn't matter that Nick loved Lisa. He was glad he did. Nick was the solid one, the family man. The one who needed a wife at his side to be complete. Neal wasn't like that. He was a loner, always had been and always would be. He liked quick relationships. Nobody got hurt because there wasn't time for anybody to get their feelings all wrapped up in the other. It was a great way to live, the best. He couldn't imagine living any other way.

"Come on, Boomer," he said wearily. "Time to go home."

Home to an empty house with a deaf cat and an old dog to keep him company.

More than you had in New York, a little voice mocked.

"Sure you don't want to come with me?" Pucky asked. "Five dollars for a spaghetti dinner's a bargain."

Lisa leaned back in the old wooden chair. Her bare feet were on the porch railing and a cold bottle of beer was in her hand. She shook her head.

"It's been a long couple of days and I'm tired," she said. "I think I'll take a pass this week."

Every Wednesday night the local VFW hall had an all-you-can-eat spaghetti dinner that she and Pucky went to more often than not. Normally she enjoyed the chance to relax and let someone else do the cooking, but not tonight. Neal had called a half hour ago to say he was coming out—with a bucket of fried chicken and a smile, as he put it.

Lisa had told him that his smile wasn't worth the trip and she wasn't hungry. Said all he had to do was give her his yes and then, since she didn't need him for another four weeks, he was on his own.

It would be safer that way in the long run. Not seeing much of him would keep those crazy thoughts from springing up unbidden. She wouldn't have to worry about her reaction to him or listen to someone singing his praises. But he'd insisted he had to talk to her, so here she was, waiting. Waiting and fuming.

It was bad enough that he hadn't agreed to father her child when she'd told him what he had to do, but now he was going to try to sweet-talk her out of it. She knew that's what he wanted. She had heard it in his sneaky little voice. All right, it hadn't been sneaky. It had been strong and forthright and just a little conciliatory. Probably was his talk-the-little-lady-into-something voice, perfected from years of experience. Nick wasn't such a smooth talker.

Although Nick had run away, and Neal hadn't. She took another pull on her bottle. At least, not yet.

A flash of blue caught her eye, and she watched Nick's truck pull into her lane. Her dogs jumped up from their cool spot under the porch and ran out to greet Neal, tails wagging furiously.

Pucky grinned at her. "Too tired, huh?" he mocked. "And to think I almost fell for that."

She glared. "He's just coming out to discuss stuff about the dinner dance," she said. "So you can wipe that knowing look off your face."

Pucky turned, glancing at her dogs jumping around excitedly. "You know, something's changed around here lately. I thought those dogs hated him."

Lisa got to her feet. "Must be the full moon," she said and walked down the steps. She wasn't going to stay around for a discussion of Nick and Neal.

But Pucky followed her. "There's no full moon for another two weeks," he said. "And it's not just the dogs. It's the way he's always around here all of a sudden. That look in his eye." He grinned at her again. "The way you're suddenly wearing sexy clothes."

She refused to look at her sleeveless, rather form-fitting knit top. She'd chosen it because it was cool, that was all. "The spaghetti's going to be all eaten by the time you get there, the way you're hanging around here."

Pucky laughed at her. "Anxious to be alone with the good doctor, are we?" But he didn't wait for an answer, going toward his truck as he waved at Neal.

Lisa waited on the stone walkway at the foot of the steps. Neal was greeting her dogs, scratching each one behind the ears. They looked so perfectly content, even Neal, like he was happy to be here. Like he belonged here. Like he was home. Which was crazy, of course.

She could hardly wait for her next fertile period. Get the deed done, then send him packing. Anxiety was making her hallucinate. It was going to be a long four weeks, and reading all sorts of positive things into his every action was going to make it all the longer. She'd do better to concentrate on ignoring him. Pretend he had no effect on her at all. Pretend that he was Nick and they were good friends. Period.

So she forced herself to smile at Neal Sheridan—veterinarian and con man extraordinaire—as he walked up the drive. The box he carried was the fried chicken, probably from the House of Cluck, but the look on his face was pure Neal.

She felt her heart start to race and her breath catch in her throat. There was a funny quiver in her stomach, like a sweet hope that that smile on his lips was due to her. That that bounce in his walk was because he was anxious to see her.

Holy cow. She closed her eyes for a brief moment to pull her heart into place. Nick and Neal were identical twins, mirror images. She never had this reaction to Nick. She would not let herself have this reaction to Neal.

"Hi."

Lisa opened her eyes and forced herself to look into his. They were sparkling with a glow that would drive the sun to tears. Damn him. He must have put a fresh set of batteries in his heart.

"Nice evening," he said.

Lisa shrugged, fighting to be strong. "It's not raining for a change."

"You know what I like about you small town folks?" He leaned against the handrail by the steps, still smiling at her. "You're so doggone friendly."

Lisa considered whacking him on the head with the bottle she held. That would be the way to fight his smart mouth as well as her traitorous heart. But there was still some beer in it and she was still thirsty.

"Would you like some beer?" she asked.

"Yes, I would. Thank you."

"Well, come on in." She walked up the steps to the door. "And bring your fried chicken with you."

"It's my best part," he replied.

She could feel him walking almost on her heels, felt his eyes on her, but wasn't bothered at all. The only reason she hurried was that she had worked hard this afternoon and was thirsty. The only reason her cheeks were flushing was because it was so stuffy in the house. Maybe she'd break down and turn the air-conditioning on tonight, though she hated the processed air.

In the kitchen, she took two bottles out of the refrigerator. "Do you need a glass?"

"No." He put the box of chicken on the table. "I want to give this country-boy thing my best shot."

Lisa frowned at him, not letting herself be pulled into any of his little games. "You want a glass, I'll give you a glass. I'm too tired to fool around."

"No," he repeated, opening the box. "Straight from the bottle is fine."

"Want place mats and napkins?" she asked, opening the bottles.

"No use going halfway."

A smile tried to break free of her restraints. Damn. This was Neal. His jokes weren't funny. His smile wasn't contagious, and his eyes did not make her knees wobble. She put the bottles on the table, sat down, pulled a drumstick out of the box and began eating.

They ate silently for several minutes, long enough for her to get rid of those weird thoughts as well as demolish the chicken and accompanying coleslaw and start on their third bottles of beer. Well, his third, her fourth, but who was counting?

"Maybe I should have gotten the extra-large bucket," he said.

"Why?" she asked. "You still hungry?"

"No. Are you?"

"No."

They fell into silence, but with nothing to eat, it was harder to keep her eyes off him. He was wearing a shirt of Nick's but he looked different in it. His arms looked stronger, his chest broader, and she could see a tiny flickering of a pulse at the base of his neck. She dragged her eyes away with difficulty.

"I know about you and Nick," he said.

Lisa glanced at him, but only for a second. "Oh?" What was there to know about her and Nick? This was part of some trick of his, part of his nefarious plan to change her mind. Well, ha! It wasn't going to work. She lifted her bottle to her lips.

"About how you guys are really and truly in love."

He caught her in midswallow and she sputtered, trying not to spray beer all over. This wasn't what she had expected. "In love with who?" she finally asked.

Neal shook his head as if he hadn't heard her. "I know he has a funny way of expressing it." He took a swallow of beer, looking everywhere around the kitchen but at her. "But I know it's true."

"You do?"

Where did he get this idea? Not from Nick, that was certain. She and Nick did not have some secret love for each other.

Heck. They'd talked about it a number of times. They liked and respected the other. But love, the passionate aching need to possess each other? No way. The spark wasn't there and never would be.

"All we have to do is get Nick to admit it," Neal was going on.

Her eyes narrowed. Just what was he talking about? Was this his great plan? Or—she looked at the empty beer bottles in front of him—was three beers beyond his limit?

"Neal—"

"Guys have these images, these pictures of what makes up an ideal woman."

It had to be the liquor. He'd be much more devious if this was a plan.

"You're one kind of a woman." He shrugged. "And Donna was another."

Definitely the liquor. "Are you saying that I'm not attractive because I'm not like Donna?"

"No, no." He reached over and took her hand. "You're beautiful. Really beautiful."

She pulled her hand from his. Not sharply, like her head told her to, but gently as if she was trying to be careful of his feelings. Which was stupid. This was Neal the smooth talker she was dealing with. Neal the ladies' man. Neal the scoundrel who couldn't handle his liquor. She shouldn't believe anything he said to her.

Why, then, were the words so sweet to hear from him?

"It's much more complicated than who is or isn't attractive," he said.

It sure was. Much more. Like, why did she care if Neal thought she was attractive? Why did she not want his words to be part of some devious scheme?

"Nick's very attracted to you," Neal went on. "He's in love with you. But you keep clashing with his picture of an ideal woman."

Maybe he wasn't the one who couldn't handle his liquor.

Maybe it was her. She'd suddenly become delusional, wanting things she'd never wanted before. Things she should know enough not to want, certainly not from Neal.

"I think you'd better go home." She stood up. "I've had a long day. We can talk about this tomorrow."

"I know what it is," he said with a sigh. "You don't trust me because of what happened in high school."

Good gracious! He was serious about this whole thing! He really did believe she and Nick were in love!

"I was fourteen," she pointed out. "And it was just a crush."

He shook his head. "I never meant to hurt you back then," he said.

"Hurt me? You didn't hurt me," she said. "I was really embarrassed and would have cheerfully killed you because of that, but you didn't hurt me."

"I was a jerk. You were so intense, so serious. It scared me that you felt so strongly. And at the same time, I was so jealous of Nick for inspiring such emotion that I couldn't think straight."

Lisa stared at him, a thousand things running through her head that would prove she and Nick were not in love, but all she could see was that scene twenty years ago.

She'd had a major crush on Nick and had decided to let him know how she felt. "I'd really like to be more than your friend," she'd told him one day as they walked to study hall, her heart in her throat.

He'd looked surprised, then grinned at her. "Cool. How about my slave?"

"Your slave?"

"Yeah. You can do all kinds of junky stuff for me. Clean my room. Take my tests. Iron my shirts."

She'd known then it was Neal, not Nick, she'd confided in. Her face had burned, her stomach had twisted, and she'd reacted in the only possible way—she'd slugged him. But now, looking back, she saw Neal from a slightly different perspective. He'd been jerky and know-it-all, but also he had been trying so hard to prove he was cool.

She picked up her beer, then stopped. "You didn't fit in any better than me," she said, just realizing it. He had pretended to fit in, where she hadn't bothered, but deep inside they had been the same.

"Damn it." He got to his feet. "This isn't about then. It's about now. You have to trust me. I can make Nick admit that he loves you. I can make you into the kind of lady he thinks he wants."

"You can what?" Lisa couldn't believe her ears. He was going to remake her? And to think she'd been warming up to this guy! "There's nothing wrong with me."

"Of course, there isn't," he agreed. "It's all Nick."

Eyeing him suspiciously, Lisa leaned against the counter, arms folded across her chest. They had finally gotten to the plan.

"It's all Nick's fault?" she asked.

Neal nodded. "I'm sure he really loves you, but he's so used to you, he doesn't see you anymore. You just need to learn a few ways to wake him up. Once you get him to look at you differently, you can go back to being yourself."

And in the meantime she was supposed to take acting lessons from Neal the great pretender? Let him teach her how to be sexy? What was Neal going to do, turn her into one of those sexy sophisticates he dated? Just because he couldn't resist them, it didn't mean—

A slow smile covered her face. That's right, he couldn't resist them. And if she was one, he wouldn't be able to resist her, either. All she had to do was time it right, and she'd have her child.

She stepped closer to Neal, resting her hand lightly on his arm. "There are so many things I could use help with."

She saw a flicker of awareness dance in his eyes, and she pressed on. "I mean, with all this girl stuff."

"Ah." He stood up and moved a step from her. "I was just

thinking of clothes. Hair.'' He shrugged. ''You know, that kind of stuff.''

''But that's so—'' she shrugged in turn ''—superficial. I'm more concerned with my ability to be a real woman.'' She stepped in close to him. ''Like those women you're always dating. Glamorous. Sexy.''

He was backing away again, shaking his head. ''I don't know anything about—''

''You're not afraid, are you?''

A number of emotions flickered across his face, but he settled on hard. Firm. Resolute. ''I'll help you any way I can.''

The sound of her dogs' frantic barking interrupted her fun. She put her beer down and hurried to the front door. A car had pulled into the drive. The two dogs were at the edge of the drive, barking.

''Chipper. Rusty,'' she called. They stopped barking and looked at her. ''On the porch.''

As the dogs scampered onto the porch, Lisa walked down the steps. A young woman got out of the car. Dressed in a summer suit, she was slick and sophisticated. Her blond hair was perfect, and her makeup added to her mysterious look of glamour. Lisa was aware that Neal was right behind her and that this woman was probably the epitome of everything he liked in a woman. And everything Lisa wasn't. The thought unnerved her, and she frowned.

''Lisa Hughes?'' The woman stuck her hand out. ''I'm Ellen Wilkinson from the Detroit *Sentinel*. I'm doing a story on the animal welfare committee the governor is about to name.''

Chapter Seven

Lisa shook the woman's hand slowly, carefully, as if it might commit her to something. "What can I do for you, Miss Wilkinson?" she asked.

"Agreeing to an interview and some pictures would be great," the woman said, stopping to dazzle them with a bright smile.

"Me?" Lisa was confused. "Why would you want to interview me about the animal welfare committee?"

"Aren't you the founder and president of the Hoofed Animal Rescue Society? We want to know how this committee would affect your society's work. And—" her smile grew wider "—we hear that Dr. Nick Sheridan works with your group, and we'd like your impressions of him."

"Uh." Lisa glanced over her shoulder at Neal. Now what? She had threatened to expose him if he didn't agree to father her child. And he really hadn't agreed. Yet...

He looked at her, his eyes not betraying one iota of his feelings.

Rats. Lisa had kind of hoped to see him crawl. Show that she had an effect on him of some sort, even if she wasn't as glamorous as the reporter. Delusions of grandeur. She turned to the other woman with a sigh.

"This is Nick Sheridan," she said.

The woman's face gave new meaning to the concept of brightening, hard as that was to believe, and held out her hand for Neal to shake. "Well, hello."

The word became a six-syllable caress, setting Lisa's nerves on edge. It didn't seem to bother Neal at all, though. He looked like a cat that had found a bucket of cream.

"Glad to meet you," he told the woman. Lisa could almost hear the purr in his voice. "I think I may have read some of your articles."

It was such a patent lie that Lisa wanted to throw up. Was this what he liked in women? She looked at the reporter with a more critical eye as she and Neal volleyed sugar-coated comments back and forth between them.

The reporter wore a cream-colored suit that was rather fitted, accenting her trim figure. Lisa could wear that. Her figure was just as good. Of course, she'd have to stay out of the barn and away from the dogs in that color.

The woman's hair was another story, though. It was curled and arranged with such studied windsweptness that it must have taken her hours. No doubt she'd earned her degree in curling iron skills at the age of two. If Lisa wanted her hair to look like that, she'd have to pay someone to arrange it for her. It would never last through even a quick cleaning of the barn.

"I'd really love to interview you about the committee," the reporter was saying to Neal.

"Wouldn't that be a bit premature?" Neal said.

His voice was low and teasing, and it sent little shivers down Lisa's spine even though he wasn't talking to her. She found herself wanting to purr at him. It was probably all the beer she'd had.

"Ask me again once the governor releases his list," Neal went on.

"I will. You can count on it," the reporter promised, and turned to Lisa. "What about you, Ms. Hughes? Can we talk about your rescue group and the committee?"

"Sure."

Lisa led her up to the porch, her heart sinking with every step. There was no way she was going to learn how to drive Neal wild with desire in four weeks. Not if she had to turn into Miss Glamorous here. Hell, four decades wouldn't be enough. This was a really stupid idea.

Neal slowed the truck to a stop by the broad porch. It was a beautiful day—bright sunshine, blue sky and green as far as the eye could see. Add a beautiful woman to the picture, and you had paradise.

He turned off the ignition and stepped out of the vehicle. But it wasn't a paradise that belonged to him. He had to keep reminding himself of that. Maybe it was a good thing they were starting their make-over program today. It would serve as a reminder to him.

Rusty and Chipper were already by his truck, doing their duty as the farm's welcoming committee. He squatted to pet them and scratch behind their ears.

"Howdy, doc." Pucky waved as he headed around the house. "You're over early."

"Weatherman said it's going to be a hot one," Neal said, standing up. "Might as well get all the chores done early." Not that seeing Lisa was a chore. No, far from it.

Lisa came out on the porch. "I don't know about you," she called. "But I have a busy day coming up."

Neal walked toward her, his brain drying up like a snowflake in this July heat. Damn, she was beautiful. She could go anyplace in the world—Paris, New York, or L.A.— and she'd still stand out.

"I have a ten o'clock meeting in Kalamazoo," she said. "That doesn't give me much time."

"So let's get started then."

She turned and strode into her house, leaving Neal standing there feeling a touch guilty. She'd agreed to this personal remake project last night but she was probably having second thoughts about now. Not that he could blame her. Hell, he didn't see a thing wrong with her the way she was right now. He'd take her as is and consider himself damn lucky.

But he wasn't the one she was in love with. And, once they got through some of his brother's hang-ups, everything would be fine. Lisa and Nick would marry and live happily ever after. He'd go back to New York and live his same old happy, uncommitted, uncluttered bachelor life.

Neal quickly bounded onto the porch and into the house. Lisa wasn't in the foyer. He slowly climbed the stairs and made his way to her bedroom.

"I figured you knew the way."

She was leaning against her dresser as he walked into her bedroom, looking so solemn, so apprehensive. She must not believe they could achieve their goal. He needed to see her smile, see the light in her eyes shine out on everything around her.

"Hmm." He looked around the room with a mock smile. "Something looks different here."

"Daylight is streaming in through the windows. Kind of brightens the place. Don't you think?"

Actually, all a room needed was her presence to be bright, but he wasn't going to make her uneasy with compliments. "No, it's something else," he said, pretending to think. Then he snapped his fingers. "I know. You're not armed."

She grimaced, but that light of laughter glimmered in her eyes again. "Would you like me to be?" she asked. "Is that something you find attractive in a woman? You think Nick would, too?"

"Somehow I can't see Donna packing a gun."

"What about all those glamour pusses you hang around with?" she asked, then grinned. "Nah, you'd never tell me the truth. You'd be afraid I'd send something to one of those gossip columnists and screw up your social life."

It was Neal's turn to laugh. "Not really. Most of my dates just want something presentable to lean against when they're out pretending to have fun."

Her smile disappeared, and Neal didn't know how to describe the expression that came into her eyes. It couldn't be sympathy—he had no need for that. He was on top of the world and could have anything he wanted. Well, almost anything.

"Let's get started on the inventory," he said.

"Be my guest," she said, indicating a door to her right.

He frowned. He'd thought she'd go through her clothes with him. Didn't she realize that this was going to help her reach her goal?

Well, he'd get started on his own. He walked into her spacious closet. Some clothes were hanging along the wall to his right, while on the left were shelves of jeans, sweaters and T-shirts. His feet faltered when he was assailed with the soft flowery scent she wore always. And he felt his skin grow warm as he looked at her clothes around him, feeling almost as if he was in her embrace.

"You finding everything okay?" Lisa asked.

He turned. She was in the closet doorway, a guarded look on her face.

"Uh, yeah. Sure."

He looked first at the dresses. There were only a few, and they were as different from Donna's as night was from day. Donna had worn soft and clingy dresses—frilly, lacy concoctions that said she needed protecting. Lisa's were plain, made of sturdy fabrics and in straight, crisp designs. Ones that were suited to her, that looked great on her. But not ones that would make Nick sit up and take notice.

"You don't wear dresses much, do you?"

"I run a horse farm," she pointed out. "That doesn't lend itself to dresses."

"But what about when you're relaxing?" he said. "When you and Nick go out evenings?"

"We both dress for comfort."

"And he doesn't notice you're a woman." Though how he could miss it, Neal had no idea. Lisa was all woman and would be no matter what she wore. There was no disguising her femininity. But rather than pursue that line of thinking, Neal bent to look at the shoes in a shoe rack in the corner. Loafers, moccasins, leather boots, sandals. One pair of heels.

"What do your women wear?" she asked.

"Oh, this and that," he said. "Whatever the occasion calls for." He tried to remember, and couldn't. His dates weren't all that memorable. Neither were the clothes they wore.

He came into the room and she moved, darted almost as if she didn't want to be too close to him. He felt something sag inside him. That old animosity was still there. He'd hoped she was getting over it.

"How about accessories?" he said. "You know, scarves, jewelry, hats."

She sank onto the edge of her bed. "I know you don't want to see my winter scarf or the baseball cap I wear when it's raining. The only jewelry I have is in that box on the dresser."

He glanced over and saw the box, then looked at her. She shrugged.

"Go ahead," she told him "It won't bite. All I have are a few pieces that belonged to my mother. Her engagement and wedding rings, a pearl necklace and a few pins."

She looked so vulnerable there, telling him about her mother's jewelry. He felt like a creep, like he was prying. He was only doing it for her, he reminded himself. For her and for Nick.

"Your mother died when you were young, didn't she?" Now where had that come from?

Lisa nodded and got to her feet. She picked up a framed

picture off the dresser and handed it to him. "When I was four. I don't really remember her."

He looked at the picture of a very young Lisa with her parents. Her father looked vaguely familiar. Neal must have met him when he'd visited Three Oaks as a kid. "You look a lot like her," he told Lisa and handed the picture back.

She looked at it herself for a long moment before putting it on the dresser. "Yeah, and how I used to hate it."

"Why?"

She shrugged with a forced laugh. "Oh, you know how kids are. You think if you were just tall, blond and tanned, you'd be popular."

He had a brief glimpse of that lost teenager, defiantly shutting out the world she wanted to embrace her. And of the hurt he'd inflicted. "I didn't help, did I?" he asked.

"Oh, you were a minor annoyance. Nothing more," she said. "So what's the verdict?"

Her tone had changed. The confidences were over, and they were back to business. "You need a few things," he said. "Some dressy dresses, some casual wear and maybe some loungewear."

"Loungewear?" she mocked.

"You know. Silk pajamas." He stopped to catch his breath at the sudden image that came into his thoughts. Silk that slid over her curves, molding itself to those luscious legs and those wonderful breasts. No wonder his voice had sounded weak and raspy.

She rolled her eyes. "You know how long a pair of silk pajamas would last if I have to run out to the barn in the middle of the night to birth a colt?"

"You don't wear them to bed," he told her.

The image of that was tantalizing, though. Too tantalizing. Lisa lying on her bed. Or on his, the one in his bedroom in New York with Central Park spread out below them. He found his heart was racing and had to fight back. He had to remind her—but mostly himself—that this was about her and Nick.

"The silk pajamas are to wear when you and Nick watch those Cubs games." He let his voice be harsh as he shook his head. "Jeez, it's a good thing we're having these lessons."

Lisa straightened. The confidences were definitely over. Her eyes flashed with annoyance, and there was no trace of a smile anywhere. "Have you finished?"

"For now." His words were sharp and his steps determined as he strode by her. He didn't let that faint flowery scent slow him a bit. "I'll pick you up around six tomorrow and we'll do some shopping. Okay?"

"Fine."

Neal hurried out of the house and into the truck, not even pausing to bid Rusty and Chipper farewell. When he was miles down the road, he pulled the truck over and let out a long, slow breath. In one way, it felt as if he'd been locked up for years and was suddenly free. Yet in another, he felt imprisoned, unable to move or think or even breathe without thoughts of Lisa.

It was a good thing he only had five more weeks. He could last that long.

"Ooh, now this is lovely," a clerk cooed.

"And with a henna rinse on her hair..." another said.

"Perfect," a third decreed.

Lisa clenched her teeth and stood still. She would not say a word. She would not rip this frilly, fussy pink *thing* off her body. She would not muss her hair up. Most of all, she would not kill Neal. She needed him alive, at least for four more weeks.

About two hours ago, they'd gotten to this little boutique in New Buffalo. Apparently Neal had warned the store they were coming. As soon as they'd gotten in the door, the store personnel had swept her into a dressing room larger than her bedroom where they'd descended on her like crows on fresh roadkill. They pulled at her clothes, yanked at her hair, pinched at her buttocks and poked at her breasts.

Under their orders, she tried on linen suits, silk pajamas and lacy cocktail dresses. Sequined sheaths and satin sundresses. Bras that pushed and squished and propped her up to unnatural excesses. And with each new outfit, they paraded her in front of Neal like a prize steer up for auction at the state fair.

She tried to tell herself that something good was coming from all of this—that she had not had one single solitary crazy reaction to Neal since they'd gotten here. No racing of the heart, no shortness of breath, no insane longings.

But that was only because her anger and frustration were growing with each minute. It was bad enough that the store personnel all acted as if she wasn't really there, but so did Neal! The whole time, she hadn't seen a single sign that he was remotely affected by any of the changes they were making in her appearance. She kept watching for some flash of awareness in his eyes. A slowing of his gaze along her leg. A quickening of his breath. Anything. But he sat there like some Roman emperor, voting yea or nay on each outfit.

Why was she doing this, if she wasn't becoming more attractive to him? That was the only reason she putting up with all this.

"I think a two-inch heel would do well," one of the clerks was saying.

"No, try the three-inch." Someone lifted Lisa's foot and shoved a shoe on. "See? Much much better turn of calf."

Turn of calf? What the hell was that? It sounded like something from a cattle ranch.

"You know, a three-and-half-inch might be even better," Neal said.

She looked at him. Was there a certain fire in his eye that said he loved the look of really high heels on a woman? Not that she could see. Was there a tremor in his voice that hinted his control was weakening? He was talking to the store manager, laughing over something—her inadequacies probably!

Suddenly Lisa had had it. She pulled off the stupid shoes

and flung them at him. They hit him in the chest and resulted in a satisfying "oomph!" from him.

"How do you like this turn of calf?" she snapped and turning, headed right out the door.

The jerk. The idiot. The absolute fool. Trouble was, she wasn't sure just who the jerk, idiot and fool was—Neal or herself.

She stomped through the tourists meandering on the street to the end of the block and found herself at the Lake Michigan beach. Why not? The warm sand felt so good on her bare feet, it helped to ease some of the anger. She walked a little way, past the families wading in the shallow water and groups of teens sunbathing on blankets, until she came to the bluff, then climbed the slope with its patchy bits of grass. After a brief moment of frowning at the flimsy pink dress she still had on, she sat and looked at the lake.

There was no getting away from it—she was the fool. Neal had offered to remake her, and she'd agreed. She'd gambled that in making herself attractive to Nick, he'd also be making her attractive to himself. She'd thought all she had to do was make herself irresistible to him and he wouldn't be able to say no when her fertile time came around again.

Trouble was, she'd never really considered the price her pride would have to pay. It was humiliating to be treated like a prize heifer. She wouldn't mind taking suggestions, but no one was *suggesting* anything. Least of all Neal. And she hadn't noticed him taking an increased interest in her with each change the clerks wrought in her appearance.

"There you are," Neal said.

Lisa refused to turn around, but a scraping sound told her he was stepping over the low wooden railing that ran along the boardwalk on top of the bluff. He'd come a different route than her but had found her nonetheless. There probably was some homing device hidden in this hideous dress so he could make sure she didn't keep it. Like she really wanted to look like some huge swirl of cotton candy.

"I was getting worried." He sat down by her side. "I couldn't imagine where you'd disappeared to."

"Into thin air," she snapped.

They sat silently for a long moment. Lisa didn't know if Neal was looking at her but she damn well didn't care. Maybe she should punch him again. It had been satisfying when she'd done it back in high school. And from all that happened since he'd come to town, it should be even more fun now.

Unfortunately she needed him. She did have other options, but she wasn't ready to give up on the Sheridans yet. No, she wasn't ready to give up on Neal yet. Looked like she'd have to leak some more pride from her balloon.

"I'm sorry," she murmured through clenched teeth.

"It was my fault."

She turned toward him. He looked almost as miserable as she felt, and her heart started weakening. She tried to hold tight to her anger, but it wouldn't let her. Damn him. Damn her silly marshmallow willpower. What happened to the Lisa Hughes who was strong and tough and hated Neal Sheridan?

She turned toward the lake. Some of the families were packing up their blankets and picnic baskets as the sun dropped lower in the sky. Moms and Pops and sleepy kids going home. She'd be going home once again to an empty house—unless she could coax the dogs or Clyde to come inside again.

That's what had happened to that old Lisa Hughes—she'd discovered that some goals required compromise. And that some old hatreds weren't worth the struggle to maintain.

"I thought we'd be going to the mall," she said softly. "You know. Pop into a few stores. I'd pick out a few things and you'd give me some advice about which would be worn where, and that would be it."

"I thought it would be more efficient this way."

She glanced at him. "I need that much work?" Fear had worked its way into her voice.

He looked appalled at her interpretation. "No, no," he said quickly. "I thought this way we could get everything done at once. Shoes, clothes, accessories. I thought it would be easier than tramping off to a dozen different stores.''

She bit her lower lip. She had to admit it made sense, much as she hated to agree with Neal on anything. "I guess it would be," she said slowly.

"So where'd I go wrong?" he asked.

"You didn't," she said and shrugged. "I just needed a break. Looking beautiful makes me exhausted."

"Would you stop putting yourself down?" he snapped.

She glanced at him, startled. She hadn't noticed how close he was to her. Or that glint in his eye. It made her nervous. No, not nervous, exactly. But there was a delicious tension in the pit of her stomach that would have been scary if it hadn't been so intriguing. She knew she should move away or at least get to her feet. She seemed unable to budge.

"Why do you think I was putting myself down?" she asked.

"Because you do, all the time," he told her. "Whenever you think someone's coming close to a compliment, you make sure they wouldn't dream of saying it aloud."

"That's crazy." But her laugh faltered.

"Is it?" He looked at her, and she had the unnerving sensation that he was looking into her soul. "You're afraid to be beautiful. You're as afraid of being beautiful as you are of letting people close."

"When'd you get your degree in psychology?" she asked. But the words hadn't come out as annoyed as she'd wanted, so she got to her feet. "I'm not afraid of anything. Well, maybe of not being able to pass the farm on to someone who'll love it as much as I do."

He got to his feet also. "Is that why you want a kid?"

"Of course not. It's much more than that." He was still too close. It made her heart race, and her brain had to strain to make sense of his words. "I want someone to share my life with."

He looked away, toward the lake, but somehow she was

sure that wasn't what he was seeing. "What if Nick isn't the one?" he asked softly.

"Huh?"

He turned to her, his eyes afire with some unreadable emotion. "How many guys have you dated?" he asked. "How many guys have you gotten to know? Maybe you're settling on Nick because he's convenient and safe."

The intensity in his voice caught her by surprise. It pulled her closer somehow, even as her feet tried to take her farther away. She wanted to tell him that she wasn't settling for Nick, that she wasn't thinking about him at all that way. But that would ruin his whole plan, and hers.

Besides, in some strange way she couldn't—wouldn't—explain to herself, it felt safer to let Neal think that. She turned and walked toward the boardwalk.

"So are they calling the police?" she asked.

He followed her. "Who?"

"The store. I didn't pay for this dress." She frowned. "Did you?"

"In a way." Neal shrugged. "I paid the store a retainer when I set this all up."

She stopped at the railing, judging how high she'd have to hike her skirt to get over it. "Well, let's hope you can get it back," she said. "I'd hate to think I was stuck with this thing."

"What's the matter with it?"

She looked at the pink ruffles, then at him. "I look like a giant swirl of cotton candy."

He laughed softly, his voice low and intimate. The sound wrapped around her like an embrace. He stepped over the railing. "I thought you looked delicious in it, but I hadn't known why until now."

"Yeah, right. You—"

He reached over the railing and swept her into his arms. Her heart stopped. Her voice disappeared. And the craziest warmth spread over her cheeks.

"What are you doing?" she squeaked.

"Getting you over the rail without further damaging the dress," he said.

Of course, it was something like that. Why else would he sweep her into his arms? Pink froth must destroy brain cells. Just like it made it hard to breathe and made her feverish.

Neal put her on the boardwalk. Her toes curled onto the dry wood as if she needed extra help in standing upright. Which she did.

"Good idea. We wouldn't want to damage it any more." She turned to walk in the direction of the store.

"Lisa."

His voice stopped her. When she turned to him, he took her hand in his.

"I think the dress looks beautiful on you," he said, his voice as gentle as a night's breeze. "Though I think you're beautiful all the time."

The fever came back, full force, and turned her cheeks to fire. She wanted to say something clever, but her mouth didn't seem to be working. His eyes had seemed to capture hers and she couldn't break away. Just as her hand couldn't get free of his.

Something stirred in his eyes, and he took a step closer. Lisa's brain told her to move back, to keep that distance in place, but she couldn't remember how. Her gaze slipped from his eyes to his lips, and a sweet wondering took hold of her heart. What would those lips taste like? What would they feel like pressed against—

Then his mouth was on hers, a light and gentle touch. The dew kissing the grass. The evening's breeze whispering in the trees. She felt as if she was just waking up. She had that slow, sleepy feeling of early morning, tinged with that bright hope of dawn. She wanted to stretch and purr and lean closer into him.

But then they both pulled away. Neal looking almost confused, chagrined. "We'd better get back," he said slowly.

They started walking, with an unnatural stiffness that came from trying to be natural.

"You can give them the dress and we'll go to a regular mall tomorrow," Neal said after a few moments.

What had come over her back there? And why did she wish it would come over her again, for a longer period this time? "We're already here," she said. "Going to a mall would just waste more time."

"Are you sure?"

Was she sure? Lisa almost laughed out loud. She wasn't sure about anything anymore.

"This is crazy," Lisa muttered to Neal as they walked across the ornate lobby of the restaurant. "We could have gotten a good dinner for much less at the Coffee Cup."

"I don't think we're dressed for a diner," he pointed out.

"That's just the point," she said. "We could be comfortable while we eat."

Rather than argue the point, Neal gave the maitre d' his name and waited while the man gathered their menus.

"This way, please." The maitre d' flashed them a quick smile as he led them through the dimly lit room toward a secluded table in the corner.

Neal followed behind Lisa. Well, he had to agree with her in one way—he wasn't exactly comfortable. Not watching how her black dress clung to her every curve or how her hair gently brushed her bare shoulders as she walked. He ran a finger around his collar to try to loosen it. No, comfortable was pretty far from an accurate description of how he felt.

They were at Miller's Roadhouse in Union Pier, about a fifteen-minute drive from Three Oaks, for a practice night out. He wasn't sure anymore who was supposed to be practicing what, but he was going to be practicing saying his brother's name over and over and over again. He had to stay focused on his mission, not get swept away like he had the other night when he'd kissed her.

He had to admit he was a little concerned, though. He'd gotten a postcard from Nick today from Paris, Illinois. It had said that Love was providing him quite an education. What did that mean? Love Pet Foods, certainly, but what were they teaching him? Maybe Neal should have gotten more details about the trip before he'd sent Nick on it.

"Would you like a drink before dinner?"

Neal looked up, startled, to find the maitre d' was still there. "We'll just have wine with the meal," he told the man.

"Very good, sir." He laid the menus before them. "Our specials tonight are beef Wellington, poached salmon in a cucumber sauce and New Orleans shrimp stir fry. Your server will be with you soon." The man practically bowed as he left.

As soon as the maitre d' was away from the table, Lisa closed her eyes and let out a low groan.

Neal felt worry clutch at his stomach. "What's the matter? Aren't you feeling well?"

"These damn shoes are horrible," Lisa replied. Her expression relaxed, and he was sure she'd kicked them off under the table. "They're absolutely barbaric. I'm sure glad I'm not a cocktail waitress in some fancy bar."

"You'd get big tips," he replied.

"And be crippled for life," she said, frowning as she turned her attention to the menu.

Since Neal had already decided on the shrimp stir fry, he sat there watching her and waiting. Her hair kept slipping forward and brushing her cheek. Absently, she'd push it back only to have it fall forward again. He wanted to reach over and do it for her. He wanted to be the one to brush that cheek, to feel the silky softness of her hair. He wanted—

Whew! He took a deep breath and looked away. Whatever Love was teaching Nick, he hoped that it brought him back here to Lisa quickly. If his brother didn't snatch Lisa up, Neal was going to put him down for terminal stupidity.

It had only been a little more than a week since he'd come to Three Oaks, and Lisa was already living in his dreams. Five more weeks of this and he'd be a basket case. This woman loved Nick, he reminded himself. Loved Nick, hated Neal. Maybe he should tattoo it on his wrist so he could reread it in moments of weakness.

Lisa put her menu down, and he pumped a few hundred extra watts into his smile. "What are you going to have?" he asked.

"Are you a waiter here?" She took a sip of her water. "I would think you'd have enough to do running the clinic."

"I was going to order for you."

She frowned. "Why?"

"Because I'm a man and you're a woman."

She sat back, her frown changing to laughter. "Wow, you're good. You sure got your money's worth out of veterinary school."

He bit back the urge to laugh with her. He was supposed to be teaching her the rituals, not flouting them. "Men like to do things for women."

"Oh, yeah?" She snorted. "I asked you to do something for me. I asked you to do the only thing that a woman needs a man for, and you got all prissy-faced about it."

She had to bring that up. "I did not," he said with the remnants of dignity.

"Did, too."

"Good evening," a voice said from beside them.

Neal stopped and glared at the waiter, who'd snuck up on their table.

"I'm Todd and I'll be your server tonight."

Lisa favored Todd with a dazzling smile, one bright enough to overpower the sun. "Todd, is it?" she asked.

"Yes, ma'am." The poor guy was almost basking in the glow of her attention.

"So you're a guy?"

The waiter paused, then stole a quick glance at Neal. Todd's eyes were flickering with uncertainty.

What was she up to? Neal was worried. "Lisa," he said. "There's no need to give the guy a hard time."

"I just want to ask him a question."

She turned her attention—and her smile—to the server, leaving Neal to feel like he'd been abandoned in the tundra. This was crazy. He didn't need her constant attention. He'd never needed that from a woman.

"So," Lisa was saying to the waiter. "As a guy, you like to do things for women?"

"Lisa," Neal repeated, his worries doubling. She wouldn't, would she?

"Ah, yeah." Todd's tone was hesitant as he clutched his little order pad. "Pretty much."

She wouldn't really shop around for a father for her child like this, would she?

Lisa's smile grew. "So—" She dragged the word out so it took fourteen minutes to say. Neal felt the sweat pop out on his forehead. "If I tell you what I want to eat, you'll get it for me?"

"Yes, ma'am."

Todd was beaming, confident and cocky, while Neal was left gasping for breath. Being with Lisa was like living on the edge of a cliff in earthquake season. He'd never met anybody who took him on such rides. And now that his heartbeat was almost down to the frantic range, he had to admit he liked not being able to predict where they'd go next.

"And what'll you have, sir?" Todd was asking him.

Neal started. He hadn't been aware that Lisa had ordered. Clearing his throat sharply, he ordered the stir fry and a bottle of wine. Todd gave him a knowing look, groveled a little more for Lisa, then left.

"See, wasn't that a lot more efficient?" Lisa said brightly.

"There are certain things that are tradition," Neal pointed out. "Certain things that make a man feel, uh, manly."

She just looked at him, a crooked grin on her lips and laughter in her eyes. "You're kidding, right? Fathering my child wouldn't make you feel manly, but ordering my dinner would?''

''I never said that.'' He felt caught up in her spell and tried to pull away. Tried to maintain his emotional distance, if nothing else. He was doing this for Nick, he had to remember.

''There are lots of things that make a man feel manly,'' he said. ''But some are safer than others.''

She eyed him for a long moment. ''I never would have thought you were the type that went the safe route.''

Safe? He looked at her lips that he so longed to taste again. He looked at her hands, wanting them to touch him. He looked at her eyes that held such depths and mystery. There was no ''safe'' around Lisa. Not as far as he was concerned.

Todd came with the wine and conversation was suspended while they played the ritualistic game of tasting it first. When Neal nodded his approval, Todd filled both their glasses half full, then left again.

Neal sipped his wine for a moment, reminding himself why he was here. ''So let's pretend I'm Nick,'' he finally said. ''What would you be talking about if you were here with him?''

Lisa shrugged. ''Well, ignoring the fact we wouldn't be here because it's too expensive, we'd probably be talking about different cases he had or the rescue group. If you were really him right now, we'd be talking about the dinner dance and what still needed to be done.''

Neal made a face. ''That's all work stuff,'' he said. ''Don't you ever talk about anything personal?''

''Like what?''

''I don't know.'' Neal thought. ''How you're feeling. What you're hoping for. Something you worry about in the middle of the night.''

''We talk about abuse cases that're worrying us. Or how we're hoping that the dinner dance raises enough money to cover some public awareness messages.''

''That's still work. You could say that stuff to anybody.

Aren't there things you can say to Nick that you wouldn't say to anybody else?''

She frowned. "I don't think so."

"Well, there should be." He reached across the table to take her hands. Their warmth shot through him, making it impossible to let her go. "You have to lean on him emotionally and let him lean on you. Come on, pretend I'm him and tell me something that's bothering you."

She looked at him like he'd lost his mind. "I did that once, remember? Actually, if you count the first few days you were here this time, I've done it a bunch."

She tried to slip her hands from his, but he tightened his hold. "Okay. I'll be Nick and I'll open up to you."

"No, be Neal," she said.

That took him by surprise, but he nodded. That would make more sense. He couldn't really be Nick, anyway. "Okay," he said. "I could talk about—"

"Tell me why you date so many women."

"I don't date so many women," he protested. "Only one at a time."

She shook her head. This time she did slip her hands from his and cupped them around her wineglass. "I thought you were going to lean on me emotionally," she said. "Or is that just too scary a thought?"

"It's not scary at all," he said and looked into his wineglass before his eyes met hers again. There was no reason not to answer her question. He had nothing to hide. "I date lots of different women because I've never met one I wanted to date a lot."

"Why not?" she asked softly. As if she really cared.

He shrugged, careful not to look in her eyes. His certainty that this was safe ground was slipping away. "Who knows? Maybe I like variety."

"Maybe you never let them lean on you."

"No, that's not true. I'm a good listener."

"But are you a good talker?" she asked. "Did you ever tell

any of them what you worry about in the middle of the night?''

He drank a good bit of his wine. "There's never time."

"There is now."

He put his glass down and before he could order them to look elsewhere, his eyes had met hers. Her look was so inviting, so willing to listen. So safe. Still...

"I don't worry in the middle of the night," he said with a brisk smile. "I'm a sound sleeper. Ah, here's our salads." Talk about great timing. Good old Todd was earning himself a hefty tip.

"Very informative," she murmured as Todd set her salad in front of her. "Thanks, Todd."

Something in Lisa's voice had been disconcerting. "What do you mean, informative?" Neal asked.

"Well, we know you're a chicken now," she said brightly. "And why your relationships don't last more than three weeks."

"I am not a chicken," he said sharply, gaining a quizzical look from Todd. Neal smiled weakly and waited until the waiter left. "I am not a chicken," he repeated.

She smiled at him, giving him a look that left him smoldering. "Hey, three weeks isn't necessarily a bad amount of time. In fact, three weeks from today sounds like a great time for me."

He didn't pretend to misunderstand. "Three weeks from today, you'll be turning cartwheels because Nick will be home soon. You wouldn't be interested in me if I came knocking naked at your door."

Her eyes glittered, but it was with laughter. "You know, you owe me a good long look at you in your birthday suit," she said. "After all, you saw me that way."

"I didn't look."

Her laughter danced in the air like snowflakes catching the sparkle of the sun. "Right."

His smile slipped out, then he began to laugh, too. "Okay, maybe a little. But only for medical reasons."

"Medical reasons?"

"Sure. To watch for signs of severe hay allergy or bug bites or even heat stroke. You might have needed CPR."

"CPR for a bug bite? You're a great guy." She settled down to eat her salad.

"Yeah." But his laughter died. Not as great as Nick, though.

As Neal turned onto the two-lane blacktop, Lisa took a deep breath of the sweet night air. She wiggled her toes on the truck's floor mat, enjoying the freedom from her heels. A nice end to a nice evening.

The moon was full, and a chorus of crickets was singing its praises, joined by an occasional bullfrog. The soft humid air was cooler, but it held enough of the heat of day to make it pleasant. It was as near to heaven as a person could get.

"Thank you for the dinner," Lisa said.

"You're welcome."

His reply was courteous enough, but he kept his eyes on the road before them. Lisa swallowed her disappointment and looked out the open passenger window.

Things had gone well tonight. At least for part of the time. She felt like she'd gotten closer to knowing Neal, and that meant closer to knowing what really attracted him. But he'd kept pulling back, trying to turn the conversation to Nick. It seemed like for every two steps forward they took, Neal jumped back about a mile.

He turned into her lane, and an army of centipedes danced in her stomach. It wasn't all that late, not quite ten o'clock according to his dashboard clock. And she wasn't the least bit sleepy.

"You want to come in?" she asked as the truck coasted up in front of her porch. "Have an iced tea? Beer? Whatever?"

"That would be nice," he replied. "But I have a heavy day tomorrow."

She turned in the seat to face him. Some light from her front porch fell on his face, but not enough to read his mood. "So now what am I supposed to say?" she asked.

He turned toward her. "What?"

"I thought this evening was a practice run. I invite Nick to come in and he's turned me down. So now what do I say?"

"Oh, right. Practice." He ran his fingers through his hair and sighed. "I don't know. Maybe just let him go tonight. Don't want to rush things."

Don't want to rush things? It was only three weeks until she was fertile again.

"So what do we practice next?" she asked.

"I don't know. I'll give you a call."

He was pushing her away. If she let him get away with it, he'd be all the way to Fort Wayne by the time she was fertile. But what was she supposed to do? Drag him inside?

"Okay," she said with a sigh and, leaning forward, brushed his cheek with her lips.

It was just a quick kiss, the lightest of touches, but she felt him stir. She felt the air become charged all of a sudden. Hunger came out of the shadows and nipped at her heels. She wanted him to take her in his arms and felt he wanted her there. The night was still, waiting on edge for the need to break loose.

"Oh, Lisa," he groaned.

Then his arms were around her, his mouth was on hers and all heaven seemed to break loose. It was as if all the laughter and sunshine and magic in the world were in his lips. Her heart cried out for joy, finding a wonder in his touch that she'd never expected existed. This was so much more than she'd ever dreamed about.

His embrace was crushing, his lips demanding as if his hungers were stronger than reason. But she wanted only to be held tighter, harder, longer. Her mouth moved against his, her hands pulling him closer and closer as they roamed over the hard muscles of his back. There was a need in her she'd never felt before, not like this. Not in this overpowering, thunderous way.

A tension grew in her, and her heart raced. Her lips sought to devour him. Just brushing his mouth with hers was no longer enough. She felt his hands move, one cupping the back of her head, twining in her hair, as the other slid to her waist. Wherever they touched, she seemed afire.

But then Neal pulled away slowly, regretfully. They were left in the semidarkness, the only sound their ragged breathing. His face was in shadow. She couldn't read his thoughts or his mood. Not that she was in any shape to discern anything. Her hands were shaking as badly as her heart.

"I'd better go in," she said.

"Right."

Stumbling, she picked up her shoes and got out of the truck. The gravel felt good on her bare feet. It hurt, and that made her feel sensible again. She shut the door and hurried to the porch steps.

"Lisa."

Her heart stuttered as she turned.

He leaned out the window. "You should wear those heels a little bit every day," he said. Though his voice was shaky, it was far more in control than she felt. "The more you practice, the less your feet will hurt."

For a moment, she considered throwing the damn shoes at him, but didn't. "I'll wear them to clean out the barn tomorrow," she promised, then bounded up the stairs.

She didn't let herself turn around until the crunching of the gravel told her that Neal was pulling out. Then she stared at the red lights disappearing down her lane. This was never going to work. It was time to get out that book again.

Chapter Eight

"Thanks, Doc. Appreciate you coming out all this way."

"Glad I could help," Neal replied as he soaped up his arms in the big cast-iron sink in the corner of the barn. "Not too often twins come along, let alone triplets."

One of the man's cows had gone into labor, but the calf that had come out had been awfully small. Neal had reached inside to see if another one was in there, and sure enough, there was. And not one more, but two! Triplets! What an experience. Neal had spent so much time in front of the TV cameras, he'd forgotten what a miracle birth was. It had been an indescribable thrill to see the three calves wobble and try to stand.

"Used to take care of that kind of stuff myself," the cattle farmer said. "Can't do it anymore, what with the arthritis and all."

"No problem." Neal took the towel the man was holding and dried his arms. "It was a nice day for a drive."

"Made you late for your meeting, though," the man said.

Neal shrugged. "Believe me, there'll always be another meeting to go to."

He picked up his bag and together they walked to his truck. The sun was shining, the birds singing and the air was as sweet and fresh as it could be. This had been incredible. Amazing. He couldn't wait to tell Lisa all about—

He frowned. What was he thinking? Lisa wasn't his to run to with stories. She was Nick's. Much as he wanted to share his excitement with her, he couldn't. He wouldn't. He'd just have to be content with telling Boomer and Pansy. They were good listeners. It didn't matter that Pansy was deaf.

He stopped at the truck to take off the coverall Nick kept behind the front seat for such jobs as this, then changed his shoes. Hell. He didn't have to tell anybody anything. He'd never been one for sharing stuff. Why this sudden urge to now?

"Boy, you and your brother both're in the news these days," the man said. "Kinda funny, ain't it?"

Neal looked up. He knew Nick had been named to the governor's animal welfare committee. The official word had come to the clinic this morning by certified mail, but what had Neal been doing?

"Neal was in the news, too?" he asked. "This about his concussion?"

The man shook his head. "Nah, that was last week. He was in some bar fight in St. Louis. Saw it on 'Worldwide's Wide World.'"

Nick in a bar fight? It seemed impossible. Had to be impossible. Worldwide was just making up stories, like they usually did. The tabloid paper and its television counterpart had never been big on accuracy. Nothing to worry about.

"Looks like we're going to have ourselves another gully washer," the farmer said.

Neal followed the man's gaze and saw the black clouds moving in from the west. Great. Another rainstorm, another round of "Neal must be in town" jokes.

"You're welcome to wait here, if you like."

"No." Neal shook his head. "I probably have time to get into New Buffalo before it hits. Maybe I can catch the tail end of my meeting."

He'd skip it without a qualm except that it was a luncheon for representatives of all the nonprofit groups in the county. Lisa's rescue group was making a pitch for their dinner dance, and he felt he should be there. Or rather, Nick should be there.

Neal tossed his things onto the front seat of the truck and climbed in after them. "Call me if there's any problems with the little guys or their mom," Neal told the farmer, then with a wave drove to the highway.

He needed to be at the meeting for another reason, too, one that only vaguely related to Nick. He needed practice seeing Lisa and not being affected. It was this nonsense of wanting to tell her about the births this morning. Or being so affected by her closeness that day last week when he'd kissed her. Or the other night at dinner, when she'd led him this way and that—and he'd loved every nerve-racking minute of it.

No, he needed to take a new stand with her. He was teaching her how to catch Nick's attention, so it was time he acted like a teacher, not a love-struck student.

The meeting was in the conference room at the Captain's Cove Inn. Just as Neal pulled into the parking lot, the rain started. He ran for the door, but still managed to get wet.

"Boy, the rain we've been having this last week or so," the reservations clerk said, shaking her head. She barely looked twenty-one, too young to have heard the stories.

Neal relaxed. "Making up for lost time," he said and nodded toward the meeting room. "I'm here for the luncheon."

"Oh, sure. Go on back," she said. "I think you missed lunch, though. You want me to bring you something?"

He shook his head, his feet hurrying him toward the room. He thought he could hear Lisa's voice. She must be speaking to the group.

He slipped into the room quietly. There were about a half-dozen round tables in the middle of the room, all filled, and a long table at the far end with the podium in the center. Lisa was standing at it, her face lit with an inner glow as she spoke about the work the rescue group did. She told a story of a horse they'd saved and spoke about the needs to reach more people with word of their organization. Her voice was impassioned, and her eyes sparkled with love for what she did.

For a moment, her gaze met his over the heads of the seated guests, and it seemed that she was talking just to him. The words were about the dinner dance, but her eyes were saying something else. Her eyes were speaking straight to his soul, daring it to come alive in her laughter. Daring him to break his three-week rule. Daring him to look at life like he never had before.

Then suddenly she was done speaking and was going to her seat. The eye contact was gone. The spell was broken. Neal felt he could breathe again, yet in another way felt he couldn't find any air. It was crazy. Must be the barometric pressure. Or the fact he missed lunch.

Another voice was encouraging people to buy tickets for the dinner dance, then adjourned the meeting. Neal was torn between fleeing and meeting his weakness head-on. Only a coward would run, he told himself, and started to work his way through the departing crowd.

"Hey, Nick," someone said. "Heard about your appointment."

"Congratulations," another called out.

"Good job."

Neal smiled and laughed and shook hands as he wove around tables and chairs and busboys starting to clear away dishes. Little by little, he got closer to the table where Lisa was standing. She looked so fresh, so much like summer in her sleeveless top—

What was she wearing? He stopped, only to be nudged into moving again by a man with a briefcase.

"Sorry, Nick," the man murmured. "But I think you're going the wrong way."

Neal laughed. "You know me, always bucking tradition."

The other man smiled and moved with the crowd while Neal strained to catch sight of Lisa again. She wasn't wearing one of the new summer suits they'd picked out last week. She was in a sleeveless knit top and denim skirt. He spotted her again and moved closer, near enough so he could see her feet. She was wearing sandals! Where were her heels? Didn't she understand how important this all was? How was she going attract Nick's attention if she didn't look more like Donna?

A panic clutched at Neal's belly, only to be displaced by that all too familiar fire as Lisa caught sight of him. Her smile set his heart ablaze, and his body followed suit. He wanted to sweep her into his arms. He wanted to kiss those laughing lips and crush that oh, so wonderful body against his.

He wanted to go back to New York. Now. Before he betrayed Nick's trust in him.

"Hi," Lisa said as he stopped in front of her.

He couldn't speak. Her hair was like silk, like the darkest midnight. His hands needed to touch it, to feel if it was as soft as it looked. He needed to bury his face in it and be lost in her scent. He took a deep breath. Nick and Lisa, Nick and Lisa, he reminded himself.

"How are you?" he managed to ask.

But then a woman came rushing over to the table and asked Lisa a question. Tickets to the dinner dance were exchanged for a check, then pleasantries were mouthed and promises to get together sometime, before Lisa was smiling at him.

"We've sold almost twenty pairs of tickets here alone," she said as she slipped a pile of checks into an envelope.

"Good." He would not get caught up in her excitement. He was a guide, a teacher. The one who would lead her to Nick's side. "Why didn't you wear your shoes?"

"Shoes?" She frowned, then looked at her feet. "These are shoes."

But they were shoes for the old Lisa. She had to become the new one. "I meant your high heels," he said. "I thought we'd agreed you needed practice walking in them."

"They didn't go with this skirt."

He shook his head. "Why didn't you wear that suit we bought?"

"This skirt and blouse are new," she said. "I thought the suit was too dressy. Besides, why waste all the new stuff when Nick isn't here to see them?"

Neal looked around nervously at the mention of Nick's name. No one was close enough to have heard. "You need to practice wearing all the stuff," he whispered. "You can't just put them on when Nick shows up and expect to feel natural in them."

"I don't think I'm ever going to feel natural in them."

Her voice had a faint hint of worry in it. He wanted to take her hands in his and tell her it would work. He wanted to give her hope and bring back that sparkle to her eyes.

He wanted to say the hell with Nick, but he couldn't.

"You can't think like that," he said.

She put her papers into a canvas briefcase and clasped it shut. "Maybe I need more specialized practice," she said, then turned to catch his gaze. "Do you think I look better in them?"

He could have sworn she batted her eyelashes at him. Or maybe it was just her nearness making him flash in and out of consciousness. He wanted to tell her she looked wonderful in anything. In nothing. But that wouldn't do. He had to think of what Nick would like.

"Of course I do," he said. "Would I have gone to all that trouble to get them if I didn't?"

Her eyes flashed, and her jaw got a stubborn look to it. "Well, I didn't tell you to go to all that trouble," she snapped.

"I didn't have much choice, did I?"

"You had lots of choices. You were just too chicken to

pick the easiest one." She grabbed her briefcase and spun around, looking ready to stomp out.

"I am not a—"

He moved as she turned, and somehow her briefcase slammed into his stomach. Well, somewhat below his stomach. Hard.

Hell. She was hitting him again! He'd known this was going to happen. No matter how nice he tried to be, she was going to find a reason to hit him.

Lisa's hands flew to her mouth. "Oh, Neal. I'm so—"

"Don't apologize." The words snapped Neal's head up in time to see his grandmother marching down on them. "Women are always apologizing. That's why the world thinks they're responsible for making everyone happy."

"I didn't mean to hit him," Lisa said.

"A lot of good that does me," Neal said.

"Oh, quit your whining, boy," Gram said. "You've always been an aggravator. You deserve what you got and more."

Lisa shook her head. "Are you all right?" she asked him.

He nodded. "I just wasn't expecting it, that's all."

"I believe that," Gram said. "You men aren't very observant."

Hell, why didn't they all pick on him? "I'm very observant," he said. "I just wasn't expecting her to slug me again."

"I didn't slug you," Lisa pointed out. "I accidentally hit you with my briefcase. Now, if you want to see slugging—"

"I've seen it. Or felt it," he corrected. "I don't need to again."

"Come on, dear." Gram pulled at Lisa's arm. "Maybe you can drive me home. That boy's getting too cranky for company."

Oh, Lordy. He didn't need to feel her slugging again. He'd done it now. He'd let the cat out of the bag.

But even as he tried to work up worry that his grandmother knew he was Neal, he only felt a keen sense of loss as he watched Lisa leave. He'd hurt her again.

* * *

"Who are the flowers for, Dr. Nick?" The middle-aged woman gave him a sly grin as she wrapped the long-stemmed roses. "Anyone special?"

Neal tried to keep his smile. Boy, the joys of small-town living. "For my grandmother," he said.

"Oh, sure. Like every young man gives his grandmother long-stemmed roses." The woman shook her head. "Isn't it wonderful how she's getting on since the cast came off? She really hated that thing, didn't she?"

Neal could only stare at her. What cast? "Uh, I don't think any of us like them," he said lamely.

The woman nodded. "You're right there. Though some breaks would be less annoying that your right wrist."

His grandmother had broken her wrist? When? Why hadn't anyone told him?

"It's so nice to see you're moving on with life." The flower lady handed him the roses. "So who are these really for?"

Oh, what the hell. Everyone found out everything anyway. "They're for Lisa," he said. He hoped he wouldn't have to go into the whole story of how he owed her an apology for his behavior at noon.

But the woman sniffed slightly as she took his money. "Fine, don't tell me," she said.

Neal didn't argue. He knew by now he couldn't win. He took the flowers and headed into the late afternoon heat.

So his grandmother had broken her wrist recently. What else didn't he know about his own family? He was used to not knowing all the little family jokes, since he wasn't around for the day-to-day minutia that inspired them. But something like her health? Did they not tell him because they didn't want him to worry? Or just because they never thought to?

Just another month in this backwater. Another month and Nick would be home and reunited with Lisa. Then Neal would be out of here. Gone so fast that they wouldn't even see his smoke. He'd had more than enough of Three Oaks. The place did nothing but upset his ordered life.

Lisa's fence came into view, and he turned into her lane. He slowed, as always, expecting the dogs to come running out, but they didn't. Was it too hot for them? He stopped the truck next to the house. When he turned off the motor, he heard barking from the back of the house. Was something wrong?

He jumped out of the truck and ran toward the sound. Chipper and Rusty were in the backyard, facing the porch, barking at something on the roof. Lisa!

"What are you doing?" he cried.

She was standing amid the overhanging branches of a big oak tree. Not that close to the edge of the roof, but not that far, either.

She looked at him. "Clyde's in the tree."

He looked through the branches, expecting to see a child up there. He saw nothing but leaves. "Who's Clyde?"

"The kitten," she said. "You know. My watch cat."

Oh, right. His good buddy who ratted on him. Neal moved under the branches of the tree. Far up, off to one side, he thought he saw a little speck of orange. He stepped out into the open.

"If he got up, can't he get down?" he called to Lisa.

"He was chasing a squirrel and went too high. He hasn't moved for an hour." She took another step into the branches of the tree. "I can almost reach him. If this roof was just another foot wider..."

"Just stay back," Neal told her. "There's got to be another way to reach him."

He went under the tree and looked at the branches. They were spaced pretty well for climbing. He should be able to get a reasonable distance up the tree, assuming he remembered how to do it. But wasn't tree climbing something you never forgot how to do? Or was that riding a bike?

"You're not climbing up, too, are you?" Lisa called. "We don't need two of you stuck in the tree."

Boy, great image she had of him. No wonder she was always slugging him. He grabbed a low branch and swung himself up. Luckily, he had athletic shoes on. He went up to one level and then the next. Before too long, he could see Clyde easily—clinging to a narrow branch, his back toward the main trunk. Not too much farther. Only a few more branches up and a few more over. Of course, those branches had to be rather puny ones. The kitten was looking over his shoulder, eyeing Neal with a mixture of apprehension and relief.

"So, Clyde, you gonna rat on me again?" Neal asked him, inching around the trunk to Clyde's side. "Or are we best buddies from now on?"

"You can't put conditions on rescuing him!" Lisa cried from somewhere to his right.

"This is a private moment between two guys," he told her. "You're not supposed to be eavesdropping."

If he slid out on that branch a couple of feet, he should be able to reach the kitten. Assuming the branch held his weight. And that the cat didn't decide to scoot farther away. Neal's hand hit some sticky sap. Well, even if his feet slipped, his hand would be cemented to the tree.

"Are you getting close to him?" Lisa asked.

"He doesn't want to," Neal said. "He said he's not into male bonding."

"Would you stop joking for a change?"

Neal slid out a step on the branch he'd chosen, holding on to Clyde's branch at the same time. His foot branch sagged slightly, and leaves brushed his back. He slid out a little more. It sagged a little more, but it didn't feel like it was cracking. Except he'd lost sight of Clyde amid the leaves and had to move farther out to see him again. Why was he doing this?

"If I fall to my death here, will you remember me kindly?" he called to Lisa.

"Would you quit joking?"

Neal looked at the kitten. "Should I take that for a yes?" The cat meowed softly. "That's what I thought. She's a hard woman to please, isn't she?"

"I heard that."

One more step. "Well, Clyde, old man. Here's what's happening. I'm gonna come closer and you're not going to run farther away. When I take hold of you, you aren't going to squirm, hiss, bite or jump, got it?"

"He's got it."

Neal glanced in the direction of Lisa's voice but saw only leaves and more leaves. Just as well. He didn't need the distraction of seeing her.

"Okay, Clyde, here we go."

He reached out slowly and carefully and then with a quick snatch, grabbed the kitten by the back of its neck. After a meow, it let go of the branch and let Neal pick it up. Except...

"Now what?"

"What?" Lisa cried. "What happened?"

"Nothing." Except here he was, twenty feet above the ground in a tree with only one free hand to get him down. He turned Clyde slightly and looked at him. He didn't look ready to nestle on Neal's shoulder while Neal climbed down. Well, the kitten wouldn't fit in his pocket. There was only one other place.

Neal pulled out the front of his short-sleeved, tucked-in shirt and dropped the kitten inside. "Now, don't bite or claw," he ordered. Clyde hunkered down against his stomach, purring.

"Did you get him?"

"Yes."

Neal inched his way to the main trunk, then carefully climbed down. By the time he reached the ground, Lisa was waiting for him.

"Where is he?" she cried, then must have heard his purring, for she began to unbutton Neal's shirt. "Oh, how clever!"

"Hey, haven't we been through his before?" He moved a

step back and got Clyde from inside his shirt himself. The last thing he needed right now was Lisa undressing him.

But once she had the kitten in her arms, she seemed to forget all about Neal. Which was what Neal wanted. He guessed.

"Oh, you bad little boy. Don't you do that again," she was saying to the kitten. "Now, we're going to have to make some chicken for dinner. You'll like that."

"Boy," Neal said. "That'll certainly teach him to never climb trees again."

Lisa made a face at him. "He needs nourishment after his ordeal."

"What about me? I was in the tree, too."

"You're welcome to have some, too."

"Okay." He wasn't really hungry, but he'd eat sand just to be with her. "Why not?"

"Come on in, then." She almost smiled as she opened the door and waved him in.

She put Clyde down just inside the kitchen, and he raced off to places he was welcome and Neal wasn't. Maybe in his next life, Neal would come back as a cat.

He followed Lisa into the kitchen, thoroughly examining the walls, floor and ceiling—anything but Lisa's gracefully swaying body in front of him. Neal was having trouble enough handling her image in his dreams. He didn't want to tackle the reality of it. Although, actually, he wouldn't mind tackling—

He forced his eyes and attention away from her. On the copper pots hanging on the wall. At the worn butcher block cabinet to one side. At the book lying open on the kitchen table. What was that a picture of?

Lisa slammed it shut and whipped the book into a drawer. "Why don't you pour some iced tea for us while I broil the chicken?"

"Okay." He poured two glasses, putting one on the counter

where Lisa was fixing some chicken breasts for the broiler and taking the other with him as he wandered around the kitchen.

It was a nice room. A homey room. A slowly spinning ceiling fan made it pleasant even in the summer's heat, but he could also see it warm and cozy in the winter, with a harsh northwest wind blowing snowflakes past the steamed-up windows.

Neal shook his head and took a healthy gulp of his iced tea. What the hell was wrong with him? He wasn't going to be here in the winter. He wasn't even going to be here in the fall. Hell's bells, he wasn't ever coming back here.

He'd return for Nick and Lisa's wedding, but that would be it. That would be the last time he'd ever show his face in Three Oaks.

Neal found his gaze had stopped on Lisa, savoring her soft, sweet presence. He forced his eyes away, but it didn't help. He could still feel everything she did. Chopping a sweet onion. Tearing and washing lettuce. Light on her feet with quick hands. Graceful and sure in all her movements. Competent in everything she did. A woman a man could grow old with.

Hell, he had to stop thinking like that. He couldn't spend a night with her. Not even a day. His job was to straighten out her and Nick's problems and ride off into the sunset, like some cowboy hero in the movies. Maybe Lisa could lend him a horse. Unless she was still mad at him.

"Oh, hell." He put his glass on the counter. "I'll be right back."

He raced out to the truck for the flowers. They looked like they'd been in an oven for the last hour. Hell, maybe he should leave them there. But he'd brought them as a peace offering and he had nothing else. He hurried into the house, silently placing the flowers on the table. She stared at them.

"They're roses," Neal said.

"Oh, Neal." Her voice was soft, so soft he couldn't read a single thing in her tone.

"I'm sorry. I forgot about them. They got wilted." One look at her, and he forgot to breathe.

She picked up the flowers, her eyes looking all teary as she put the roses to her face and breathed in their sweet scent. Her smile lit up every dark corner of a man's soul. Chased the sun from the skies. Made the moon hide and the stars weep in shame.

She suddenly threw her arms around him, catching him up in the fever of her emotion. The scent of the flowers mingled with the soft scent of her soap, combining for a heady mixture that left him without air to breathe. Or the ability to breathe it. He let his arms wrap around her for just a split second, just a quick glimpse of heaven, as his body burst into flames of desire. And then she pulled back.

"It doesn't matter that they got wilted," she said. "You were saving Clyde. I think that was more important."

He forced his heart to beat more slowly and tried to make sense of her words. "I'm sorry about this afternoon."

"You have nothing to be sorry about, except that you didn't duck in time." She looked sadly at the flowers as she put them on the counter. "I don't suppose it would help to put them in water."

"No more than it would help to water a corpse."

She started to laugh, and the spell was broken. Or one spell was broken—her laughter seemed to weave another around him. It danced around, darting out of his reach even as it bound him firmly in its grasp. It wasn't just her body he wanted to hold—it was her laughter, her smile, her wit and her pain.

He made a move to regain his soul. "Am I supposed to be doing something for this dinner dance?" he asked her. "Nick certainly must have had duties, but you haven't told me what they are."

"We preferred to save Nick's time for treating the animals we rescued. He only came to meetings to stay abreast of possible rescues." She paused, then shrugged. "Well, he was helping me with the facilities committee."

"Okay. So what should I be doing?"

"Everything's pretty much set. I just need to go to Tabor Hill tomorrow and make the final arrangements."

His brain said not to get involved in yet another part of Lisa's life, but his conscience said it wasn't fair to let her do all the work just because he and Nick switched places. Just because his will turned to mush around her.

"Want me to do it?"

"You could come with me," she said, putting the salad on the table.

"Sure." He'd thought he could do it alone, but he could handle together.

"Tomorrow evening all right?"

"Fine."

He watched as she took the chicken out of the broiler, suddenly conscious of how homey this all felt. And how that meant he was losing focus. He had a goal he was aiming at here.

"Now that we've worked on your clothes," he said, "I thought maybe next we should work on hair and makeup."

Lisa brought the broiled chicken over and they sat down to eat. "I think we need to work on me being sexy," she said.

"On what?" he asked.

She couldn't have said what he'd thought she said. She was the sexiest woman he'd ever met. She just had to look at him to have him sizzling. One touch from her, and he was a goner.

"Being sexy," she repeated. "Buck naked didn't do it for me, so I must be missing something."

He wondered if she'd ever undressed for Nick. He hoped she hadn't. Suddenly his whole face grew white hot.

Why the hell should he care what she did for his brother? Damn it, they were in love with each other. Boyfriend-girlfriend. Soon to be man and wife.

"I thought maybe we could start with flirting," she said.

"Maybe you could give me some direction on what kind of flirting a man likes."

"Okay."

Neal put his head down and spent several moments shoveling food in his mouth, getting his nerves under control. Getting his whole body under control. Steeling himself to look into those beautiful blue eyes.

"Okay." He kept looking at his plate. "The eyes are key. They're the main vehicle for good flirting."

"Okay."

Yeah, okay. But now what? It was going to be hard to work with Lisa on flirting if he didn't look at her. But looking at her could be fraught with danger, too. Damn. He lifted his head and glared.

"First thing you should do—" he cleared his throat "—is blink a lot more."

She frowned. "Blink a lot."

"And use mascara," he said, still speaking quickly. "Mascara helps. It highlights your eyes."

"Okay."

He ate in silence for several minutes. Damn, she didn't need mascara or blinking or even all those fancy clothes to be sexy. She was beautiful. Gorgeous. Sensuous. All without any help from him. His feeble attempt to make her into another Donna was like putting glitter on a star. Her natural radiance outshown any weak suggestions he made.

"Could we practice now?" she asked. She blinked once. "How was that?"

He felt his cheeks warm as she stared straight at him. God, he loved those blue eyes. They were going to follow him the rest of his life. Lull him to sleep at night and wake him in the morning. All without Lisa ever being there.

He tried to focus on the topic at hand. "Ah, you're supposed to smile. You always have to smile."

Lisa closed her eyes and took a deep breath, then she opened her eyes. She batted her eyelashes at him with a smile on her face that would have done the Mona Lisa proud. Neal felt his stomach quiver.

"Good." The word came out a bit scratchy. "Real good."

"How long do I have to do this?" she asked. "My eyelids are starting to hurt."

He wished it was his eyelids that hurt. "You should do it in spurts."

Lisa went back to her normal direct gaze. "Now what?"

Damn. He wished he'd never started this. "Then you get close to the guy."

"Okay." She moved her chair closer to his. "Like this?"

Oh. Her soft, sweet fragrance surrounded him as her leg gently nudged his. Fire shot through him, and he wanted to scream in pain. "Yeah, that's fine." He gulped. "Then you lean forward a little. Show some cleavage."

"Wouldn't it be better to show everything?"

"No! No! No!" Neal was surprised to find he was standing and slowly forced himself to sit down. "I mean, ah—" he cleared his throat "—you don't want to overwhelm a guy."

"Okay. Don't overwhelm." She looked so calm. So beautiful.

"And you should touch a lot."

"Any place special?" she asked, leaning toward him.

A million and one places jumped to mind, but he stuck his arm out. "On the arm," he quickly replied. "On the arm is good."

Lisa moved closer and began stroking his forearm, pushing the hairs against their grain. He began breathing deep.

"How is that?" she asked.

"Good." He was proud that he didn't squeak. "Very good."

"Hmm."

She was moving closer, but he could take that. He was doing good, staying tough.

"And how about this?"

Neal had barely felt her bare foot moving up his leg when

he found himself on the ceiling. Or almost. Everything in his body was primed. All systems were go. And he was about to explode.

"I gotta go."

Lisa frowned at him. "What?"

"Boomer's calling me. He's hungry."

"Calling you?"

His passion tumbled into a state of confusion. "We use mental telepathy."

"Mental telepathy with a dog that doesn't even like you?"

"Hey, we're close. Real close." He edged toward the door. "I'll see you tomorrow evening."

"So just what are we doing at Tabor Hill?" Neal asked as he turned onto Mount Tabor Road.

"Just checking the menu," Lisa said. "Confirming the head count and stuff like that."

"Oh."

Stuff that could have been handled over the phone, but then she wouldn't have had a chance to spend more time with him. Of course, when she'd planned this, she'd thought she would practice flirting with him some more. Bat her eyelashes, touch his arm, lean in close. She'd had him going last night, she knew she had. And she'd thought she'd raise the pitch even more tonight. But now that he was here, now that he was close, she felt so unbelievably self-conscious. She turned to look out her window.

They passed gently rolling hills covered with grapevines, lush greens in the deep evening shadows as far as the eye could see. Hawks soared overhead, and she thought she caught sight of a deer near a stand of pines before the road curved, giving them a new vista.

Neal slowed and turned into the drive for the Tabor Hill winery. It was an ordinary-looking cedar-shingled building, seemingly on the small side since it was built on the edge of a hill, but everyone seemed to think it was the perfect spot for romance. She'd never thought about it before, just enjoying the locally made wine and the delicious foods. But now, driving out here with Neal, she began to get a sense of what had been meant. It was so pretty here, so remote. She could almost believe that she and Neal were the only ones around.

Which shouldn't make any difference to her, anyway. If she was looking for romance—which she wasn't—Neal would be the last person in the world she'd focus on. There was a lot more she'd want in a relationship than someone whose company she enjoyed. Mostly, she'd need to trust he'd be around longer than three weeks.

No, the only thing she wanted from Neal was help in getting pregnant. She had a little more than two weeks before she was fertile again, a little more than two weeks to make sure she knew how to get him to cooperate. Which is why she made up that story about Nick and her being on the facilities committee.

It had taken some doing on her part last night to juggle the committees. She'd had to get Myrna to take Ben from facilities and put him on her entertainment committee. Ben agreed easily, but Myrna was a harder sell. She preferred not to work with Ben, but agreed—in exchange for the services of Lisa's prize stallion for two of Myrna's mares.

That was pretty steep, but Lisa didn't begrudge it. She only wanted to get pregnant once.

"I'd been hoping we could have dinner here, too, as long as we were going to be here anyway," she said as Neal pulled into a parking spot. "But I couldn't get reservations."

"It's popular, is it?"

"Extremely."

Neal got out of the car, and Lisa forced herself to wait for him to come around to her door. After all, she'd worn one of the dresses he'd picked out, and the Horrendous High Heels from Hell. She needed to give him a good chance to appreciate her appearance. It was suggestion number fourteen in her book. *Let him open doors and hold your chair. Look him in*

*the eye when he does, and make sure he's seeing nothing but
you.*

When he opened the door, she got out slowly. *Move slowly
and sensuously. Let your clothes flow around you.* Suggestion
number seventeen.

Giving him her hand, she put one foot on the pavement,
then the other. She moved like she'd seen women do in the
movies, only they'd been getting out of limousines, not trucks.
No matter. The guy was looking at her, not the vehicle.

"You look very nice tonight," Neal said as she stood.

"Thanks." She tried not to wobble in her shoes as they
walked across the parking lot. "I've been trying to follow all
your suggestions." Well, that was almost true. She had been
following somebody's suggestions.

"It'll just be until Nick sees you in a different light," Neal
reminded her.

No, it would just be until Neal succumbed. But she didn't
correct him. She walked at his side to the entrance.

"Is that where we're going to eat?" Neal asked. To their
right was a deck that overlooked the vineyards.

"No, we'll eat inside. Then we'll move out here for dancing
and mingling."

"Guess we're hoping for good weather, then." He smiled
at her. "Maybe I shouldn't come."

A quick sense of loss gripped her. "You have to come,"
she said, then thought that sounded a bit desperate. "Nick
already bought a ticket."

He opened the restaurant door for her. "I wasn't going to
ask for my money back."

How did she handle this? She was too worried to remember
to make him watch her as she walked in. He had to come to
the dance. She'd been looking forward to going to it with him.
She'd even recruited more people to do the chores at the dance
so she'd have more free time. What was she going to do with
it if he wasn't there?

Somehow Lisa managed to remember what she was supposed to discuss with the manager, and somehow all the final arrangements were made. They checked over the menu, got to taste a new zucchini side dish the chef was making and picked the wines that would be served. All the while Lisa was trying to come up with a way to insure that Neal would come to the dinner dance.

She'd already put him on a committee after telling him Nick wasn't on any, so she couldn't say he had to take tickets or work the cleanup crew—which would be pretty farfetched anyway, since they were having it at a restaurant. Maybe she had to appeal to his sense of duty.

As they were leaving the manager's office, she turned to him. "You need to come to help me practice," she told him. "After all, we picked out a dress just for the dinner."

"You'd do fine without me."

But don't you want to see me in it? she wanted to ask, but didn't.

They walked outside. It had gotten dark, and in the distance, heat lightning danced across the sky. Above them, though, the stars glittered like a handful of diamonds.

"Everyone'll be concerned if Nick isn't there," she said. "It's the day before the anniversary of Donna's death, so they'll think he's off somewhere mourning."

"They'll see me around and know I'm fine. He's fine."

Why was he being so stubborn? They started across the parking lot toward the truck.

"Let's walk around the back a little," she suggested. "People like to wander here, and we should see what it's like."

"It's dark," Neal said.

She put a stupid perky smile on her face—suggestion number twenty-one. "Just a quick look," she replied, grabbing his arm.

Without saying anything more, Neal led her down the stairs and onto the lawn. Her heels immediately sank into the ground.

"You okay?"

She wanted to tell him she'd be fine once she'd gotten rid of these damn shoes. But suggestion number twenty-two said, *Never show irritation. Men are very sensitive to negative vibes and scare easily.*

"I'm just fine, thank you."

They walked away from the building across the narrow strip of lawn. Once in the deep shadows along the grapevines, they turned to walk in the deep, rich scent. Cicadas sang in the darkness, and an owl hooted in the distance.

To their left and above them was the restaurant, light spilling out of the long expanse of windows. Though Lisa preferred the darkness that enveloped her and Neal, she was drawn to look at the diners. It was like watching a movie without the sound. People laughing and talking, living their lives right before her eyes, yet so far away at the same time.

"Doesn't life sometimes feel like that?" Neal asked.

"Like what?" she asked. He couldn't be seeing things the same way she was.

He nodded toward the restaurant. "Like you're on the outside looking in."

She shook her head, not knowing what to think. "You can't feel that way," she said. "Not with the life you lead."

He laughed and they walked farther, staying in the darkness close to the vines. "What kind of life do you think I lead?" he asked.

"Well, not like mine," she said. "You don't clean out barns or fight those awful biting flies or worry whether the hay's dried properly." She looked at the gaiety in the lighted room above them. "You're one of them. In there having a glamorous good time."

"Am I?" he asked, then was silent for a long moment. "Funny how we see someone's life so differently from how they see it. You have a home that really is a home, filled with animals that care about you and in a town filled with people who know and respect you."

She said nothing, surprised by his view of her life. Did he

see those things missing from his? Maybe his life wasn't as great as she'd imagined. A breeze ruffled the leaves on the acres of vines around them, making it sound like a thousand little voices whispering to her. But she couldn't understand the words.

She took his hand in hers as they walked in the uneven grass. He wasn't all that different from that know-it-all fifteen-year-old she'd slugged—he still liked to pretend he was invulnerable, even while he desperately wanted to belong. But she had changed in the past twenty years. Changed enough to see beneath his surface and feel his silent yearnings.

Her heart was giving her advice on what to do about his yearnings, but she couldn't seem to understand the words. Or maybe her own yearnings were getting in the way.

All too quickly, they reached the end of the lawn. It was either turn around and go back or climb the slope to the parking lot. Lisa didn't want to leave, didn't even want to move. She stood still, leaning her head back to look at the stars. There were thousands of them up there winking at her.

"After my mother died, I thought she was up on one of those stars, making it blink at me," she said.

"So did you wish on them all the time then?" he asked. His voice was soft and all too close in the darkness.

"No," she said simply, still staring at the sky. Not daring to turn toward him. "I never could. I somehow got the idea that she would grant me whatever I wished for, but only if I found the right star to wish on. So I had to wait until I was sure I'd found it."

He sighed, and she felt him move away from her. If not in body, at least in spirit. "And have you ever?"

"I've never made my wish," she said and turned away from the stars. "It sounds crazy, but I always used to think that I'd know the star when I knew the man of my dreams."

"Sounds too fantastic for me," he said.

She shook her head and took his arm. "For me, too, and I'm not nearly as cynical as you."

"The word is realistic," he said.

"Yeah, right."

They started up the slope to the parking lot. "Will we get a chance to dance and party at this dinner dance or will we be working the whole evening?" he asked.

"There's not much work to be done," she told him. He must be planning on going, she realized and tried another tactic. "I don't dance, but you're free to if you'd like."

"Why don't you dance?" he asked.

She laughed. A little sadly, she hoped. "I don't know how."

"You don't know how to dance?"

She stopped walking and shook her head, then decided he probably couldn't see that. "No," she said. "I hated all that stuff in high school and just never got around to learning."

"I could give you a few lessons." His voice was thoughtful.

"Could you?"

"For Nick's sake," he said softly.

"For Nick's sake," she agreed.

Chapter Nine

"Hello," Lisa called as she opened the screen door.

"Be down in a minute," Neal said.

She came into his kitchen and stopped to pet Pansy. Boomer paused in the doorway, then came forward to greet her.

"It's just me," she told the old dog. "Yeah, I know I don't look like me, but I am."

When she'd seen Neal at his office that afternoon, he'd told her to wear a dress with a loose skirt and heels, so that's what she was wearing. She felt like a kid at Halloween, right down to that quiver of anticipation in the pit of her stomach. She heard Neal coming down the stairs and went into the hallway.

"Well." She forced a bright smile to her lips—suggestion number twenty-one again. "All set to teach me to boogie?"

He nodded. "I thought we could practice in the basement. It's cooler and there's no rug to worry about."

"Sounds good to me." Perky, perky, perky, she reminded herself. Surprisingly, it wasn't that hard. She felt as giddy as a girl with her first crush. "I've brought some CDs."

"Great."

His smile did funny things to her knees, made them all wobbly and weak. Time to get on with things. She turned to the basement stairs and started down. Unfortunately, her knees hadn't quite recovered, and somehow the heel of her left shoe caught on the top stair. She grabbed quickly for the banister while falling to one knee. The bag of CDs tumbled all the way to the basement floor.

"Are you all right?"

Neal was by her side so fast Lisa hadn't had time to take a breath. He was on the step below her, a strong arm around her waist. Her right hand found its way to his shoulder. The whole thing felt so good. She loved the scent of his cologne, a piney woods smell.

"Yeah, I'm fine." She tried to push herself away. It was one thing to mate with him. It was another to like it. "I just stumbled a little."

"Are you sure?"

His brown eyes were two deep wells of concern. No man had looked so worried about her since she'd been eight and had fallen off her horse, making her father age ten years in the process. She shook her head.

"I haven't been practicing enough," she said.

"What?"

"You told me to practice walking in my heels," she replied. "And I have. But only on a flat floor. I haven't been doing stairs."

"Well, this is not a time to push things." He put an arm under her legs and in one smooth movement stood up, carrying her in his arms. "Nick would never forgive me if I broke anything."

"Hey," she cried.

But it was a halfhearted protest, at best. She liked being in his arms, liked the sense someone cared about her—even if it was just keeping her safe and in one piece for his brother. For the few moments it took to go down the stairs, her heart sang and the world was filled with smiles. Then they were down and he was letting her feet drop to the floor.

"How was that?" he asked.

For the first time since she'd arrived, Neal smiled, really smiled. His eyes lit up, and she felt warm in their glow, warm and wanting to stay close. Her silly knees wobbled some more. That song in her heart was down to a murmur, but still there.

"Just fine, sir. Thank you."

Their eyes crossed the great divide between them and held. Held on tight, pulling toward each other. Something was trying to bloom between them, making Lisa almost believe that she could reach for other dreams. That she could have more than a child someday. But then Neal looked away, and sanity returned.

What was she thinking of? Hadn't she learned long ago not to entrust her happiness to someone else? Especially someone as dedicated to roaming as Neal.

"Let's get going," she said.

"Fine." Neal's manner was brisk, his movements sharp as he went over to pick up the CDs. "We'll start with a fox-trot."

After he put a CD in the player, he came to where she was standing. He put his right hand on her waist and took her right hand in his left. She felt a warmth spread from his touch, trying to melt all the common sense encircling her heart, encouraging her to believe in dreams and fairy-tale endings.

This was crazy. She was smarter than she was acting. Relationships based on emotions brought nothing but pain. All she wanted from Neal was sex. They wouldn't be making love. There would be no happily ever after. Neither of them wanted it.

"The fox-trot is a four-step dance," he told her. "Listen for the underlying drumbeat."

She nodded.

"And don't look down," he told her. "You need to put yourself in touch with my body and follow my lead."

Put herself in touch with his body? Isn't that what she'd been trying to do for weeks? But she took his *follow my lead* as the perfect opening for a seductive remark—suggestion fifty-four—and moved closer to him. "Are you taking me anyplace interesting?"

Neal seemed to have no reaction. "Don't forget to relax."

She melted in his arms, making him grimace. Not quite the reaction she wanted, but better than none.

"How about somewhere in between?"

They spent a lot of time on the fox-trot, then the waltz. Lisa smiled and melted and leaned and touched, suggestions twenty-four, twenty-seven, thirty-three and fifteen. The little bit of dancing experience she'd had helped her, and she picked up the steps quickly. But she had a new worry.

None of those hundred and one suggestions seemed to be doing a thing for him, but they were sure putting a flame in her furnace. She liked his hands on her, guiding her movements, and liked her hands on him even more. It felt natural to lean against him, to rest her head on his chest and let the dreamy music swirl around them. The smile that had been so forced before was now as natural as breathing. She could only hope that it was all having a residual effect on him and, one day about two weeks in the future, it would sweep down on him with such force that it would rip him from his moorings. And right into her arms, of course.

"Did you know my grandmother broke her wrist recently?" he asked her suddenly.

She looked at him. His lips were so close she found herself wanting to brush them with hers—she was sure that had to be a suggestion somewhere in the book—but the shadow in his eyes stopped her. There was something behind his question, some hurt.

"Yes," she said. "It wasn't all that recently, though. Late winter, I think."

"But you knew about it?"

His voice had such a vulnerable quality to it. Maybe it was

her own background of feeling on the outside, but she was sure she heard pain behind the words.

"Yes, I did," she admitted. "Why?"

He looked at her as the music came to an end. "Because nobody saw fit to tell me."

She wanted to pull him back, to tell him he didn't have to be alone. "Maybe they didn't want to worry you."

"They still could have told me. Nobody seemed to have cared enough to bother." He went over and snapped off the stereo. "We can stop now. You'll do fine at the dance."

Lisa was delighted to be able to kick off her doggone heels, but she wasn't quite so eager to lose the excuse to have his arms around her. All the more reason for the lesson to end, she told herself. She was wandering into too many silly fantasies tonight.

"Same time tomorrow night?" she asked.

"I don't think we need another lesson." He looked away, putting the CDs into her bag. "Besides, I'm having dinner with my father tomorrow, and I don't know how long it'll last. Since I don't really know him all that well, I can't say."

That pain was in his voice, and there was a stiffening of his shoulders that said he was trying not to care. There was no way she could leave him like this. She knew only too well how easy it was to imagine slights, build them into hurts and weld them into walls.

"Neal," she said softly and put her hand on his arm.

His gaze came around to meet hers, and she reached up to touch his cheek. Just a gentle touch, the whisper of the wind. She had to tell him not to hurt, not to feel so alone.

But he took her hand and brought it to his lips, repaying her gentle touch with the softest of kisses, the most tender of touches. And that's all it was until their eyes met again and suddenly a charge passed between them, wild and strong. Like an explosion, it rocked the air, throwing them off balance and into the other's arms.

His lips came down on hers with such a force, such a hunger

that she could not breathe or think or wonder. She felt his need, his passion, and met them with a desire of her own. Her arms wound around him, tighter and tighter, so that she was almost part of him. So that their hearts could beat in unison as their lips spoke words of magic.

His mouth moved against hers, taking all that she had to offer and more. This was a heaven now twice visited. It was a delight she thought she could only dream of. It was riding a horse that ran like the wind. There was laughter and sunshine and a thousand firecrackers exploding in the air. She never wanted it to end.

They pulled away slowly, as if it was an effort to move. He just stared into her eyes. Her heart tried to read the shadows there, but she was too wobbly and shaken by the storm that had now passed.

"I think I'd better go," Lisa said. Her voice was a whisper.

"Yeah," he said.

Somehow she made it home, but she wasn't sure how. What in the world had happened to her? She shouldn't be having that reaction to Neal. Not to Neal, of all people!

"What has it been now?" Joe Sheridan asked, fiddling with the barbecue grill. "Three whole days without rain?"

"Yeah, I guess," Neal replied.

He'd been a little too preoccupied with his reactions to Lisa to notice the weather. He spent his nights dreaming about her and his days fearing he'd see her and worrying that he wouldn't. Nothing made sense anymore.

His father put the cover of the grill on. "Another few minutes, then we can put the burgers on."

Neal nodded.

They were sitting behind his father's house, out on the southeast edge of town. Leaning back in their lawn chairs, they watched the large marshy pond to the south, red-winged blackbirds flitting among the cattails. A gentle breeze cooled them and drove the mosquitoes off.

It was a postcard-perfect country evening, Neal pointed out to himself. So why was he in the dumps?

"So how's Lisa?" his father asked.

"Fine," Neal said slowly, carefully. "Busy with plans for the dinner dance."

"You should have brought her along. She could have used the night off."

Did Nick bring her here for dinner? Another thing Neal hadn't considered. "I wasn't sure you'd have enough," he said. Besides which, he needed to limit his time with her. Yesterday had been dangerous. He'd almost lost his head there, almost forgotten who and what she was.

"I always have enough." His father put his lemonade on the small table between them. "Time to get to work. The usual okay with you?"

Neal didn't know what the usual was, but he smiled. "Sure."

Joe put some hamburgers on the grill, then glanced at Neal. "Why don't you go get the salads? The burgers will be done in a few minutes."

"You're going to make me work for my supper, huh?"

"Nothing's free in this world," his father replied.

That had always been one of Dad's favorite sayings. Neal suddenly remembered a discussion they'd had years ago about the concept of free love. His father had argued that there was no such thing, that a man sometimes got free sex, but love was too precious to ever be free.

Neal threw himself out of his chair, trying to bury his aggravating thoughts as he picked up his glass. The preciousness of love was a lesson Nick should be learning. It had nothing to do with the here and now. All Neal was troubled by was his physical response to Lisa.

"You want more lemonade?" Neal asked his father.

"No, I'm fine."

Nodding, Neal hurried through the sliding door into the family room. His father had moved into this house after Nick and Donna had married, giving the big old house to them. It looked like he'd gotten rid of a lot of his old furniture, too. The only piece Neal recognized was the big desk in the corner. It had been in his father's office since he'd started his medical practice and—

Neal smiled. All these weeks he'd been tortured by thoughts of Lisa, and who better to help him quiet that physical torment than a medical doctor? Neal's smile grew broader as he hurried into the kitchen for the salads.

"Thought I was going to have to send the dogs out for you," Joe said as Neal came onto the deck. "Afraid you'd gotten lost."

"Don't you wish," Neal joked. "You just want all the food for yourself."

Grunting noncommittally, his father put a burger on each plate, the buns already liberally coated with condiments. He handed Neal a plate, then took the other to the table and sat down.

Neal did the same, pausing only slightly when he bit into his hamburger to discover it had been topped with a generous helping of pickle relish—the only seasoning he hated. He tried not to make a face.

"You know—" Neal put down his hamburger "—I could use some medical advice." No, he'd said that wrong. "Actually, it's a friend of mine who needs the help. He has this problem with a woman."

"Oh?" Joe said.

Neal went on. "The problem's kind of, um, sexual."

"He's impotent?" his father asked.

"No, no." Neal felt his cheeks glow with a white hot heat. The words had come out a lot sharper than he intended, and he took a deep, settling breath. "No, he doesn't have that kind of a problem."

"So, ah, this friend. He's not looking for an aphrodisiac?"

Neal closed his eyes in agony. That was the last thing he needed. "Absolutely not. This guy's problem is just the opposite," he said. "He's very attracted to this woman, but he doesn't want to be."

"What kind of involvement is it?" Joe asked. "Emotional or physical?" He took a sip of lemonade. "Or both?"

"Physical." Neal looked away. That was all it was. Well, all right, there was a little emotional involvement, but he could handle that. "Purely physical."

"You know who you should be talking to about this?" his father asked. "Neal."

"Neal?" For a moment, Neal forgot he was supposed to be Nick, then the world righted itself. "Why would I talk to Neal about it?"

Joe leaned forward. "It sounds like him. Trouble making a commitment. A fear of getting close. A tendency to keep people at a distance." He shook his head. "You know, I worry about him."

Neal stared at his father. "Why? He's perfectly happy." Or he was until he came to this place.

Joe's eyes grew shadowed. "I think the divorce was a lot harder on him. Your mother and I tried, but he just seemed to pull away from us all. Maybe I should have insisted he come here instead of going off to boarding school when he was going into high school."

Neal shifted in his chair uneasily. "As I recall, he didn't want to come here."

"I'm sure he would have if I'd asked him."

Neal couldn't believe his father was stewing over something that happened almost twenty years ago. It was over and done with. There was no reason for anyone to feel guilty. His hamburger lay before him, daring him to leave it there and add to his father's guilt. With a sigh, Neal picked it up.

"Dad, Neal is very happy with his life. Not everyone needs to be married to be happy."

"An endless series of three-week-long relationships isn't happiness."

"He doesn't have time for more right now."

"You don't choose a time for love. It chooses you."

"Well, it hasn't chosen me."

There was a dead silence as his father stared at him. "I thought we were talking about Neal."

"Uh..." Neal smiled. "Yeah, we were. But I was just saying that I'm not in love, either." What about Lisa? Wasn't Nick in love with Lisa? "At least, I don't think I am," Neal added with a laugh.

"You know what I think?" his father said. "I think it's love."

Neal felt a spurt of fear. "What is?"

"This obsession your friend has with this woman." His father sat a moment, shaking his head. "I think your friend's in love and denying it."

Why had he ever started this? "No," Neal protested wearily. "No, he isn't. And it's not an obsession. He just needs a little something to dampen his enthusiasm."

His father looked at him for a long moment before shrugging. "Physical exertion sometimes helps. So does keeping your mind occupied elsewhere. Alcohol's a depressant, too, though I don't recommend he get in the habit of using it."

"So what should I tell him?" Neal asked with a sigh.

"He should admit his true feelings."

Neal sank back in his chair. This was no help. Nobody really understood. He didn't have any feelings toward Lisa. He couldn't. She belonged to Nick.

She looked at the moon, the couples mingling on the huge deck attached to the Tabor Hill winery, and took a deep breath. Clenching her jaw and shaking her head. It was a perfect night for romance. But she didn't care. Not in the least.

She wasn't looking for romance from Neal, not at this dinner dance, not anywhere. Though she wished she didn't have to keep reminding herself of that. Over and over and over again. She picked up the door-prize tickets she'd been selling and went inside.

Every time she was near him, her heart raced and her stupid brain shut down. So what was she supposed to do—avoid him and stay clueless as to how to attract him, or get to know him and risk insanity?

"Great party," someone said to her in passing.

"Thanks."

She should never have worn the pink cotton candy dress from the boutique and the heels that gave her a great turn of calf, or spent an hour on her hair and makeup. She'd tried too hard to look good and seemed to be constantly searching for Neal and that glint in his eye that confirmed it.

"Nick's in the gift shop." It was Nick's grandmother, her matchmaking smile alive and well.

"Okay," Lisa said, but she headed into the restaurant.

"I think he wanted you to come there when you had a chance."

Lisa shrugged. "I still have some more tickets to sell."

The older woman pulled them from her hand. "Not anymore, you don't. Now, go see what the boy wants."

Lisa made a face, but went into the wine-tasting room and started up the stairs to the gift display on the balcony. It had been bad enough sitting next to Neal all through dinner and having his arm brush hers accidentally, his leg touch hers every once in a while. Now she was supposed to seek him out?

"I love your dress," a woman coming down the stairs told Lisa.

"You look fabulous," another said.

Lisa smiled. She had to toughen her silly heart. She had to keep her mind fixed on her goal. Two more weeks, that's all she had left.

Her breath faltered as she topped the stairs, even as her cheeks burned with heat. Neal was at the far side of the balcony, and she had to fight to keep hold of her determination.

"Lisa." Neal moved quickly toward her and took her arm as she came close, making a painful awareness shoot through the length of her body. Forbidden dreams danced uninvited through her mind—dreams of those hands holding her close. Of those hands—

"You know Andrew Baker, don't you?" Neal was going on.

Good gracious! Neal had the wealthiest man in southwestern Michigan in tow, and she hadn't even noticed. Bad didn't even begin to describe the shape she was in. "I've never had the pleasure," Lisa said smoothly, and shook the man's hand. "It's nice to finally get the chance to meet you."

"The pleasure's all mine." The man took her hand. He was probably only a little older than she was, no more than his early forties. He was handsome with a great smile, but a nicely laid out buffet would have had more of an effect on her.

Neal went on, "Mr. Baker wants to help out the rescue group."

"Oh?" Lisa forced herself to concentrate. "Good. We can always use more help."

"I've already given Nick here a check," the man said. "But I'd like to do more. I have room in my stables to house horses you've rescued, but I thought you probably had plenty of space between your volunteers."

"Up until now, we have," she agreed. "Though you never know what the future will bring."

"Well, certainly the space is there if you should need it," he said. "But Nick suggested a way I might help that others couldn't. He suggested I produce a public-service announcement in one of my studios to be aired on television stations across the state."

Lisa was stunned. This was beyond her wildest dreams. "That would be wonderful," was all she could mutter.

Andrew pressed a business card into her hand. "I'm going to be out of town for the next month. Give me a call after Labor Day and we'll work out the details." He reached over to shake Neal's hand. "Pleasure meeting you, Nick. Now I'm going to enjoy some of the great hospitality this place is famous for.''

With a wave, the man turned and went down the stairs, leaving Neal and Lisa alone on the balcony. Lisa stared at the business card in her hand.

''I can't believe—''

''In here,'' Neal whispered and, taking her hand, pulled her into a small office that was clearly marked Private. ''Look at this.''

He put a check into her hands. It was for twenty-five thousand dollars. Her heart stopped.

''Holy cow,'' she gasped. She turned it over as if somehow expecting it to be a joke, but it looked real. ''He gave this to us? Really and truly?'' She looked at Neal and burst into laughter. ''This is fantastic!'' she cried and threw her arms around him.

He joined her laughter, grabbing her in his arms and swinging her off her feet. ''Can you believe it?'' he said.

''We've never gotten a donation like this.'' She was so excited, it felt like Christmas.

''I knew you'd be thrilled.'' He set her down slowly.

''There's so much we can do with this.''

She smiled at him, reveling in her joy, when the mood suddenly shifted. She became aware of his arms around her. Of the intimacy of the tiny room. Of his lips so very close to hers.

Then they were kissing. His lips were on hers, and sparklers were going off in the night. Roman candles were exploding above the vineyards, shooting stars were racing across the heavens. The light was dazzling, blinding as the sun shattering into a million pieces.

She clung to him, running her fingers through his hair and delighting in the nearness of him. Her mouth on his wasn't enough. She needed to be closer to him, to make him a part of her. This was a moment that she wanted to last forever, a moment suspended in time that would never end.

''Lisa? Nick?'' Myrna called. ''Are you up here?''

Sanity sent them crashing to earth, throwing them apart. Somewhat. He still had her hands in his, and she thought that was all that was keeping her wobbling knees from letting her fall to the floor.

Neal's eyes were shadowed, or maybe it was just the poor lighting in the office. She couldn't read anything in them, though, and that, more than anything, put the steel in her bones.

"You all right?" he asked. His voice was only the slightest bit hoarse. Obviously, he was just fine.

"Of course," she said. If he was, she was. She pulled the door open a bit more. "We're in here, Myrna."

Myrna's eyes widened when she looked into the office, her gaze landing squarely on their clasped hands. Lisa moved away from Neal, dropping his hand as if it were red-hot steel.

"Wait till you see the donation we got," Lisa told her. "Nick was just showing me."

"How nice."

Myrna's voice said more than her words, but Lisa chose to ignore her tone. "It's from Andrew Baker, and we're going to have to write a really nice thank-you note."

"Oh?"

Seeing that Myrna still wasn't convinced, Lisa handed her the check.

"Oh! Oh, my!" Myrna's eyes grew as wide as saucers, and she hugged Lisa hard. "This is so great!"

"Isn't it?" Lisa agreed. "I'm still having trouble believing it."

"There's so much we can do with this." Myrna handed the check to Lisa with shaking hands. "Gracious, I think I'm going to have a heart attack."

"Don't do that," Lisa said with a laugh and gave the check to Neal along with the business card. "You want to keep these? I'm fresh out of pockets."

"And chain it shut," Myrna added.

"Consider it chained." He put both in the inside pocket of

his suit coat. "I'd better get back downstairs. I've got some ticket stubs I need to put into the door-prize drawing."

Myrna held out her hand. "Actually that's what I came for, but you both should get down there. We've got a lot of acknowledgments to make."

"Good idea," Neal said and lightly put his hand on Lisa's shoulder.

It felt so right, so much like they were a couple. Suddenly she found the whole place claustrophobic. She needed some air—by herself. "I'll meet you both down there," she said. "I've got a couple of chores to do first."

Before they could do anything but agree, Lisa was past Myrna and in the gift shop. Rather than go down the main stairs, though, she slipped through a storage area and down the back way. It left her just outside the kitchen, where she got a few curious glances from the staff, but was left alone.

Taking a deep breath, she leaned against the tiled wall and closed her eyes. This whole thing with Neal was rapidly becoming a nightmare. She wasn't in control of anything anymore. Mostly, she was out of control. At least every time he was near.

So what was she going to do? Her plan had seemed so simple. Let Neal think he was helping her attract Nick, when in reality she was watching to see what attracted him. And it should be working. Except that she hadn't counted on her own heart being weak and unpredictable.

What she hadn't counted on was liking Neal. A whole lot.

"Can I help you with something, miss?"

Lisa opened her eyes. The assistant manager stood before her, a worried look on his face.

"No, I'm fine," she said quickly and found a smile. "I was just resting a minute."

"Oh."

But he stood there looking at her, giving her no option but to leave. Well, how much time did she need, anyway, to know she had no idea what she was doing? She went through a side door and wandered out to the deck.

It was fairly crowded with couples dancing slowly under the stars. There was a soft breeze, just enough to bring the sweet scents of the vines.

"Should we give it a try?"

She turned to find Neal at her side. Everything, everybody else seemed suddenly in the shadows. "We really need to talk," she told him.

Ben, clutching the notes he always carried when he emceed these events, appeared next to Neal. "Oh, Lisa, can—"

But Neal had swept her into his arms. "Sorry," he called to Ben. "She'll catch you later." He looked at Lisa. "This is probably the best place to talk. Anywhere else and we'd be interrupted a million times."

"I guess." But his hand on her waist made her brain stumble.

He pulled her closer to his chest so his breath tickled her ear. "And I know what you're going to say. I want you to know it won't happen again."

"It won't?" He might have been talking about his kiss or the large donation or even Ben's interruption. She didn't care. She could feel his heart beating, and that was enough for the moment. Closing her eyes, she let the music lead her.

"I've gotten carried away a few times and I shouldn't have," he said to her.

She found her heart wanting to be carried away again, swept off to that magic land where all she knew was Neal's touch and all she hungered for was his caress.

"I know your feelings for Nick," he was going on. "I won't betray them again."

She opened her eyes and found herself staring at his lapel. She was so incredibly happy it was mind-boggling. It was stupefying. It was very, very scary. She had to keep reminding herself that she didn't do these kinds of relationships. She didn't do anything that meant she needed someone else in her life. Especially long term.

"Are you saying we're going to stop this little make-over of yours?" she asked.

"No. Why would we do that? You and Nick belong together."

She sighed. "So what now?"

"I'll be more careful," he said. "I'll keep my distance better."

Like he was now? But she didn't say the words aloud. She hadn't asked, "What now?" expecting him to answer. She'd been asking herself, but the words had slipped out. What was she to do now? Go on with her plan and hope he'd slip once more, big-time? Or did she confess that she and Nick were not in love and never would be? But if she did that, she'd lose Neal altogether. Not that she actually had him. Not that she actually wanted him. The music stopped, leaving her no closer to an answer.

"Ladies and gentlemen," Ben intoned. "Before we draw for our grand prize—two tickets for next Saturday's performance of the revival of *Fiddler on the Roof* in Chicago, plus meals and overnight accommodation—we have some people we'd like to thank."

While Ben introduced various volunteers and donors, Lisa's mind wandered. She was attracted to Neal, no getting around that. It complicated her plan somewhat but it didn't mean she had to abandon it. She just had to force herself to stay focused. She had to concentrate on getting a reaction from him and ignore any reactions she might have.

Over the next two weeks, she needed to make a full attack. She needed to smile and coo and simper and sway until she was ready to collapse and Neal was ready to give in. A child was her goal, and that was all. Neal could go back to New York in a month, and she wouldn't miss him. Not really.

Her heart wavered, but she refused to listen to its whining. She was not falling in love with Neal. It was ridiculous. Unthinkable. Impossible. As idiotic as the idea of him falling in love with her. There were some things that defied the laws of reason, and her falling in love was one of them.

She looked toward the small stage and saw that Myrna was shaking the feedbag full of ticket stubs as Ben read off the list of donors for the Chicago weekend getaway prize.

A weekend away might be a great idea, Lisa thought, if she could get Neal to agree to one. They could go someplace where there'd be no expectations from anyone. No one telling them what a cute couple they made or making assumptions about the staying power of their relationship. No one planting the dangerous seeds of fantasy in her mind. It would be just the way to get her back on track.

"And lastly our own Bryer's Motors for donating the transportation to get the winner to Chicago and back," Ben said. "Now are we ready for the big moment?" He reached in the box and pulled out a ticket, pausing to heighten the tension. "And the winner is…Nina Sheridan."

The group burst into applause as Neal's grandmother moved toward the stage. A few voices called out offers to accompany her. After a moment, she climbed up and Ben gave her the envelope with the gift certificates. She held up both hands for silence.

"As most of you folks here know," she said, "I'm an old biddy and don't have nearly the amount of energy a wild weekend in Chicago would require."

There was some laughter. Lisa felt a twinge of anticipation in her heart.

"So I'm going to give my prize to somebody else," the old woman went on. "Somebody who's able and willing to put a weekend in Chicago to good use."

The crowd grew quiet. Lisa clenched her hands in sudden hope.

"I'm giving this prize to Lisa and my grandson."

Yes! Lisa cried to herself.

Mrs. Sheridan smiled at her. "Here's hoping you young folks put it to good use."

Oh, she would, Lisa assured her silently. She would put it to excellent use.

"I'm really sorry," Neal said as soon as he pulled the truck out of the restaurant parking lot. The very idea of the trip was both ecstasy and torture. Two days with Lisa in the city, no one else around to claim her attention. Alone in a hotel room—

He bit back the thought with a frown. "I had no idea Grams was going to do that."

"It's all right," Lisa said.

"No, it's not," he said. "It's just part of this whole stupid masquerade. They all think I'm Nick and that this would be something the two of you would love." Well, actually, he'd love it, too. He just wasn't allowed to.

"I think it would be fun," she said. "I haven't been to the theater in ages."

"You should take it, then," he said. "Ask a friend to go with you."

"She gave it to both of us."

"And I'm giving my share to you." He stared into the darkness, watching as the headlights swept the road.

"I can't accept it," Lisa replied. "Your grandmother will start asking questions if the two of us don't go."

"Damn." He slammed the wheel with the palm of his hand. Every place he turned he was running into something.

"Besides, why can't the two of us go?"

Because he had enough trouble staying sane when she walked into the clinic. How was he going to control himself when they were sleeping in the same room? Because the more time he spent with her, the more time he wanted to spend with her. Because in the normal course of his life, he should be ending this relationship about now, not looking to drag it out longer.

"You aren't thinking this through," he told her. "This is two days and one night together. All the time. Awake and sleeping."

"I know that," she said. "What's the big deal? It's one little night. Probably not even eight hours, what with going to the play Saturday night. What can happen in a few hours?"

Chapter Ten

"What am I going to do?" Neal asked Pansy. The cat yawned and curled up in a patch of sunshine. Her solution to every problem.

"I can't spend a weekend in Chicago with Lisa," he told Boomer. The dog scratched his ear.

"Thanks for nothing," Neal muttered and went into the backyard. Since Nick had a neighbor kid cut the grass, there wasn't much yard work to do, but he could weed the garden. That should relieve some of his frustrations, especially since it was about ninety degrees already.

He got a bucket from the garage and started yanking weed after weed from the dry ground. It was a week since it had rained. The Neal rainy season had slowed to a halt. Did that mean he was turning into Nick? And if so, did that mean—

He frowned and moved to the tomato plants. The issue at hand was what to do about this trip to Chicago. He couldn't go. No way. No how. Absolutely not.

But after Grams had announced to the whole state that she

was giving them the weekend, he'd have to come up with a damn good excuse not to.

"Boy, here's a sight I never thought I'd see."

Neal turned. His father had come into the yard. "What do you mean? I keep this weeded." He assumed Nick did, anyway. Somebody did.

"Sure." Joe picked up one of the molded chairs on the patio and carried it to where Neal was kneeling. "So how come you're pulling out your radishes?"

Neal looked at the weed in his hand. It did indeed have a tiny reddish bulb at the base. Damn. How was he supposed to know what a radish plant looked like?

"I was thinning them," he said and tried to replant the one in his hand. It looked sad.

"I see." Joe sat down. "So I hear you hit the jackpot last night."

Neal went back to his weeding so his father couldn't see the panic that surely had crossed his face. "Depends on your viewpoint," he said.

"What viewpoint is there that doesn't see a weekend with a beautiful woman as a positive?"

"It's not that simple," Neal pointed out. He pulled some dead leaves off the tomato plants then moved his bucket to the pepper plants, taking his clue from the tiny peppers on them. He pulled a few little sprouts from the dirt around them, then moved to the overgrown patch behind them

"You've always had a tendency to look for the problems in life," his father said. "So what makes this so complicated?"

How about that Lisa was in love with Nick? "It's just not the right time for something like this."

"Not the right time?" His father sounded genuinely puzzled. "You mean because of the anniversary of Donna's death?"

Actually, Neal hadn't, but it was as good an excuse as any.

"Think how it would look," he said. He started pulling out some of the grassy-looking weeds.

"Like you were getting on with your life." His father paused. "Don't pull those. That's your asparagus."

"I knew that." Neal picked up the bucket and got to his feet. Damn, there weren't even any weeds here for him to pull. "I just think it would be better to get on with life in a few weeks, not now."

"I don't know what's wrong with you, boy," his father said, obviously exasperated. "You've got yourself a nice weekend in Chicago with a beautiful woman—who definitely has eyes for you—and you're moping like someone stole your Michael Jordan jersey."

Has eyes for you. The words went through Neal's heart like a knife, and truth flashed before his eyes. Deep down, he'd had a little niggle of hope that maybe there wasn't anything between Lisa and Nick, that he'd misread the whole situation. But his father's words ground that hope into the dirt.

Lisa was in love with Nick, and it was obvious to everyone. It was also for the best. Nick was the stable, relationship-type guy. Neal was the loner.

"You're a lucky man," his father was saying. "A very lucky man."

Yeah, right, Neal thought. *Real lucky.* If he were any luckier, they'd resurface the *Titanic* and he'd win tickets for a cruise to the North Pole.

"I can't believe you and Nick are going to Chicago," Myrna said.

"It was nice of Mrs. Sheridan to offer it to us," Lisa agreed. "Do you have the receipt for the postage?"

Myrna sorted through the papers on her side of the dining room table and pushed one across to her. "It's so strange how this thing between you and Nick has blossomed so suddenly," Myrna went on. "Just in the last few weeks."

Lisa tried to not scream in frustration. It was bad enough

that everywhere she went the last few days—the grocery store, the butcher shop, even walking to the road to pick up her mail—she met somebody who wanted to congratulate her on the weekend in Chicago. Hell, she wasn't even safe in her own dining room, going over the preliminary reports of the dinner dance.

"There's nothing new between us," Lisa said wearily. "We're friends. That's what we are and that's what we always will be."

"Friends?" Myrna was laughing at her. "Well, I guess. You sure looked friendly last night when you were cuddling in that little office."

"We were not cuddling," Lisa protested. "We were celebrating that donation."

"Sure." Myrna got to her feet. "Except even a blind man could see the spark between you two. You need me for anything else? I've got to pick Mickey up from his swimming lessons."

"I think we're just about done." Lisa slipped all the receipts into a file folder. "We had a very successful evening."

"In more ways than one."

Lisa said nothing, but walked with Myrna to the door. The late afternoon shadows were getting long. It should start to cool off soon. If only her emotions were as easy to predict.

"Hey, I didn't mean to give you a hard time," Myrna said, reaching over to give Lisa a sudden hug. "I just think it's so great that you've finally found somebody."

Lisa hugged her back, unable to say anything. Damn Neal and his stupid plan. Look what it made everyone think. Of course, she was just as much to blame. She had agreed to it. Plus she had talked him into going on the weekend! How did she keep forgetting that everyone else in town was putting a different spin on things? A spin that her heart kept trying to echo even though it knew the truth! There was no grand romance and never would be.

But once Myrna had left, Lisa was unable to go in the house

and wandered around to the paddocks. Ariel was in the near one with some other mares and came trotting over.

"Hey, beauty," she told the mare. "I didn't bring any carrots. I'm sorry."

"Maybe she wants a souvenir from Chicago," Pucky said.

Lisa made a face and brushed some mud flecks from the white star on Ariel's forehead. "I'm not sure I'm going to go." She had no idea where that thought had come from, but maybe it was the right one.

Pucky just clucked at her. "Never thought you were a chicken," he said.

"Being sensible isn't the same as being afraid."

"It is if you're too sensible all the time."

"How can I be too sensible?"

"You're always trying to think things out rather than listen to your heart."

That was just the point. She was listening to her heart, and what it was saying was scaring the hell out of her. If she went to Chicago with Neal, she'd maybe learn what she needed to get him to father her child. But she'd also be feeding her heart's stupid fantasies.

"Nick and I are just friends," she insisted. "I hate the way everyone's trying to make it more than that."

"Maybe you owe it to yourselves to find out who's right."

She knew who was right. There was nothing to find out. She had to stick to her guns. She was never going to have another chance like this. In less than two weeks, she'd be fertile again. She had to stay committed. She turned and she started to walk to the house.

"What made you so afraid of love?" Pucky asked, falling in step beside her. He sounded worried. Apparently he was in another of his it-was-my-fault moods.

"I'm not afraid of love," she argued. "And there was nothing that you and Dad did wrong. I just don't feel the need to base my happiness on someone else's whims."

"It was hanging around all those Hollywood people as a

kid, wasn't it? Nobody's marriage lasted more than a year or two, it seemed.''

She shook her head. "I don't remember how long anybody's anything lasted," she said.

"But it was there and must have affected you."

"Pucky, stop trying to make this into a problem. I like my life." And she'd like it even more once she had her child.

Neal figured it out Wednesday night while watching heat lightning off to the north. They'd been having a lot of that lately. No rain, just lightning. But for some reason one spectacular flash made him see the light, as it were.

It was so simple, he didn't know why it took him four days. He was a doctor, and a doctor couldn't leave his patients. Lisa would understand. The town would understand.

His euphoria lasted into the morning—through some routine surgeries and up to his first real appointment.

"Now remember, Mrs. Barnes," Neal told the elderly woman as he walked her to the door. "If Ruckus has any kind of a reaction to those shots, call me immediately."

The woman frowned, looking from Neal to Sara and back again. "Didn't you just give him his regular shots?"

"Yes," Neal replied.

"The same shots you've been giving him for five years now?"

"Yes." Though it hadn't been Neal.

"Well, then you should know he never has a reaction." Mrs. Barnes was frowning.

Neal maintained his professional smile. "That's good, Mrs. Barnes. But you never can tell what might happen."

The woman traded a quick look with Sara and rolled her eyes before heading for the door.

"You can contact me over the weekend," Neal called to her rapidly retreating back. "I'll be here."

"No, you won't," Sara said once the door had slammed shut. "You're going to be in Chicago with Lisa."

"I don't think so," he said as he made a few notes on Ruckus's chart. "I can't just up and leave my patients."

"Dr. Jim will be available all weekend, like he always is."

Neal shook his head. "Jim's getting on in years."

"He's in great shape."

"And I'm not so sure he can handle everything."

"He always has before."

Neal walked toward his office. "I've made up my mind," he said. "I'm staying in town this weekend."

"We have everything under control," Sara called after him.

He stopped and turned. "We?"

"Dr. Jim is primary backup. Secondary backup is his niece who's visiting this weekend."

"A rookie, I bet." Neal sniffed. "Someone's who's just graduated."

"She's young but she's talented."

"You have that on good authority, I presume?"

"Her husband will be third backup," Sara went on. "He teaches at the School of Veterinary Medicine in Lansing." She smiled at him. "I'd say we can spare you for two days."

Neal didn't bother glaring at her as he stomped into his office.

"Party time! Party time!" Baron cried.

"Oh, shut up," Neal snapped and threw himself into his chair. On top of his mail lay the most recent copy of *Worldwide News,* featuring a story about Neal Sheridan with a photo of Nick slugging some guy.

Great. Nick was going crazy. Just what Lisa needed to find out.

Lisa zipped into the clinic parking lot, the tires of her truck squealing as she turned in, but once she'd parked and turned off the ignition she just sat there. She really had to go inside and check the rescue group's mail, but her feet didn't want to move.

She hadn't seen Neal since the dinner dance, but sooner or

later, she had to. They had to finalize their plans for the weekend. Taking a deep breath, she got out of the truck and hurried into the clinic.

"Hi," Sara said, looking up from the computer screen. "All excited about the weekend?"

"Oh, sure," Lisa said.

Fortunately the waiting room was full, and she didn't have to elaborate. She slipped in behind the counter and pulled the mail from the bin where Sara put it.

"It's so good to see Dr. Nick's gotten over Donna," Mrs. Jefferson said.

Lisa looked at the older woman. "Yes, it is," she said brightly. "I imagine soon he'll be dating every single woman for miles around."

The woman laughed and waved off Lisa's comment. "No, no, that's his brother. Dr. Nick is the type to settle down."

But I'm not, Lisa wanted to point out, *and neither is Neal.* She didn't voice the thought, though.

"Mrs. Jefferson, you want to take Bootsie in room three?" Sara said.

The woman took her dog as directed, leaving Lisa with a half-dozen smiling faces staring at her. All with expectation in their eyes.

"I think I'll take a look at the mail in Nick's office," she told Sara, and fled in that direction.

"Thief! Thief!" Baron cried.

"Yeah, I know." She dropped the mail on Nick's sofa and plopped down next to it. She wasn't sure what she was stealing, but she was sure she was. "I just don't know what to do, Baron."

"Fire! Fire!"

"You're no help," she muttered and picked up the mail.

About an hour later, after she'd sorted all the mail and used Nick's computer to answer a half-dozen letters, Neal came in. He looked tired, with little lines of weariness around his eyes and tension in his lips. A little quiver raced down her spine.

"How are you?" she asked. "You look like hell."

He grinned as he sank into a chair. "Thanks. Anybody ever mention how you have a way with words?"

"Not recently." She came around back of him and rubbed his shoulders. His muscles were all knotted up. "Have you been busy here? Why don't you have Sara call Jim in?"

Neal leaned back in the chair and caught her hand in his. For a brief moment, he held it then suddenly got to his feet, moving across the room. "No, we haven't been all that busy," he said. "It's just this trip thing."

He still didn't want to go. She could read it in every inch of him. He was trying to find a way to back out. But he couldn't. Should she let him off? She couldn't.

"You're anxious, too?" she said and grinned at him. "I can't wait. It's been ages since I've had a vacation, even a short one. And I love Chicago. I wouldn't care what we did. It'll just be so great to be there."

She felt like an idiot rambling on, but she wasn't going to give up this chance without a fight. His shoulders sank, leaving Lisa's stomach to flinch with guilt.

"Yeah." He smiled at her. "Real excited. It'll be fun."

Her conscience screeched at her. She tried to offer an olive branch to both it and Neal. "And just think, you won't have to pretend while we're there. You can be yourself and no one will know the difference."

"There's that," he agreed.

Her conscience was choking on the olive branch so badly she had to perform a moral Hiemlich. "Look, Neal, if you really don't want to go, we don't have to." She forced the words out, pushing them past her own disappointment.

"How would we explain it to everyone?" he asked.

"What do you care? You don't live here."

"But you do."

She shrugged. "The hell with everyone. This town is too damn nosy as it is."

He shook his head. "Why do I feel like that's straight from your high school script?"

"Maybe because some things haven't changed."

"They care about you, Lisa," he said. "Just as they care about Nick. They really want to see you two happy together."

She looked away, gathering the mail she had scattered on his desk. A hundred million emotions were dancing in her stomach but she could only identify one—disappointment.

"Maybe we have different ideas of what'll make us happy." She clutched the mail to her chest and looked at him. "Are you telling your grandmother or should I?"

Neal looked at her. She tried to turn away, tried to lock up her heart and keep all her silly emotions from spilling over into her eyes. But she wasn't that strong.

"Tell her what?" he asked, his voice soft. "That I'm picking you up at ten Saturday morning?"

Neal paused at the stop sign and rubbed his eyes. This was the longest six weeks of his life, and it was barely half over. By the time he got back to New York, he'd be so decrepit, they'd cancel his show. He forced himself to drive the truck through the intersection.

The plumbing truck in the drive registered on his brain as he turned onto his street, but he didn't really process the information until he parked in front of the house.

What was a plumber doing here? He'd mentioned to Sara the other day that the water pressure in his shower was non-existent. Had she called the plumber for him? That was nice of her. Maybe there were some advantages to small town living.

After dragging his weary body up the driveway, Neal found the plumber fiddling with the door under Boomer's relaxed supervision. That is, until Neal came into view. Then the damn dog began barking and growling as if a pack of wolves had come onto his territory.

"Hey, Doc," the man said with a quick glance over his shoulder. "Your door was locked."

Neal almost groaned aloud. He'd been so agitated lately, he'd made another stupid mistake. It was a wonder the whole town didn't know that he was Neal, not Nick.

"I had to spring the lock to get in," the plumber said. "But I'll have it fixed in a minute." The man paused and laughed. "Although maybe I shouldn't bother. Locks are a real pain in the butt when you want to get in."

Neal saw the name sewn on the man's shirt. "Howdy, Zack. What's the word? I'm guessing that you didn't come here to break a lock so you could fix it."

Zack laughed. "Don't you wish." He gave a screw some final twists then straightened up. "You got yourself some big problems."

Neal felt himself sagging. The man didn't know the half of it.

"Your shower fixture's all corroded inside. Needs to be replaced, and soon, before those pipes burst. It's gonna be expensive, though."

Replacing a shower fixture wouldn't break either him or Nick, but it was just one more thing going wrong. "When can you do it?"

"It'll have to be this weekend," the plumber said. "You can't leave it like that."

For one long moment, Neal stared at the man. This was an excuse to cancel the trip that no one could argue with. That no one could doubt or question or remedy with the wave of a hand. Just as Zack said, it had to be fixed without delay. But then Neal remembered that look in Lisa's eyes. That quiver in her voice. He didn't think the trip really meant all that much to her, but canceling it would. It would be a public rejection, no matter the reason. Especially coming after that newspaper article that she knew was about Nick. No, he couldn't abandon her the way it looked like his brother had.

"This weekend'll be a problem," Neal began.

"I don't need more than Saturday to finish the job," Zack said. "It'll be a long day, but it won't take more than that."

Neal shook his head. "It doesn't matter how long it takes. One day, two days. I can't get it fixed this weekend."

"Hey, if it's the cost, you're worrying about…"

"No, it's not the cost. I'm supposed to go to Chicago with Lisa this weekend. I can't stay here."

Zack frowned. "This is a tricky job," he said. "I might have to take out part of a wall. And then there's the fixture itself. You'll be wanting to pick it yourself."

"If you want me here, we'll have to pray the pipes hold over the weekend and you fix it Monday. If you think they won't, then you'll have to pick out the fixture for me."

"The missus never lets me pick anything out."

"Then ask the missus's advice," Neal said. "Or my grandmother's. Ask anybody. If you're doing it this weekend, you just can't ask me."

"Okay," Zack said, though his doubt was draped over the word.

"It'll be fine," Neal told him. "I'll like whatever you put in. Even better, I'll pay for whatever you put in."

Somehow his feet carried him into the house, though his heart was heavy. Regret mingled with just enough anticipation to make him thoroughly confused.

Once thing was certain, though—he'd had his chance. Fate had waved the opportunity in front of him, tempting him to grab for it. He could have stayed in town to oversee the work, and everyone would have understood. After all, an emergency was an emergency. But he couldn't. He was taking Lisa to Chicago, where they'd have a wonderful time. No matter how much it hurt him.

And he would follow his father's advice—he would physically exert and mentally distract until he collapsed into a useless blob. But he would not touch Lisa. Not at all.

Chapter Eleven

Lisa fiddled with the dial, then leaned back in the car with a contented sigh as the cool air rushed at her. She felt like Cinderella going to the ball.

"I thought you didn't like air-conditioning," Neal said.

"I didn't used to, but now that you've made me such a genteel lady I can't live without it."

He laughed and turned onto Interstate 94, the expressway linking Chicago and Detroit. Lisa felt herself relax. This was going to be great. No need for pretending he was Nick on either of their parts.

"I'm really looking forward to this trip," she said.

"Yeah. Me, too."

She wasn't sure that had been true all week, but she thought it just might be now. His voice was easy, his laughter light. This trip was going to be good for them both. He'd be free to be himself, and she'd be free to pursue her goal without letting other people's ideas distract her.

She found herself watching Neal's hands on the steering

wheel. They were nice hands, strong hands. She hoped their child would have his hands. *Their child?*

She dragged her gaze away and lay her head against the headrest, closing her eyes. She had to stop thinking that way. She'd already vowed down one side of the hill and up the other that she wouldn't make any claims on her child's father. It would be just *her* child.

But was that fair to the child? Or to the father? What if Neal wanted to help raise his son? Or wanted to be part of his daughter's life?

She'd be denying him all the moments that would be so special. Their child's first step. His first word. Her first day in school. And she'd be denying their child the chance to take pride in his father. To be part of the Sheridan family and all it meant to the town. Shadowy misgivings began to appear on the edges of her plan.

"You get to Chicago much?" Neal asked.

She sat straight up, feeling as if she'd been woken from a sound sleep. "Oh, once or twice a year. Not enough to be bored with it."

"That's the best way for it to be," he said. "Get just enough of it to make you hungry for more."

"Sort of like watching a teaser ad for a movie," she said with a laugh.

"Or hearing the end of a song."

"Finding the first crocus in spring."

"Dreaming of that first kiss."

That stopped them both, and an uneasy silence filled the air.

"Look, Lisa, I just want you to know that nothing's going to happen this weekend," he said. "I know this is really an awkward situation, but you have nothing to worry about."

"I wasn't worried," she said.

"In fact, I was just going to get us two rooms for the night."

"Two rooms?" Her stomach fell, and she tasted uncertainty. Maybe she should take this as a sign and give up this whole thing. But then the idea of growing old alone mocked her, tore at her insides and left her eyes stinging. A child would give her someone to love, someone who would love her.

"I'll pay for my room," he said. "You don't have to—"

"I don't care about the money," she snapped.

This whole thing was just getting to be too hard. What had seemed so straightforward a month ago was turning into a royal mess. The hell with all this mushy nonsense. She'd made her decision months ago, and she wasn't giving up now. In one week, she was going to be fertile again, and come hell or high water, Neal was going to get her pregnant. Since he'd resisted all her attempts so far to drive him crazy with desire, she was going to have to double her efforts.

"I don't care about the money," she said more softly. "It'll just be harder to coordinate things with two rooms."

"We'll manage," he assured her.

"Sure." She turned and looked out the window. He'd be a gentleman, she knew. He'd walk her to her room. All she had to do was make it impossible for him to leave. She must know enough about him by now to be able to do that.

She stewed the whole rest of the ride, fretting and plotting, but luck was with her. The hotel had no more rooms available.

"I'm so sorry, sir." The desk clerk was all apologies when Neal tried to get another room. "But we have a convention here, and there just are no more rooms."

Lisa tried not to turn cartwheels, but Neal looked stunned. "I see," he said slowly. "Perhaps I could stay someplace nearby."

The desk clerk coughed quietly. "Uh, there really is no place too near, I'm afraid. And I fear you'd find the same situation all over."

"It's all right," she said. "The one room will be fine."

"It's very spacious," the clerk assured them.

"It'll be fine," Lisa said. "We'll just love it."

A bellboy carried their bags up. Neal still looked like he

was trying to concoct a new plan, while Lisa tried not to gloat. Whatever he was planning, she was certain she could foil it. She was on a roll. In control and in the money. She was so sure of herself, she let go a bit, oohing and aahing over the gold-trimmed mirrors in the elevator and marveling over the richness of the carpet in the hallway. She was sure she sounded like a country bumpkin of the bumpkinest quality, but she didn't care.

"Here you go," the bell boy said. "The television, VCR and stuff is here. The kitchenette is around the corner. It has its own ice machine and microwave."

Lisa stopped in the doorway, staring with glee at the piece of furniture in the middle of the room. A king-size bed! There'd be no way Neal could avoid her tonight.

Neal hung up his suit and dress shirt, which took all of about two seconds, all the while trying not to look at the bed. Lisa seemed totally unconcerned as she knelt on a chair by the window, looking north along Chicago's lakeshore.

He walked behind her, his hands firmly locked behind his back. "Quite a view," he murmured.

"Sure is."

They weren't talking about the same things, but he didn't point that out. Her hair was slightly curled and tied back with a green ribbon, and her understated cologne gave off a fresh country scent, a scent that he would carry with him to his grave and beyond. Her soft body called to him, the bed right there adding urgency to that cry. But he was strong. Like Hercules, he refused to listen to the siren call of her beauty.

"Think you'd like living here?" he asked.

She laughed, turning those bright blue eyes toward him. His resolve trembled under her onslaught. "No way," she replied. "There's no room for my horses, dogs or cats."

She was a country girl and always would be. That was the good news. And the bad news. He sat on the edge of the bed.

"So what would you like to do?" he asked. He didn't care, as long as they got out of the room.

She turned from the window and slumped in the chair. "I'd like to go to the aquarium and the zoo, then eat at a really nice place before we go to the play."

"Your wish is my command," he said with a bow.

A slow, lazy smile filled her face. "I'll have to remember that."

He'd only meant he'd take her to places she wanted to visit, but suddenly all too many possibilities jumped into his mind. The far reaches of the universe, traversed in each other's arms, was only one. He looked into her deep blue eyes and knew this was not the time or the place for such a discussion. Truth be told, there'd never be a time for it.

"Why don't we do the aquarium first?" he asked, getting to his feet. "Afterward we can grab a late lunch."

"Okay."

So they took a cab to the Shedd Aquarium and bought tickets for all exhibits, all shows.

"Do we have enough time to see everything?" Lisa asked, doubt in her voice.

"Sure," he said. "We just can't dawdle. Here, let's slip around these people. If we hurry we can catch the next dolphin show."

Though Lisa grumbled, Neal kept her moving through the aquarium. Then he bustled her off to lunch and the zoo.

The sun was baking hot outside, but Neal barely noticed as they wandered past the sea lion pool, around the hoofed animal enclosure and over to the large cat house. He didn't feel like he was tiring out his body or distracting his mind. Not nearly enough, anyway.

They ended up in the great ape exhibit, where Lisa stood a long moment, trading stares with an older male gorilla who was leaning against a wall in his glass-fronted enclosure.

"He looks like a lifer in a prison movie," she said, her voice sad.

"In a way he is," Neal replied. But in a way, Neal felt he was, too.

Lisa turned from the enclosure with a sigh. "When we were kids, a friend and I used to plot how we'd free all the animals in the zoos," she said. "We were going to take them to live in the jungles where they belonged."

"A lot of these animals wouldn't exist any more if it weren't for zoos," Neal said.

"I know."

She looked up and flashed him a smile. He wondered how something so soft could strike him with such force.

"That's what so great about being a kid," she said. "You don't have to be all that practical or sensible."

"Speaking of sensible." He needed to look anyplace but at those blue eyes, so he studied his watch. "We should be getting back. We need time to clean up for dinner and the play."

Though once at the hotel, Neal wondered why he had been in a rush to get there. He could have sworn the room had shrunk while they'd been gone. There was less air to breathe, less space to walk in and much more bed.

"You want the bathroom first?" he asked.

"If you don't mind."

"Not at all." He sank into the chair by the window. "I'll just read the newspaper."

But the sight of her taking her toiletries out of her bag was just too much. His mind's eye could see her in the shower using that shampoo, stepping out of the tub and putting on that lotion. He could see her coming over here—

He leaped to his feet. "I think I'll go down and use the exercise room for a while," he said.

"The exercise room?" She stared at him like he was crazy. "We must have walked ten miles today."

"You can never get enough exercise," he said and hurried to the door. "I won't be long."

When he dragged himself to their room after about forty-five minutes on a rowing machine, Lisa was all dressed and reading. She jumped to her feet when he came in, and slipped her book into her suitcase.

"You're back," she said.

"Told you I wouldn't be long."

She was wearing a green evening dress and white high-heeled sandals. Her hair was tied back with a green ribbon. She was beautiful enough to give life to a dead man. Fortunately, they had dinner reservations, so he had to hurry.

All in all, dinner went reasonably well. Neal didn't jump on the table and proclaim his passion for Lisa. He didn't fall to his knees and ask her to run away to Tahiti with him. He didn't clutch her to his chest and kiss her until both were breathless. He kept his head down, ate his food and drank most of their bottle of wine.

Unfortunately, it wasn't quite that easy during the play. Her leg kept brushing his. Her arm was resting against him. He was aware of her every breath, her every sigh, her every smile.

And mostly he was aware of that bed waiting in the hotel room.

It was the fastest rendition of *Fiddler on the Roof* ever produced. He had barely worked up an immunity to the touch of Lisa's hand when it was over. Hell, he thought as they got to their feet. Come all this way for a play and have it end in— he pulled back his sleeve to check his watch—three hours. He let his sleeve fall. Stupid watch must be wrong.

"Didn't you like the play?" Lisa asked, once they got outside.

"Oh, sure," he replied. "It was great."

"You seemed preoccupied," she said and tucked her hand in his arm. "Must be all that exercise putting you to sleep. We'd better get you back to the room."

"No way. It's not even midnight yet."

"It's late enough for me," Lisa replied. "I'm about to turn into a pumpkin."

"Hey, you're in the big city. There's a lot of party time left." He hailed a cab and helped her in. "The Steel Drum, please," he told the driver, then leaned back in the seat. "It's a West Indies nightclub. It'll be fun."

"But just for a little while. Then we're taking this mare back to the barn." She leaned close and took his hand in hers.

As they sped north up Clark Street, Neal prayed that Lisa would enjoy the nightclub. That she would find it so fascinating they wouldn't leave until four o'clock. That they'd stay there until the place closed and they were so exhausted they could barely totter to the hotel.

But no such luck. She watched the clock like somebody who didn't like her job. By one o'clock, barely an hour after they arrived, they were standing outside, waiting for a cab. And Neal's luck being what it was, they didn't have to wait more than a couple of minutes.

"I can't wait to get back to the hotel," Lisa said, then yawned.

"Tired?" He allowed himself to put his arm around her shoulders. "Bet you'll be asleep before your head hits the pillow."

"I'm not that tired," she assured him, a soft smile on her lips.

Neal hoped his groan was quieter than it felt. Just how late was that exercise room open, anyway?

Lisa felt bad about leaving the club, knowing Neal wanted to stay longer. She had enjoyed the music. But the longer she sat there, the more weariness settled in on her, starting at the edges and moving toward her center. Melting her resolve in the process. Making her afraid she'd be totally worthless if they stayed any longer.

Deep down she knew she'd need her wits about her to bed Neal Sheridan. And, given that Neal hadn't said a word the entire ride to the hotel, Lisa was worried they had already stayed out too long.

By the time they arrived at the hotel, Neal's weariness

seemed to double. "Oh, man. Am I beat," he moaned, once the elevator door had closed on them.

"If you're so tired, why did you want to stay at that night-club?"

"I thought you'd enjoy it," he said. "I wanted this trip to be memorable for you."

Her guilt wanted to quadruple. Here he was trying to do things for her, and she was consumed with ulterior motives. She turned to look at the restaurant listings on the elevator wall for a moment. After a deep breath to relax those guilt muscles, she reminded herself he wasn't doing this totally for her. He was quite happy to stay out just to avoid sleeping in the same room as her. She turned to him with a smile.

"It has been memorable," she assured him. "But there are other ways we could make it so."

"I didn't want this to be a weekend we could've spent in Three Oaks," he said. "No point in coming all this way for that."

They were at their floor, and the discussion stopped, as if there were gremlins hiding in the corners waiting to eavesdrop. Not that they'd hear anything exciting, Lisa thought. He unlocked the door and let her go in.

"You can change first," he told her.

He'd picked up the television guide, which didn't bode well for a romantic end to the evening, but she got her overnight bag and said, "Okay."

Once in the bathroom, she sorted through the bag. She'd brought a lacy nightgown and her usual cotton shorts and T-shirt pajamas. Her pajamas were a lot more comfortable, but she wasn't looking for comfort tonight. She was looking for—

There was a knock at the bathroom door. "I'm going downstairs for a minute," Neal said.

For what? To exercise some more? "All right," she called as she picked up the nightgown. It was time for her to bring out the big guns.

A few minutes later, she was out of the bathroom, but Neal wasn't back. That was all right. It gave her time to get everything ready.

She dimmed the lights in the room, pulled back the covers on the bed. She checked her book for a few suggestions and found there was something missing. She took a bottle of wine out of the refrigerator, then turned at the sound of the key in the lock.

Neal came in holding two book-size black boxes. He stopped at the sight of her, his eyes widening and his face flushing. "Wait until you see what I got," he said, his voice hoarse.

She smiled at him, feeling a little bolder at his reaction to her. "Movies?" she said. That was a great idea. *Gone with the Wind. Casablanca. The African Queen.*

He handed them to her. *The Best of the Roadrunner,* part one and part two.

"Cartoons?" she asked. "Roadrunner cartoons?"

"Sure," he said with a grin. "They're the greatest. I used to watch them all the time as a kid." He paused. "Nick didn't, much. He used to feel sorry for Wiley Coyote."

Lisa stared at him. This was to be her big romantic evening. The night she was going to sweep him off his feet and into unbridled passion. It was going to be her triumph after the long weeks of studying him. And he thought he was going to watch cartoons!

She knew what he was up to. He figured that no one would make love during cartoons. Well, little did he know that suggestion twenty-seven was made for a situation like this. "Don't fall into a rut as to what's romantic and what isn't. Make the most innocent pastimes romantic with your attitude."

So she smiled at him as she took the videos from him, trailing her hand slowly over his arm. She could feel him start, heard him inhale sharply. "You go change into something more comfortable," she said softly. "I'll get the cartoons ready to go."

"Okay." His voice sounded a little stronger, but wary.

As soon as the bathroom door shut behind him, she searched among the goodies in the kitchenette. She found a packet of microwave popcorn in the refrigerator. Great. That should be just the thing to confuse him.

As she waited for the popcorn and poured the wine, a delicious sense of anticipation swept over her. This was going to work. She could feel it in her bones. They'd eat popcorn, watch cartoons, he'd let his guard down and, like floodwaters rolling downhill, nature would take its course.

He'd admit his attraction to her and sweep her off her feet with passionate caresses and kisses to die for. He'd tell her he couldn't live without her, that—

The microwave buzzed and derailed her train of thought. Just as well, she thought as she took the bag of popcorn out. The train had definitely taken a wrong turn somewhere.

Neal stepped out of the bathroom just as she was pouring the contents into a bowl. He was wearing running shorts and a T-shirt and carefully keeping his gaze averted from her. But then he stopped and wiggled his nose like a rabbit.

"Popcorn?" he asked.

She grinned. "Sure. How can you watch cartoons without it?"

She went to the bed and propped their pillows against the headboard, then sat against them, patting the spot on the bed next to her.

"Come on over," she said. "Let's get this show on the road."

He brought the two glasses and, after handing her one, sat down. A bit farther away from her than necessary. She scooted closer and gave him a warm kiss on his cheek.

"Thank you, kind sir," she said, the words carried on a breath.

"For what?" His voice trembled.

"For everything," she said. "The day out, the wonderful evening." She smiled her most seductive smile at him. "And especially the glass of wine."

She was feeling giddy and not a little nervous, wondering if she'd be able to pull this off. She sipped her wine, then took a longer drink of it. Bubbles tickled her nose and made her laugh. He was watching her, and his eyes seemed to be ready to swallow her up.

"So are you going to start the movie?" she asked.

"Uh, sure."

Using the remote control, he flicked on the television and then started the video. She snuggled close to him, resting her head on his shoulder. Her heart was racing and that thrill of anticipation got tenser or tighter or higher somehow. Her hands had a sudden ache to touch him, to feel his tight muscles under her gentle touch. She gulped her wine, confused by the heat of her thoughts. He filled her glass as the video ran through some copyright information.

The cartoons didn't start right afterward, though. There were ads for all sorts of Roadrunner stuff. Jackets, shirts, sleepwear, even pens and notebooks. She tried to get her mind in control, instead of her wayward senses. He was the one needing seduction, not her.

"How come you never have stuff on your show advertising different rescue groups?" she asked him.

"You watch my show?" he said. "I'm flattered."

"Of course I watch it, but that's not how I know you don't." Unable to keep her hands off him, she ran her fingers lightly over his arm, just barely mussing the hairs. It sent a shiver down her spine, and his, too, apparently, since he moved to put his arm around her. That made her body hunger for him even more.

She tried again to hang on to her sanity. "We had T-shirts made a couple of years ago, and someone suggested we send one to you. But Nick said you never promote individual groups."

He stiffened. "I promoted some in the beginning," he told her. His voice was tight, and she could feel tension all through him. "I wanted to help all the little rescue groups."

It had seemed like a safe, easy topic, but there was pain in his voice. It tore at her, making her regret starting the conversation, but she was unable to let it go. "And?" she prodded gently.

"And I got stung." He shrugged as if it didn't matter, but she knew better. "I pushed a group that was really a scam. People trusted me and thought they were helping puppies rescued from a testing laboratory. They were helping to line some jerk's pockets."

"How were you to know?" she asked and slid her hand down his arm to take his hand. "It could have happened to anybody."

"No, it couldn't," he said. "It happened because I was stupid and naive. I didn't realize that most people are looking to use you. Everybody's got their own agenda."

"That's not true," she cried, letting go of his hand. Guilt jabbed at her.

"Sure, it is. Oh, I don't mean you," he said quickly. "I know you aren't after me for anything. And neither are most of the people in Three Oaks, but just about everybody else is. The women I date want to be seen with me. My business manager wants me to keep selling the sponsor's food so they'll keep wanting to sponsor my show. My neighbor wants me to get him Knicks' basketball tickets, the clerk at the dry cleaners wants me to get her boyfriend an audition as an announcer on the show. And my doorman wants me to diagnose every ailment of every animal in his family for free."

Lisa didn't know what to say. She stayed leaning against him but felt like the biggest fraud ever. She was glad he couldn't see her face. He'd surely see the guilt and treachery in her eyes and know.

"Sometimes I think I come back to Three Oaks every once in a while just to be around people I can trust," he said softly.

She couldn't do it. She couldn't trick him into making love to her. There was no way in hell she could prove him right—that everyone did want something from him. He'd opened up his soul to her. She couldn't repay that trust by tricking him. All her big plans were for nothing.

She slowly pulled away from him and lay against her own pillows, then closed her eyes and tried not to cry.

The cartoon color disappeared, replaced by the mottled gray that said the video had reached its end. Neal picked up the remote and turned off the television, then looked at Lisa. She lay on the bed next to him, sound asleep.

He had done it. With the help of three hours of the Roadrunner dropping anvils, boulders and bombs on Wiley Coyote, Neal had made it through the night without making love to Lisa. It hadn't been easy, it hadn't been something he ever wanted to go through again, but he had done it.

He gingerly got out of bed, picked up the blanket from the chair and laid it over her. She stirred slightly but didn't wake. She looked so beautiful lying there, so utterly wonderful, that he couldn't help himself. He bent down and brushed her cheek with his lips.

Then, afraid that that slight touch would only lead to more, he went to the other side of the bed and grabbed the other blanket. He wrapped it around himself and laid down.

"Brother of mine," he muttered as he turned off the light. "If you ever make this lady cry, I will personally make your life hell."

Chapter Twelve

Lisa woke with a groan. It surprised her, and she gingerly stretched her arms and then her legs. Nothing hurt. Why had she groaned? She moved her head slightly. No hangover headache.

She groaned again, or rather, the groan was heard again, but it hadn't been her making the sound. She rolled over and found Neal lying on the other side of the bed.

Everything came rushing back to her. They were in Chicago. And she was a rotten, selfish individual.

Neal sat up, leaning on his elbows, and groaned again.

"What's the matter?" she asked.

He shook his head. "My back is all stiff."

"A little too much exercise, maybe?"

"Couldn't be. I must have just slept funny. I'll be fine once I'm up."

Lisa watched while he made his slow way into the bathroom, then got up herself. It was early, just past eight, but late compared to when she normally got up at home. Sunlight was streaming around the closed drapes. She went over and opened them, blinking against the sudden brightness.

It was time to go home for more reasons than Neal's sore back. She had a lot of thinking to do and she couldn't do it here with him close by. How had things gotten so complex all of a sudden? She had wanted a child. That was all. Women got pregnant all the time, a good number of them by men who had no interest in a child. Why had it turned so complicated when she wanted it?

All she knew was that she couldn't go ahead with her plan to seduce Neal. She didn't know where that left her in her desire to have a child, but she knew Neal would not be the father. Not unless he agreed openly and honestly, and that was something he would never do.

Neal came out of the bathroom, moving as if all the vertebrae in his back had fused together.

"I think we ought to go home," Lisa said.

"No, that's crazy. I'm fine. We have a whole day left. Where do you want to go?"

"Skating along the lakefront." Then her heart melted at the pained expression that filled his face. "Look, we had a great day yesterday. We don't need to spend another few hours here to have had a good time."

"I just need to move around a bit," he said. "Really. Give me a little time and we can do whatever you want."

Yesterday that comment would have brought a teasing smile to Lisa's lips, but not today. "All I want is to go home," she said, unable to keep a certain weariness from creeping into her voice.

He looked at her, frowning. His eyes grew guarded. "If that's what you want…"

"It is."

In an hour, they were on their way. Lisa insisted on driving over Neal's protests. He was moving much better, she had to admit to herself, but refused to admit it to him. She needed to drive, needed to keep busy in some way to stop her thoughts from haunting her. To stop the memories from becoming more than she could bear.

"Bet you'll be glad to get home," she said as she headed down Lake Shore Drive.

"I guess," he said. "Zack was supposed to be fixing the pipes in the bathroom, and I'm not sure what I'll find."

Lisa glanced his way. "I meant back to New York," she said. "You know, your home."

"Oh." He laughed. "Forgot for a moment who I was."

Lisa laughed with him, or tried to. If only she could have. If only she could have forgotten what a rare gift his trust was and how she didn't deserve it.

"So will you be glad to get back?" she pressed, not eager for the silence to return.

"Yeah. Sure." He shifted in the passenger seat. "It'll be good to get back where I belong."

Where he belonged. It was all too easy to forget that he had a whole other life in New York. Friends. People who depended on him. "That's what I thought," she said, fighting to keep the disappointment from her voice.

What had she wanted him to say? *Oh, no, I don't want to go home. I want to stay here with you.* Dreaming was all well and good, but only when done alone.

Somehow the silence didn't seem as frightening as the conversation had been, and she concentrated on her driving. She got onto the expressway. There was hardly any traffic. They'd be home in no time. A couple of hours at most.

"I imagine you'll be glad to have Nick back," Neal said.

"Yep. There's lots to tell him." Though she couldn't think of a thing.

"And lots to show him," Neal added.

Huh? She looked his way, frowning in confusion.

"The new you," he prompted her. "You know, all we worked on to make Nick see you in a new light."

Oh, Lordy, was he still on that kick? It seemed years ago that she agreed to his stupid plan. She should tell him the truth once and for all, let him know there was nothing—and never would be anything—between her and Nick.

But to tell him the truth was to tell him about her deceit. How she'd only agreed to his plan so she could get closer to him, find ways to weaken his resistance to her so he'd father her child. Maybe the truth wasn't such a good thing.

Traffic picked up slightly, so she was able to use that as an excuse to avoid more conversation. Not too much more than an hour later, they pulled into Three Oaks.

"Why don't you go out to your place?" Neal suggested. "I can drive the car to the dealer from there."

She couldn't take being with him any longer, not even the ten minutes it would take to go to her farm. She hurt too badly, and that irritated the hell out of her. She'd never let a man get to her like this.

"Would you stop trying to be so damn macho?" she snapped. "You've probably stiffened up from sitting. And besides, we're almost at your place."

He looked surprised by her tone, then annoyed. "What's wrong with trying to be gentlemanly?" he snapped back. "Maybe if you let guys do things for you once in a while, Nick would have noticed you by this time."

Not this again. "Who says I want Nick to notice me?" she said and turned onto his street. A little fast perhaps, for he was flung against his door. "Who says I want any guy to notice me?"

"Right. I forgot. You haven't been mooning over Nick for the last twenty years."

Good gracious! What kind of an idiot did he think she was? "Oh, go to hell." She screeched to a stop in front of his house.

"I have," he snapped. "I'm here in Three Oaks, remember?"

He got out of the car pretty briskly for someone with a bad back, grabbed his suitcase from the back seat and slammed both doors.

"I hope Boomer bites your butt," she muttered and stepped on the gas.

The car spurted forward and she was around the corner in the blink of an eye. Out of sight, out of mind.

Well, the out-of-mind part was certainly right. With all the stupid things she'd done lately, she had to have been out of her mind.

"It's just more heat lightning up north," Neal said, leaning against the deck railing and looking at the night sky. "Three Oaks's idea of a wild Friday night. Nothing to worry about."

Boomer's reply was to yip a couple of times and scratch at the back door. Either the dog didn't believe him or he was tired of Neal's company.

"Okay, okay." Neal pushed himself away from the railing and went to open the door. Boomer went inside, leaving Neal all alone again. Story of his life. He should be used to it by now.

It was almost midnight, but there was no sense in him going to bed. He sure as hell wasn't going to sleep. The whole weekend with Lisa had been a fiasco from start to finish. Yeah, he had achieved his goal—he hadn't made love to her. But he also picked a fight with her when she was only trying to be nice.

Stupid macho pride. And now he didn't even have her friendship. Every time he'd tried to call her over the last several days, she'd hung up on him.

Enormous, jagged flashes danced across the sky. He tried to concentrate on his lightning watch. There was some story about heat lightning, something about the angels playing catch with fire. Nick had told it to him when they'd been kids. When wise adults ran the world and silly little pranks never hurt anybody.

"Oh, hell," he groaned. He wished he'd never suggested trading places.

Another bolt of lightning—a huge one—split the sky.

"Damn," he muttered. He hoped Lisa was all right. It was hard to tell from here, but the lightning seemed close to her farm. Too close.

He gave up his sentry post and hurried inside. He picked up the phone and dialed her number without even listening for a dial tone. He'd heard all the advice about not using phones during an electrical storm, but he was willing to take the risk. All he got was silence, though.

Damn. He hit the button for the dial tone and listened this time. Nothing. The phones were out.

Double damn. So if she was in trouble, she couldn't call for help.

Maybe he should go up there. He could drive by her house and check that everything looked all right. She'd never even know.

He changed his shorts for jeans and his sneakers for work boots, then checked out the emergency pack Nick kept in the back of the truck. Judging from the size, it had to have everything but the kitchen sink in it. He hoped he wouldn't need any of it.

Neal went barreling out of the driveway, tires screaming. There was a definite change in the air about two miles north of town. It was hot and heavy and still. Too still. Like the whole atmosphere was charged and ready to explode.

There was no light at any of the farms along the way, so the power lines had to be down along with the telephone. An overcast kind of darkness hung over the road, one his headlights had little effect on. If it hadn't been for the almost constant flashes of lightning, Neal wouldn't have been able to see at all.

Suddenly his heart tensed, and Neal could feel his blood pressure skyrocket. He could sense a change in the air. Something different was—

Smoke.

He stepped on the accelerator and went roaring along, finally turning into Lisa's drive. No dogs came running to greet him. The house was dark. So was the yard.

He stopped the truck and leaned on the horn, but there was no answer. The air seemed too thick to carry sound, or else it was all being swallowed up in a distant roar. He grabbed a flashlight, got out of the truck and ran to the front door. It was unlocked, of course, and he leaned in.

"Lisa!" No response. A quick sweep of the room with the flashlight showed nothing amiss.

He ran to the truck, put it in gear and followed the drive around back. That's when he saw the tree—Clyde's tree. He hit the brakes and stopped.

In the flashes of lightning, he could see the huge old oak by the house had been hit by lightning, splitting an enormous piece off. It had fallen away from the house, though, into the near paddock. The fence was down, the area around the piece charred and smoking.

"Lisa!" he called out the truck window.

Nothing. Just the frightened nickering of the horses in the other paddocks.

"Lisa! Pucky!"

Nothing. Not even a single woof. Where the hell were the dogs? But Lisa's truck was parked by the barn. They were here somewhere. The smell of smoke was stronger.

He drove down the old dirt lane, around the barns and up the hill where, once he reached the top, he saw the fire. It looked like a stand of trees, maybe a quarter of a mile down the lane, had been hit by lightning and was giving off sparks and smoke. Something told him that's where he'd find Lisa.

Speeding past the exercise areas, he flew down hill and up a small rise. There was a group of horses near the fence on his right. They were agitated but seemed all right, so he didn't bother stopping. Nor did he call for Lisa or Pucky. He'd never hear or be heard over the horses plus the fire.

Something told him to keep on driving ahead, so that's what he did. All the while sweat poured down his face. The air was so damn heavy and hot. Closer and closer to the burning trees he drove. Breathing became harder.

He wanted to push the truck faster, but he couldn't see much in front of him. The light from the burning trees threw distorted shadows over everything, and the brief flashes of lightning only seemed to make the dark darker. The bouncing told him he was riding a rough road. If he hit a hole hard enough, he could break an axle. Clenching his jaw tight, he proceeded at a steady pace.

Suddenly the air shifted, and he could hear the dogs up ahead and slightly to his left, howling as if the denizens of hell were emerging from the woods around them. Shadows caught his eye, and he leaned forward, squinting.

"Lisa? Pucky?" he called.

The shadows moved, waving him closer. Two people—Lisa and Pucky—and a horse. And Pucky's truck off to one side. Neal could see the dogs, hear them over the roar of the fire that was maybe the length of a city block beyond Lisa and Pucky. The dogs raced to greet him. The stench and the smoke were awful here. He could barely see. Breathing was done in gasps. All he could hear was the crackling, hissing sound of the flames devouring trees.

He drove the truck as close as he could without knowing the terrain, which still left him a good distance away. He got out and raced toward them, Chipper and Rusty at his side. Lisa was standing at the horse's head, obviously trying to calm her. Pucky was running to meet him.

"What happened?" Neal cried over the din as they met halfway.

"It's Ariel," the older man shouted as they hurried toward Lisa. "She was in the paddock where the old tree fell. Spooked her something fierce, and she took off through the broken fence."

"Is she burned?" Neal asked. "Break a leg?"

Pucky shook his head as he gasped for breath. "Tied up, I'm thinking."

Damn. In her panicked flight, her rump muscles had spasmed and contracted uncontrollably. It wasn't that she wouldn't move—she couldn't. Neal saw Lisa's old pickup to one side. He stopped Pucky and nodded toward the truck.

"Go get a horse trailer," he told the older man. "Even if we get her moving, we'll never get her to the barn on her own."

Pucky hesitated. "Are you sure? Maybe I ought to stay..."

"No, get going." He looked at the dogs. "And take them with you. I don't want any more patients right now."

Pucky nodded, called to the dogs, then took off for his truck as Neal hurried to Lisa. She looked up from Ariel, and he could see the terror in her movements. Somehow it gave him added speed.

"Neal," she cried. "You have to do something."

He could hear the tears in her voice even if he couldn't see them. It almost broke his heart. Anything, he cried silently. Walk through those burning trees. Put out the fire with his bare hands. Carry Ariel to safety in his arms. If only he wasn't a mere mortal.

He got close enough for Lisa's eyes to beseech him, stirring his heart more than any caress. He took a deep breath and tried to steady his nerves. Damn this stupid masquerade. Nick should be here. He would have done this under pressure before. Neal hadn't. Oh, he knew all about it, probably reported on more unusual cases, but it wasn't the same. Still, Nick wasn't here. It was up to Neal.

Even with the smoke filling the air, Neal could smell the sweat on the mare's body. And up close in the light of the flames, the animal's wide-eyed panic was obvious. He ran his hands over the animal, feeling the quivering terror in her muscles.

"How long has she been like this?" Neal shouted. If it had been too long, her kidneys could be starting to fail.

Lisa shook her head. "I don't know. Five minutes? Half an hour? I've lost all sense of time."

"We've got to start her on fluids right away." And pray that it was in time. He looked over the path he'd just run. It looked smooth enough to drive over. And he didn't care if he broke an axle now—the truck had gotten him as far as he needed to go. It was expendable. "I'm going to try to bring the truck as close as possible. It'll be quicker than trying to carry everything."

She nodded, then grabbed his hand quickly. "Neal, thank you."

He gave her a smile, then pulled away to hurry to the truck. He wanted to tell her to wait until he'd done something, but he couldn't plant doubts if she had none.

The truck was warm from the heat of the fire and got warmer as he drove slowly closer. His skin seemed to dry and shrink, but it was more an annoyance than a problem.

He got within maybe twenty yards of Lisa and Ariel and stopped the truck. He didn't want to spook the horse even more. Reaching into the back, he pulled out Nick's emergency boxes and sorted through them for an IV pack and bags of fluids. There was a good store of both in the box. Neal hoped it would be enough.

Neal went to Ariel's side and handed Lisa the flashlight. This would be a challenge, setting up an IV by fire and flashlight. He cleaned off a patch of skin as best he could with a disinfectant wash, then held his breath as he started slipping the needle in. A shower of sparks fell around them, and even though Lisa brushed them away, he felt a few burning spots on the back of his neck. But the needle stick felt good. It felt right.

He attached a bag of saline solution, then handed it to Lisa to hold as he taped the needle in place. Then he moved around to the horse's other side to insert another. If they were going to save her—and themselves—they needed to get her moving fast. But he had to treat for potential kidney trouble first. That couldn't wait.

"How long do you think we have until the fire gets here?" Neal shouted over the horse's back to Lisa.

She looked at the burning trees and the dried grass at their base and shook her head. "How long do we need?"

A spark landed on his arm, and he smelled burning hair. Or was it sparks landing on poor Ariel? He watched the fluid slowly drain out of the bag. Move faster, he willed it, move faster.

"You should go." He looked at Lisa. "We don't both need to stay here."

But she shook her head. "I'll go when we all go," she shouted. "Ariel's in foal. I'm not losing her or her baby."

Neal wasn't going to waste his energy arguing. With luck, there'd be no hard decisions. More sparks showered them. "Can you hold both bags?" he asked her.

As she took hold of his bag, he went to the truck for an old blanket. It looked like the fire-retardant one he'd featured in a spot on a show, then had sent to Nick. Maybe he was doing some good, after all.

After throwing the blanket over Ariel's back, he changed the bags, then gave her injections to relax her muscles, then changed the bags again. Was it his imagination, or did her eyes look less panicked? A little bit of hope crept into his heart.

But even as he admitted its existence, there was a huge crack to their left. One of the trees had fallen. Though it had landed more on the other trees, it shook a storm of sparks onto the grass. Neal watched in horror as the sparks grew into flames and the flames began to eat at the grass.

"Neal!" Lisa cried.

"Come on, Ariel," he muttered. "Come on, girl." He squeezed the bag, forcing the liquid out faster. The fire inched closer, its crackling sounding almost like laughter.

"Where's your rain, Neal?" Lisa cried, her voice filled with tears. "Damn it, Neal. You always bring rain. Why can't you now?"

"If I knew how to make it rain, we'd be swimming by now," he told her. Through the smoke and haze, Neal saw headlights approaching. It would be Pucky coming with the truck. "Go wait with Pucky."

Neal changed the bags again. If Ariel didn't move soon, she wouldn't make it, and it wouldn't be the fire that did her in. Her muscles would be degenerating, leaking myoglobin that would collect in the kidney tubules and cause renal failure.

"No!" Lisa cried. "I'm not leaving you. Be Neal. Make it rain."

Be Neal. Was that the reason the rains had stopped over the last week or so? Because he had stopped being himself and was being more and more like Nick? What did it mean to be Neal?

He closed his eyes and tried to think. No relationships longer than three weeks. Well, he hadn't really had a relationship with Lisa, so he hadn't violated that. "I'll be glad to get home," he said. "I've been here too long."

Lisa'd been petting Ariel and stopped to frown. "You what?" she asked.

Cynical. Okay, he'd been a little too trusting these last few weeks. He'd stop that. "Where's the fire department anyway? They stop for doughnuts on their way out here?"

"What are you talking about?" she asked. "They're probably at another fire."

A loner. He'd failed miserably there, but it wasn't too late. He could revert to his loner stage. All he had to do was tell Lisa she was holding the bag wrong, tell her he worked better alone. Tell her he didn't like the way she was helping. But the words wouldn't come out.

"Maybe you should hold the bag a little higher," was the best he could do.

But he would go back to being Neal, he vowed silently. He'd go back to being a cynical loner who jumped from relationship to relationship. He was looking forward to it, actually.

"What in heaven's—" Lisa stopped speaking.

The sudden overwhelming, complete silence surprised him. Then there was another sound. A sizzle. A sputtering. He turned his face to the sky. Something fell on his cheek. He expected the sting of a spark, but it was soft. Cool. Wet.

It was raining! A few more drops hit his face, then suddenly there was a downpour.

"Neal!" Lisa cried and threw her arms around him.

He hugged her tight, or as tight as he could while holding onto the bags of saline solution. Rain streaked their faces, soaked their clothes, but it had never felt better. It cooled. It christened. It gave life. Smoke still hung in the air, but the fire was going out. The angry hiss of drenched sparks told them it was.

Neal looked into Lisa's radiant face, glistening with the rain. Into the laughter that held such joy and promise, and knew only that her eyes reflected the joy in his heart. For this one moment, he'd been blessed with a pure and true contentment. He was at rest, at peace, at home, even.

He slowly bent to touch her lips with his. He wanted to thank her for her trust, for giving him the chance to come alive here with her. He wanted to promise to remember it always. But the kiss became so much more than that all of a sudden. It was a celebration. A dance. A symphony of their two souls winding around each other like curls of smoke rising to the heavens.

He tasted desire and delight. Hunger and happiness. Forgiveness and forever. There would never be a moment as perfect as this. There would never be another time as sweet as this. Her body pressed against his, they were in perfect unity. Then something tugged at the saline packs in his hand.

"Hey!" he cried in warning, then stopped. Ariel had moved. "Hey!" he cried in excitement.

"She's moving!" Lisa shouted.

And she was. Slowly and tentatively. But damn, she was moving.

Pucky was there then, holding the mare's head while Neal pulled out the IV lines and covered the spots with gauze and tape. Lisa was collecting the used bags and lines.

"Never saw a storm come so in the nick of time," Pucky said with a laugh.

"It was a miracle," Lisa agreed.

"It was luck." Neal patted Ariel on the rump. "Take her into the trailer and to the barn. I'll pack up and meet you there."

"Come on, old girl," Pucky was crooning to the mare as he led her away. "In just a little bit, you're gonna be snug in the barn. We've had enough excitement for tonight, don't you think?"

Lisa sighed as she dumped all the used equipment into the emergency box. "I can't believe she's all right," she said.

They didn't know if she was, but Neal couldn't bring himself to remind Lisa of that. Just because the horse was moving, there was no guarantee there wasn't some kidney damage. But he hoisted the emergency box into the truck.

"Why don't you ride with Pucky?" he suggested. "Or even in back with Ariel. She'll probably do better with someone keeping her as calm as possible."

"Okay." She grabbed his hand for a quick squeeze then raced off.

He let his eyes follow her for a moment, but she was lost in the shadows. Just as well, he thought as he went around to the driver's side of the truck. His work wasn't over yet.

He went ahead of Pucky and Lisa and the horse trailer, getting to the barn to see lights were on. Either Pucky had turned on the auxiliary generator or the power was back. Neal pulled the truck to the side and brought the box of supplies into the barn. By the time he'd settled on a clean stall where the light was good, Pucky was pulling the horse trailer into the yard.

Lisa led Ariel into the barn and into the stall where Neal

hooked up another IV. The idea was to flush out her system, getting rid of any myoglobin.

"Now we wait, right?" Lisa said.

He nodded. *And pray.*

Lisa got a couple of blankets and spread them on bales of hay in the stall across from Ariel. It took Neal back to that first day when Lisa had spread another blanket in another stall. Had it been only a month ago?

Pucky left briefly to check on the other horses, and Lisa went to make coffee. Neal kept checking and changing the IV bags. Hours passed, feeling like days as the three of them kept watch over Ariel, waiting for her to urinate. If the urine was brown, it meant Neal hadn't gotten there in time and her kidneys were failing. If it was yellow, she was home free.

"I hate waiting," Lisa said suddenly.

Pucky laughed. "That ain't nothing new," he told Neal. "Never could wait for Christmas or her birthday or the carnival to come to town."

She made a face at the older man, then got to her feet. "I need some more coffee," she said. "Anybody else want some?"

"Not me," Pucky said. "I'm still hoping to get some sleep tonight."

"I'd love some," Neal said. The longer he sat here, the more drained he felt. It was as if he'd used about twelve years worth of energy in the last three hours. He was too tired to think, too tired to feel. Or at least feel anything but tired.

"I won't be long," Lisa said.

Neal watched as she left the barn, then walked slowly to the door to watch her cross to the house. It was still raining, but not nearly so hard.

"Shame about that oak tree," Neal said.

"Been there a long time," Pucky agreed.

Neal went into Ariel's stall to check her for the eight hundredth time. They'd stopped the IVs about an hour ago, having given more saline solution than normally needed, but Neal wasn't sure that—

What was that? He looked under the horse, then grabbed the cup on a pole used to collect urine from horses.

"How's it look?" Pucky wanted to know.

"Yellow," Neal said with a grin. "It's yellow."

"Hot damn!" Pucky said and came over to slap Neal on the back. "Ya did it, Doc! Good job."

"Yeah." Neal stood there, leaning against the support pillar. He could barely believe it himself. Ariel was going to be fine.

"You go tell Lisa," Pucky said. "And get her to get some rest. I'll stay up a bit longer with Ariel here, and then I'm hitting the sack myself."

Neal nodded and hurried into the rain. He kicked off his boots as he climbed the porch steps, then burst through the kitchen door. Lisa was changing Clyde's water dish.

"It's yellow," he cried.

He didn't have to say anything else. She ran across the room and threw her arms around his neck. "Oh, Neal. You're wonderful."

"We were lucky," he said.

She pulled back to smile at him. "You were good."

He looked into those blue eyes that seemed to have captured the flames and smoke from the fire in the woods and was lost. She was such a beautiful woman. Such a strong woman. She was probably more than any man deserved.

But the only thing Neal Michael Sheridan was sure of was that she was more than any man could resist.

Chapter Thirteen

The kitchen, the worries about Ariel, the rain outside—they all faded as Lisa looked at Neal. The world was slowing its revolutions. Time was standing still, losing all meaning as she took in the songs in his eyes. Songs of love and desire and needs and passion.

She met them with an answering touch of her lips to his. She let her fingers speak to his soul as they brushed his cheek and sent tingles all through her.

"Lisa, Lisa." His voice came from deep in his throat. "Why do you have to be so damn beautiful?"

She'd spent the last three hours fighting a fire and for her horse's life, but she felt beautiful. In that fiery gaze of his, she felt loved and cherished and radiantly beautiful. She was everything he wanted her to be, everything that wonder and passion could make her.

"We've won," she told him, whispered into his chest as his arms folded around her.

But what was the battle? She couldn't remember anymore,

not with his hands roaming over her back, not with his lips seeking all the life and breath from her. She could remember Ariel, but there was more than that. There had been a battle between her and Neal, between what they wanted and what life was offering them. Somehow they had cheated fate. They had slipped in the back door and had routed the enemy.

"There are some things a man can't bear," he told her, his words dancing in her hair and falling away into the night.

"Don't go," she told him, though he'd made no move to part from her.

It was as if they were already joined, as if their souls had merged and one could not exist without the other. They were already one. She could not think of life without him, couldn't imagine taking a breath of air he did not share.

"Oh, Lisa." It was cry of pleasure, a moan of despair, a shout of victory.

It was a whisper of love.

He let go of her, but just for a moment as he scooped her up in his arms. She lay against him in his embrace, their hearts beating as one. Racing with one hope, one thought, one desire in mind. He carried her through the darkness to her room, where he put her slowly onto her feet.

The windows were open, and the sound of the rain echoed around them, but it was a gentle caress, a part of the night that cocooned, protected them from the cares of the day and the terrors of the storm. There was enough light coming in from the shadowed moon for her to see Neal's face, for her to feel the need in his touch and see the hunger in his eyes. And the soot and grime that was covering them both.

Lisa took his hand and led him into the bathroom. Still moving by the light trickling in from outside and her soft night-light, she turned the shower on. Without a word, they stripped off their clothes and went under the water.

It spluttered and splashed over them, running into her eyes so she could barely see him, but his arms came around her again, and sight was unnecessary. His mouth took hers, and she breathed in his life and his scent and his hunger for her touch. Her hands slid over his skin, slick with water.

They broke apart slowly to breathe and Neal took the soap, lathering his hands then running over every inch of her. Over her shoulders, around her breast, down her stomach, across her back. Her heart was pounding, her body tense and ready for him as she did the same for him. Her hands slid over him, their breathing growing ragged and hoarse with need. His chest, his tight buttocks, the very maleness of him.

Then his arms were around her again, their hungers too raw for patience and slow dancing. His mouth was rough, his hands demanding. Slippery from the soap and water, they moved against the other. Desire, longing, craving and need. Raging aches that sent the darkness soaring, spiraling upward into flames and wonder and forever.

It was too much, the waiting. He was hard and she was throbbing with want of him. She leaned against the wall of the shower stall, and he entered her. Hard and strong and wild as the fire they'd fought against. Waves of passion washed over them, shaking them and shattering the peace of the night. Over and over and over again, they came until the darkness burst into shooting stars and they knew release.

For a long moment, they rested in each other's arms, the water still racing over them as they fought to catch their breaths. She almost hated to move, though she knew they could hardly stay there forever.

"I guess we'd better get out," she said softly. "We'll turn into prunes otherwise."

"Suddenly one of my favorite foods." He kissed her lightly on the lips, then reached around her to turn off the water. "I have better ideas, though."

They got out and dried each other off, slow need creeping back with each touch of the towel. Soon the towels were abandoned, forgotten altogether as they went into her bedroom and lay on the bed.

For a long moment, they drank in each other with their eyes.

Not daring to move or speak, as if this was all a dream that movement would awaken them from. As if it was a spell mistakenly cast by some witch not knowing its beauty and power.

Then he reached down and touched her cheek. With the softest of caresses, he let his fingers trail along her skin. It was too slow, too gentle to strike a spark, but she felt the force of it race through her, leaving no part of her unscathed. It seared and burned and consumed everything in its path, but left her wanting more. Needing more.

She touched him, running her fingers through his damp hair. It wasn't enough. She let her hands glide over the back of his neck, the iron muscles of his shoulders, the bulk of his upper arms. But in touching him, she seemed to set loose the hunger, the need in him, for his hands began their possession of her.

Her arms, her neck, her breasts, her stomach. He touched and caressed and made her come alive with a wonder that life and love could be so splendid. Her heart seemed ready to burst again. Her skin seemed about to melt. A tension grew in her, a sweet, delicious sensation that promised more miracles to come.

"Oh, Lisa, Lisa," he moaned and brought his mouth down on hers.

He was all hunger and need. Passion and fire. He swept over her like the wind, carrying all her hopes and dreams and desires along with him and stirring them once more into a wild, unimaginable blaze. His hands pulled her ever closer as his lips devoured her, pulling all the fears and shadows from her soul, turning them into the music of the night.

There was so much she had never experienced of love, so much she'd never even guessed existed. Here, in his arms, she could feel the power shake her, the fire rush over her, but she wasn't afraid. They had cheated fate that night. They had made their own destiny. They could do anything, win any battle and tame every storm.

"I've never felt like this before," she murmured, her hands

as hungry as her lips for the feel of him. "There must be something in the air."

He smiled at her, so gently, so lovingly that it made her want to cry. "We taste of soap," he said.

"And water," she added.

She reached up to wipe a stray drop from his forehead, but he grabbed her hand and brought it to his lips. "It's the storm," he said. "It's made us crazy."

"It's made us be ourselves."

And this was so truly what she wanted, what she'd wanted for a while now. To know the magic of love in his arms, to be one with him, if only for a few moments in time.

His mouth was on hers again, driving out all reason and sense, leaving only sensation. Her body rose and fell with each breath, with each caress, rising to a higher and higher mountain, climbing each moment closer to the stars. His hand gently cupped first one breast then the other.

His touch was wonderful. She craved more of it, wanted his hands all over her body, warming each part with his caress. With his love. Her heart was pounding so hard she could scarcely think. There was an urgency to the throbbing, a growing need demanding to be met. A yearning for this moment to be all touch and hunger and lips melting into lips.

Then Neal seemed to slow down. While Lisa's heart and body were crying for his, while that tension was ready to explode with wonder, he was letting his hands explore her with gentle fascination.

"You are so beautiful," he murmured.

His lips took the tip of one breast, softly at first, then tugged and licked and pulled at it until she was trembling with want. Then, just when she thought she would scream with the ecstasy of it, he moved to the other breast and repeated the exquisite torture all over again.

"Neal," she cried.

"No." His voice was a breath, a whisper in the night. "I've

dreamed of this too long. I want to get to know every inch of you.''

His lips tasted her stomach. His tongue trailed along her skin, slowly working down until her body quivered and her soul cried out. She gripped his shoulders, needing to hold on to him, needing the strength and solidness of him to keep her from flying into space.

Then once again that raging hunger seemed to take hold, and the slow sweetness was replaced by overwhelming need. They touched. They kissed. Their bodies intertwined.

She moved and took him inside her once more, pulling him in and in and in even farther until she thought they surely could never be apart. They moved as one, riding into the stars, cheating the fire one more time. No, they were the fire, consuming everything in their path. But rather than leaving destruction, they left beauty and splendor and wonder all around.

Then they clung tightly, the fire in them exploding into sparks and magic. They were caught in a whirlpool and pulled deeper and deeper into the love. They were caught in the storm and tossed about in the winds as lightning burst and thunder crashed around them.

Then the storm was still, and peace came back. Wrapped in each other's arms, they lay and let the night swallow them up. Neal's lips brushed her forehead lightly, then he sighed as sleep seemed to overcome him.

''Didn't need long to reload, did I?'' he murmured.

She smiled and kissed his lips with a soft touch, then lay in the dark, watching him. Her heart was fairly bursting with love for him. Real love, not just the aftermath of sexual pleasure. She felt like she ought to be worried or scared or even cautious, but for the moment she was too happy.

''I love you,'' she breathed into the darkness, her words too soft to be heard even if he had been awake. ''I love you.''

Neal opened his eyes with a start. It was light outside, and not just the first light of dawn. He could hear traffic on the road. Damn. He'd never intended to stay this late. He'd never intended to stay at all.

He rolled onto his back, but that allowed him to look at Lisa, lying at his side asleep. She was so beautiful, so serene, he wanted to tear his heart out. What had he done?

He carefully rolled onto his side, then slowly sat up, trying not to disturb her. He'd robbed. He'd cheated. He'd lied. He'd spent the dark hours of the night making passionate love to his brother's woman. He was the scum of the earth.

Be Neal. Wasn't that what Lisa had wanted of him? Well, that's what he had done. He had been himself. Selfish. Self-centered. Self-indulgent. What happened to self-control or self-sacrifice? Being Neal had brought the rains, and now it would bring the tears.

He wished he had never come here, never traded places with Nick.

"Neal?" Lisa said.

Her voice tugged at him, pleaded with him, but he didn't answer. He couldn't answer. Instead, he reached for his jeans. Once he'd pulled them on, he turned to face her. Her blue eyes were troubled.

"Want some breakfast?" she asked.

He knew those weren't the real words in her soul, but he couldn't stay around to hear truth. "No, I need to get going."

She sat up, pulling the sheet around her chest. "It wouldn't take long."

"No, I can't." His words had come out harsher than he'd meant, and he tried to soften his tone. "I really can't."

She pulled back as if she'd been struck, confusion and hurt flashing across her face. He couldn't leave it like this. He had to be a man and take responsibility for his actions.

"You don't have to worry," he assured her as he pulled on his shirt. "I'll explain this all to Nick."

"Oh, don't start on that again," she snapped, and got out of bed.

She dropped the sheet as she reached for a robe on a nearby

chair. It was covering her in half a second, but for that brief moment, Neal had a glimpse of paradise again. A quick look at what he had had for one magical night. And what he had to forget.

Lisa tied the belt around her waist, then turned to face him. "Nick and I don't have that kind of a relationship," she said sharply. "We go fishing together and sometimes we play poker. We are friends. That's it."

"But you told me—"

"I told you twenty years ago I loved Nick. Twenty damn years ago!" Her voice was close to a shriek. "I never said I still did. You jumped to that conclusion all on your own."

"Why didn't you correct me?" A little glimmer of hope flickered in his heart for a moment.

"I tried. You were so hell-bent on making Nick fall in love with me, you wouldn't listen."

He thought of the new clothes and new experiences. The flirting advice and the dance lessons. It didn't make sense. "Then why go through with everything?" he asked. "You hated all the new clothes and shoes and everything, yet you wore them."

She turned away, walked slowly to the window. The sun spilled in, bringing out the fiery red in her dark hair and silhouetting her slender frame under the robe. Neal felt his hungers stir. But then she closed the blinds, cutting off the brilliance of the sun, and shadows fell over his heart.

"You were being difficult," she said, turning to face him. She lifted her chin as if trying to be defiant. "I wanted a child and wanted you to father it. I thought if I went along with your plan, I would see what you found attractive, and then I could be that."

"You could be that?" he repeated in astonishment. Be what? Didn't she know that she only had to be herself to have him burning with desire? She only had to be herself to have him wanting to spend every waking moment at her side.

"Then, when I was ovulating again," she went on, her

voice more hesitant, "I would really come on strong. We'd make love, and I'd get pregnant."

This didn't make sense to him. Oh, he knew what the words were saying, but somehow they couldn't seem to get in the right order in his brain. Only a few facts seemed to be standing out, pounding themselves into his consciousness.

She wasn't in love with Nick.

She'd been using him to get pregnant.

"I see," he said slowly. One more nagging fact shouted to be recognized. "And just when are you ovulating again? Or is that when *were* you?"

She stiffened but didn't look away. "I'm not sure."

"You're not sure?"

"Well, it's not exact," she said. "And I stopped taking my temperature each morning."

He felt weary all of a sudden and it had nothing to do with sleep or lack of it. He felt strung out emotionally. Felt as if the storm last night had battered him as well as the countryside.

"But your best guess is..."

"Yesterday." Her voice was small, quiet. "But I wasn't thinking about that last night. It never crossed my mind."

"Yeah, right." He turned toward the door. Why had he thought it would be different somehow? That she was different? "Don't bother to see me out. I know the way."

But she was at his side, pulling him to face her before he reached the top of the stairs. "What about you?" she cried. "What about this great love you thought Nick and I had for each other? I'm willing to believe that it never crossed your mind last night. Why aren't you willing to believe me?"

Because, in the long run, it didn't matter what she thought about while they were making love. All that mattered was that she had wanted Neal—the real Neal—and in the midst of all this masquerading and game playing he had forgotten just who that was. Until last night. Until this morning.

She'd wanted what he'd always boasted he was—a temporary, no-strings-attached loner. And he'd proven that's what he was by making love to her with no thought of Nick. There was a reason he'd never felt a part of things in this town, but the reason had nothing to do with the town. It had everything to do with him.

"Hey, you wanted me to be Neal, remember?" He worked a major cold front into his voice to cover the pain in his heart. "You wanted me to be Neal and bring the rain. Well, that's who you got. Old Love 'Em and Leave 'Em. The master of the three-week-romance. The big city guy who can't wait to shake the dust of Three Oaks off his shoes."

She backed off a step. "Well, don't let me stand in your way."

"Don't worry. No one ever does."

He went down the stairs and outside. The sun was so blinding it brought tears to his eyes. Damn, he'd be glad to get home to New York.

Lisa waited while the woman from Donnelly's Tree Service walked all around the old oak. She was shaking her head when she came back.

"We can try cutting off the broken branches," she said. "But I don't really think it's going to help. That piece that came down tore most of the trunk in half."

Lisa looked at the old oak tree. In the three days since the storm, the tree had gotten droopier and more battered-looking as damaged leaves and branches died. Pretty much how she felt. She'd had a moment of euphoria over being in love, but that hadn't lasted past her confession to Neal a few hours later, and the realization that he didn't want any ties. He was quite happy with his three-week relationships.

She told herself it was for the best, that she didn't do long term, that he wasn't the right man for her anyway. But she hurt nonetheless.

"You don't have to do anything right now," the tree service

woman said. "Think about it if you want. If you want to fight to give it a chance, we can do some trimming."

Lisa stared at the straggly remaining branches. She loved the old tree. It had been a place to hide when she'd moved here, then a friend who lent its shade to the yard and its grace and beauty to the house. It had kept little Clyde safe until Neal could get him down. She'd fight if there was a chance to save it, but she'd never been one to waste time on lost causes. She blinked back the tears.

"Nothing lasts forever," she told the woman. "Better you take it down than it gets weak and comes down in another storm."

"Okay." She nodded and went to her crew.

She'd get over the loss of the tree just as she'd get over losing Neal. Not that she'd really had him.

Lisa watched for a moment, then turned away as the equipment was moved to the broken tree. She wiped impatiently at her eyes.

Damn Neal. She never cried before. Never. Since he'd stormed out of here Saturday morning, it seemed she was ready to cry at the craziest things. At the tree coming down. At Ariel eating with gusto. At a sappy Love Pet Foods commercial, for goodness sakes!

The only good thing about the last three days is that she was ovulating today. She would not get pregnant from that stormy night of love. And even that she had mixed feelings about—the idea of not having Neal's child left her all weepy and hurting. But she certainly hadn't wanted to trick him into fathering her child. Well, maybe at first she had, but not at the end. At the end, she'd wanted... What?

Damn. She didn't know what she wanted anymore. The sound of the phone ringing sent her hurrying into the kitchen.

"Colleen," Lisa cried when she answered the phone. "I've been trying to reach you for weeks."

"You know, then." Her friend's voice was sharp, filled with anger. She must have found out about the switch.

"They're scum," Lisa said.

"Vermin."

"Snakes, both of them."

"All of them," Colleen said. "They're no different than all men."

"That's for sure." Lisa paused a minute. "You okay?"

"Hey, I'm fine." Colleen was trying to sound perky but didn't quite make it. "I'm so mad I could spit nails, but I'm fine."

Maybe she was stronger than Lisa was. Maybe she really did know how to keep her heart under control. "No emotional involvement?" Lisa asked.

"Me? Emotionally involved? I know better than that. How about you? How are you doing?"

"Just great," Lisa said. If Colleen could be strong, so could she.

"No baby?"

"I'm rethinking that whole plan."

"Might be best," Colleen said. "Hey, I'm going to drop by one of these days. I have so much to tell you and I'd love to see—" She stopped, no doubt realizing who else lived there. "Maybe we could meet in Chicago. Or you could come out to L.A. for a vacation."

"Sounds great," Lisa said. "Men are jerks."

"Pond scum."

They hung up, and Lisa wandered to the front of the house. She heard the buzz of a chain saw starting up, then the muted sound as it bit into wood, and felt her heart contract. It was for the best, she told herself. It was broken. It was time to cut out what was bad and replace it with something new. And that's what she'd do. She'd maybe put in a fruit tree, one that would fill the yard with its sweet scent in the spring and fruit in the fall. That's what she wanted—something that served a lot of purposes.

Not like Neal. Oh, he'd been a great lover, but he wasn't interested in any other roles. And she wasn't looking for him to fill any other roles, either, she told herself quickly. Nope, her life was just fine as it was. And it would be even better once he went back to New York.

The stupid tears started again.

Neal stopped at Sara's desk. "Did that reporter ever return my call?"

"Why do you want to talk to her, anyway?" the woman asked. "She's not your type."

Neal bit back a sigh and handed Sara the file folder for the last patient he'd seen. "She wants to do an interview," he told her. "I'm not looking for a date."

"That's good. Things will work out with Lisa, you'll see."

No, he wouldn't see. He wouldn't be here in another week. This great fiasco of a masquerade would be over, and he'd be back where he belonged. One more week. Seven days. One hundred sixty-eight hours. That wasn't too long.

Though actually that was how long ago Ariel had tied up during the storm. How long ago he and Lisa had made love. And that had seemed lifetimes ago—lifetimes lived in slow, agonizing wretchedness.

He had to stop thinking like that. "So who's next?" he asked

"You're free until four o'clock," Sara said. "You've got time to give Lisa a call."

"What for?"

"Well, the mail is piling up. You could use that as an excuse."

"I don't need an excuse to call her." He only needed to have something to say to her. And he didn't.

Everything had been said a week ago. There wasn't a single thing he could say differently. It didn't matter that she wasn't in love with Nick. It had no bearing on anything. Her life was here, and he was no part of it. Couldn't be, even if he wanted it. He had chosen his life, now he had to go back to it.

"I never thought you were so stubborn." Sara got to her feet and took a stack of folders to the file cabinet.

"Just goes to show you don't really know a person."

"Hmph." She yanked a drawer open. "Just goes to show some people aren't as all-fired smart as they think they are."

Neal stomped into Nick's office.

"Thief! Thief!" Baron screamed.

Another copy of *Worldwide News* lay on the desk with another picture of Nick on the cover.

"Atta boy," Lisa murmured to the horse as he took a low jump for her. "Wasn't that fun?"

Juniper wasn't too sure, if his reluctance to try it again was any indication. Maybe she'd been working him too hard, Lisa thought. She was in this frenzy to stay busy, and maybe she was overdoing it.

"Lisa!"

She turned toward the voice and saw Myrna leaning on the fence. Might as well call it quits, she thought. Lisa dismounted and led Juniper over.

"Hi," Lisa said. "What are you doing here? Did I forget about a meeting?"

Myrna opened the gate for her, then stepped aside to give her and the horse room to come out. "I stopped in at the clinic for some eye drops, and Sara said the mail had been piling up. I brought it out."

"Oh, thanks." Lisa led the horse toward the barn. "I haven't had a chance to get into town this last week or so."

Myrna fell into step beside her. "How's Ariel?"

"Great." Lisa smiled at her. "Just perfect. You'd never know she tied up."

"Lucky Nick came out when he did."

"Yeah."

There didn't seem to be much else to say. The heat was getting oppressive again, but there were no rain clouds in sight. Maybe they'd used up their allotment of rain for the year. She and Myrna went into the welcome shadows of the barn. Lisa put Juniper into a stall—not the end one, never the end one—with some water, then got a brush to brush him down.

Myrna leaned against a post and watched for a long moment. "You can tell me if I'm out of line, but do you want to talk about it?"

Lisa didn't pretend to misunderstand. "No. But thanks for the offer."

"I really thought you two had something going."

"Nope, not really. Just a little fun."

"Then why are you avoiding him?"

Lisa moved to the horse's other side, suddenly concentrating carefully on his coat. "I'm not. I've been busy."

"You've been busy before, and it never stopped you from picking up the mail."

"Maybe my priorities have changed."

"Maybe it's not him you're avoiding."

Lisa looked around Juniper to frown at Myrna. "What's that supposed to mean?"

"Maybe it's your feelings that you're avoiding, not the good doctor."

"My feelings!" Lisa cried and went back to Juniper. "I just wish I could avoid my feelings for a while. Believe me, they'd be a pleasure to avoid. There is nothing remotely fun in feeling miserable and angry and annoyed and exhausted and lonesome all the time."

She stopped. She hadn't meant to say all that. "Maybe I'm coming down with the flu."

"Maybe you're in love. The symptoms are pretty much the same."

Lisa came out of the stall and put the brush away before she looked Myrna's way. "My feelings don't matter," Lisa said. "He's not Mr. Right."

"What, did you take one of those magazine tests and it said he wasn't?" Myrna asked.

Lisa shook her head. "It'll sound really silly."

Myrna sighed. "Honey, nothing can be sillier than the things we do for love."

Lisa shrugged. "No, I guess not."

They walked outside and sat on the bench in the afternoon shade. It was pleasant here. Cool and safe feeling.

Lisa leaned against the barn wall, staring at the spot where the old oak had been. It looked so empty there it hurt. She felt a little bump on the bench and looked down to see Clyde had joined them. He crawled into her lap, and she petted him slowly.

"My mom loved to sit out after dark every evening and watch the stars," she told Myrna. "I remember her always telling me to make a wish. When she died, I got to believing she would grant me some big fantastic wish. But only if I found the right star to wish on."

"And how would you know the right star?" Myrna asked.

"The man I loved would help me find it."

Myrna laughed, but it was soft and gentle and filled with compassion. "And have you and the doc been doing any star-gazing?"

Lisa shook her head. "Nope."

Myrna got to her feet. "Well, maybe you'd better look harder for that star, or faster. I gotta go."

Lisa stared after her. Faster?

Neal frowned at the calendar as if he could will the days away. Though they had been moving with agonizing slowness, they had been moving. Only four more days, and he'd be gone. Any day now, Nick would be calling to arrange the switch.

The office door flew open with a bang. Neal snapped his head up, thinking it might be Lisa. Hoping it might be Lisa? It wasn't. Just as well.

"Thief! Thief!" Baron cried.

His grandmother ignored the bird as she marched into the room. "We need to talk," she snapped.

"I have a one o'clock—"

"You ain't got nothing." Gram was definitely on a tear. "I told Sara to call Jim in. He's taking the rest of today's appointments."

"What?" Neal was on his feet. "You can't just march in here and—"

She glared at him. "Shut up for a change." She sat in the chair in front of his desk. "Now when are you going to patch things up with Lisa?"

He glared right back at her. "There's nothing to patch up."

"You saying you two are all made up?" she asked.

Boy, this place was filled with busybodies. "I'm saying that we have nothing to patch up. We were friends and we still are."

"You were more than friends," she insisted. "I may be old but I'm not blind. I saw the way you two've been looking at each other."

"Well, we aren't looking that way now," he said. "We gave it a try. It wasn't right."

"Wasn't right? Hogwash!" She leaned closer, her eyes narrowed in suspicion. "What'd you do?"

"What did I do?" he cried. "If that isn't just like this place, always believing the worst of me."

She sat back with a frown. "Neal, it ain't the town's fault you're alone."

He felt his mouth work, but no words came out. He fell back from the desk, the energy pouring out of him. "Man," he murmured. "How many people know?"

"Everyone."

He looked at his grandmother. "No, they don't," he protested. "They can't."

"Two, three days was all it took." Gram snorted. "Four, max."

"No."

"Yes."

He stared at her, then looked away slowly. "Why didn't

anybody say anything?'' he asked. "They all like making a
fool out of me?''

His grandmother made an impatient noise. "When was the
last time you came here as yourself, asking to be accepted for
who you are?''

"I don't think it's that simple,'' he snapped.

"Nothing worth having is,'' she said. "The greater the
value, the more you need to put yourself at risk.''

"Maybe I'm not into putting myself at risk.''

"Then maybe you'll always be alone.''

"What are you doing up there in the middle of the night?''
Pucky called to Lisa.

She leaned against the side of the house and continued to
stare at the sky. "It's not the middle of the night. It's barely
past midnight.''

"I thought you outgrew sulking on the porch roof years
ago.''

"I'm not sulking, I'm sitting,'' she called to him. "With
the tree gone, you can really see the stars from here.''

"They're the same stars you can see from down here, and
you ain't got the chance to break your leg by falling.''

"I'm not going to break my leg,'' she said. "The window
is right here. I'm not going to climb down the trellis like I
used to.''

"Hmph. Seems you could find better uses to put tonight
to,'' he said, then went off.

"What's that supposed to mean?'' she called after him, but
she could hear his footsteps on the dirt, getting quieter as he
went into the barn.

She sighed and leaned back, looking at the sky. It was a
beautiful night. The moon was full, bathing the farm in a wonderful glow. The sky was loaded with stars, all twinkling and
promising her magic if she would pick one. How was she
supposed to know which one was the right one?

She closed her eyes. How was she supposed to know which man was the right one? What if it was Neal?

Did it matter if she thought he might be the one when he didn't share that feeling about her? It wasn't like he'd acted like she was special. Well, all right. He did act like she was, but he didn't act like she was *the* one or anything. It wasn't like he had told her what he worried about in the middle of the night.

She opened her eyes with a frown. Or had he? What was the thing that bothered him the most? That everyone seemed to want something from him. She felt a twinge of guilt. And she had been no exception, at least not in his eyes. But did she dare believe that that meant he loved her? Maybe he'd found her a sympathetic ear.

She heard Pucky in the barn, and his last words nagged at her. Giving a quick glance toward the barn door, she scooted to the trellis and scampered down it.

"Pucky?" she called as she went into the barn.

He was changing the water dish for the barn cats. "You done stargazing?"

"What kind of use should I be putting tonight to?" she asked.

He shrugged. "Just seems to me that it would have been much friendlier to welcome Dr. Nick back in town than sitting around here by yourself."

She just stared at him as his words sunk in. He knew that that had been Neal, not Nick! How long— But then his words sunk in again. "Nick is back?" He couldn't be. That would mean Neal was gone, and Neal had only been going to Portage—

"Saw him with my own eyes," Pucky said. "He was at his dad's when I went over for our poker game."

What had she been thinking of? Portage was where Neal and Nick always made their switch!

Neal was gone! Lisa felt fear clutch at her, twist inside her until she could scarcely breathe. She thought she'd have more time. She thought she'd have at least a few more days to decide what to do. A few more days to find her star. Now what?

Now she knew how stupid she'd been, that's what. Waiting around to find some star! What a timid little mouse she'd become. She had a wonderful man she loved and who might possibly love her—if he'd just admit it—and she was letting it all slip away while she played some silly, superstitious game.

Well, she'd been a fool, but maybe she wasn't too late. If Neal was gone, Nick would be back. She would go to his house and demand that he tell her where Neal was, then she would track him down. Maybe he was staying in Chicago overnight. Or else she'd get his address in New York from Nick and pound on his door.

Neal was not going to escape from her.

She hurried out of the barn toward the house. When she stopped short. Ariel was in the near paddock, prancing in the moonlight like she was dancing. The moon made her brown coat look deep and rich, and the star on her forehead looked—

Ariel's star!

It had been there all along, but somehow Lisa had never connected it with *her* star. But it was. It was her wishing star, as sure as she loved Neal Michael Sheridan. It was a magical star, given to her by Neal when he saved Ariel the night of the storm. There could be no greater proof than that.

"Just don't let me be too late," she breathed into the night, then raced for the truck.

Chapter Fourteen

Neal rolled over, forbidding his eyes to look at the clock. What did Nick keep in his mattress—rocks? He was never going to get to sleep on this lumpy bed. How had he managed to sleep here the past five and a half weeks?

Well, he hadn't. Not every night of the past five and a half weeks. There were two nights spent—

He rolled over, disturbing Pansy one too many times. She jumped off the bed and stomped away. He lay back and closed his eyes. It was dinner haunting him, that was all. He'd wanted to get away from everybody's watchful eyes for a while and had to drop that blood sample he'd taken from the Mitchells' collie at a lab in Portage, so he'd gone to dinner there. Major mistake.

He'd chosen a restaurant at random, and the place had been filled with couples, all lovey-dovey and all making him feel even more alone. He'd barely eaten, and what he had managed to get down was sitting like lumps of lead in the pit of his stomach.

What should he do about Lisa? He knew for her sake he had to give her up, but it was hard. Damn hard.

An owl hooted outside, screeching loud enough to wake up the whole state. What was the big myth about small towns? They must have a great PR service. Small towns weren't peaceful or restful or quaint or safe. He'd be glad to get back to New York where he could get a decent night's sleep.

He heard a truck driving by. It sounded like Lisa's. Damn. He groaned and rolled on his back. He really had it bad if he was hearing her truck in every vehicle that passed by. He turned and buried his head under the pillow. This was good. He wouldn't be able to hear the wretched owls, either.

He forced his breathing to slow and told himself he was getting sleepy. And that the vibrations he felt were Boomer coming up the stairs.

"Where is he, you lying, scheming bum?" a voice cried out.

Neal sat up so fast he was almost dizzy. Boomer was nowhere in sight, but Lisa was standing just a few feet away. His heart leaped at the sight of her, though even in the darkness of the unlit room, he could almost see the angry fire shooting from her eyes. What was she doing here?

"Where's who?" he asked.

She grimaced and moved. It let the streetlight spill some light on her face, and his soul wept at her beauty. If only...

"Who else?" she snapped. "Your brother."

"My brother?" Why was she looking for Nick now? Couldn't she wait until he came back in a couple of days? He felt particularly dense. Maybe he had been asleep, after all. "What do you want him for?"

"To make mad, passionate love to him."

He knew she was being sarcastic, but still her words cut into him.

"I don't see why I have to explain anything at all to you." She walked to the window and crossed her arms over her chest in obvious impatience.

"No, of course you don't," he said and swung his legs over the side of the bed. He wanted to invite her to sit down. To talk. To maybe work out their differences.

But if she sat on the bed next to him, they wouldn't talk. And they certainly wouldn't work out their differences.

"I'm not sure just where he is at the moment," Neal said slowly. It shouldn't hurt so much that she preferred Nick's company to his. It was what he had thought, what he'd wanted the past five weeks.

"You must have some idea where he is."

"Only vaguely."

"Well, then tell me vaguely where he is, and I'll take it from there," she said. She was annoyed with him, antsy to be on the move, he could tell.

Lordy, but he wanted her so bad it hurt. It hurt a thousand times worse than it had that first day in the barn. Then it had only been lust. Now it was so much more than that. Maybe he should stay longer, beg Nick for a little more time. Just enough to get tired of her. Just enough for his heart not to race at the thought of her.

"Is he in Chicago?" she demanded.

Neal looked away. Why was she doing this? Did she know what torture it was for him? "Probably," he said.

"Where?"

"Where?" he repeated. This was insane. He couldn't let her do this. "What are you thinking of? You're not going there tonight, are you?"

"After all you've pulled, I don't see where you have the right to say anything," she said.

She was right, of course, but that didn't mean this wasn't tearing him up.

"Just tell me one thing," he said carefully, knowing he would regret asking this all his life. "Do you love him?"

Sighing, she walked slowly to the bed and sat next to him. "You can't imagine how many times I've asked myself that question," she said. "How many nights I've lain awake wondering if I had the courage to be honest."

Her voice was so low, he could scarcely hear her. Or maybe it was her nearness that drove coherent thought patterns from his head. He wanted to reach over and touch her. He wanted to pull her into his arms and shower her with kisses until she couldn't remember Nick's name.

"But yes," she said. "I love him. I know it's crazy. I know it's stupid. But I do."

He wanted to die.

"I see." It felt like someone had stabbed him with a butcher knife, then twisted it around. He could barely push the words out, he was in such pain. She loved Nick! The most perfect woman he'd ever met was in love with his brother. "So did you find your star, then?"

She turned to frown at him. He could feel her confusion through the darkness. "I didn't think I ever told you about that," she said.

She didn't remember the night under the stars? It was a memory he treasured—her confidences, her laughter, her hand in his. He hadn't thought his pain could grow, but it did.

"I wouldn't know about it otherwise, would I?" he asked.

"No, of course not." She got up from the bed as if too restless, too full of energy to waste time near him. "The thing is, I think he loves me, too. I think he's so used to being alone he hasn't admitted it to himself."

How could any man alive not love her? "You may be right." He wanted her happy, above all else, but part of him wanted Nick to turn her away so he could have her.

"So will you tell me where I can find him?"

He stopped, suddenly torn, suddenly angry. "I wish you'd think this over," he said, his voice coming out sharper than he intended. "He doesn't deserve you."

"Oh, get off your high horse," she snapped. "Who are you to say who deserves who?"

He watched as she paced from deep shadow to the splotch

of light from the window. If she loved Nick, he should help her find him. He should do what he could to get them together, but the words wouldn't come out.

"If he cared about you, he wouldn't have left," Neal told her.

"I drove him away."

"A real man doesn't let himself be driven away from the woman he loves."

"Oh, give me a break!" she cried and threw herself into the easy chair in the corner. "I didn't exactly give him a reason to stay."

"If he loved you—really loved you—he couldn't have left."

"You don't understand," she snapped. "He's not like you. He's not so confident and self-assured. He hasn't had all the chances you've had."

"All what chances?" he asked. Her defense of Nick, her loyalty to him ticked him off. Nick had everything, and now he would have her. What did Neal have? Nothing. Nothing that mattered. "I haven't noticed that my life is all that great."

"How can you say that? He wanted what you have so bad, he was willing to trade places with you for six lousy weeks."

"I think he would have been better off trying to fix the problems in his own life."

"Maybe the problems are there because he's afraid to reach for love."

"All the more reason for you to steer clear of him, then," he said. "He'd only make you unhappy."

"You don't get it, do you?" she cried. "I love him! I'm willing to fight with him until he's not afraid to love me."

He stared at her through the darkness. Everything was clear all of a sudden. Everything—his anger, his jealousy, his overpowering hunger just to be near her—it all made sense.

He loved her.

He loved her more than life itself, and he could not bear the thought of her with another man. He wouldn't help her find Nick, not without trying to keep her for himself first. He didn't care if she laughed at him. Slugged him or turned him down flat. He had to try.

She was what he had been waiting for all his life. She was the one he could trust with his love, his life and his happiness. She was all he would ever want.

And who knew? Maybe one day she'd even love him back.

"I'm not going to let you go chasing after that idiot brother of mine," Neal told her and got to his feet. "He rejected you."

"I don't care," she said.

"He doesn't love you like I do." He felt desperation creeping into his soul. "I'll father your child if you'll agree to marry me."

"Nick!" she cried in astonishment and flew to her feet.

Silence dropped into the space between them.

"Nick?" he repeated slowly. Nick? What was she talking about? Then his confusion dwindled. The fog lifted. Oh, hell. All this time, she'd thought—

She flicked a switch, flooding the room with light. "Neal!" she shrieked. "You rotten, two-bit—"

She grabbed a shirt off the back of the chair and threw it at him. It only went about two feet. "You low-down sneak!" She threw a shoe at him. "You did it to me again!"

"Did what?" he asked, ducking the other shoe. "I didn't do anything."

"You tried to trick me. You pretended to be Nick and let me pour my soul out."

"I didn't pretend to be anybody," he protested. He took a step closer to her, but she'd grabbed a book from the dresser.

"You didn't correct my mistake!" she shouted and threw the book at him.

He caught it. "I didn't know you'd made one."

"Oh, right, like it wasn't obvious!" She looked around with a certain franticness that made him nervous.

"Well, it wasn't obvious to me," he said. "All you were doing was talking about how you loved Nick."

"I never said that." She turned from him and stomped into the bathroom.

"Wait a minute," he said. "You thought I was—"

She'd come out of the bathroom with Boomer's water bucket. "You slime," she cried and flung the water at him. "You lying snake."

It hit him square in the face, drenching him, the shorts he had on and the rug at his feet. He wiped water from his eyes. "You know, it doesn't really make much sense for you to be upset," he told her. "When you think about it—"

"Think about it?" she screamed. "I never want to think about this again. I am forever baring my soul to you, only to be humiliated."

She threw the bucket at him, then fled. He heard the door slam before he'd made it out of the bedroom.

Lisa got about halfway home before she started thinking again, and by the time she got all the way home, she was ready to crawl under her bed and hide. Why was she always making such an idiot of herself around Neal? What was this power he had over her?

So now what did she do? She wouldn't be surprised if he left town tonight, rather than have anything to do with her again.

He had said he loved her, though, hadn't he? Had he meant it, or had her drenching brought him to his senses? He'd also said he'd father her child if she'd marry him! She obviously had been hallucinating.

She parked the truck and trudged into the house. Clyde was waiting for her, but snuggling the little guy didn't do much for her heavy heart tonight. There were no messages from Neal on the answering machine. No headlights streaming into the house from a truck coming up the drive. She had screwed up beyond believing this time.

She changed Clyde's water and put out some fresh food, then went outside. The moon was still bathing the farm with light, but it seemed more lonely than lovely now. She walked slowly across the yard to Ariel's paddock. The horse came to greet her, nudging her hands as she looked for treats.

"Sorry, baby," she said. "I'm all out of treats tonight."

The mare stayed, though, as Lisa petted her, touching the star on her forehead with one finger. That was her star, she knew, and Neal was her love. So what did she go do now?

"I think I've got the routine down now," Neal said.

She spun. He was standing a few feet away. Her heart jumped for joy. "Damn, I'm going to start locking my gate." A smile slowly crept along her lips. "You never know who's gonna come wandering in the yard."

"You know, I was thinking that same thing about my door a half hour ago." He took a step closer. "You don't have your gun out, do you?"

"I can get it real quick, if you'd like."

"That's okay. I've already been assaulted several times tonight."

"I'm sorry," she said.

His smile was slow and sweet. "I'm not."

A wonderful certainty spread through her, a knowledge that happiness was her destiny. "Come over here. I have to show you something."

She reached out her hand, and he took it. So firmly, so strongly, so like he would never let it go. She blinked away a sudden wetness in her eyes and turned to the paddock.

"Ariel," he said.

"Wait until she turns this way," Lisa said. "Then look at her forehead."

Even as she spoke, the horse turned their way, as if she knew they were watching her. The moonlight caught her face.

"Her star," Neal said.

Lisa nodded and wrapped her arms around his waist. "That's my star. It was there all along, but I didn't see it until you gave her back to me."

"I never noticed it." He put his arms around her, holding

her tightly against his body. "I guess it works better than my suggestion."

She had her head against his chest. His heart was racing. Or was it her heart she was hearing? "And what was that?"

"That I was your star," he told her with a smile. "I am a big TV star, you know."

She laughed and looked into his face. His mouth was laughing, but his eyes reflected all the hope and pain and hunger her heart felt. All the love.

"I love you so much," she told him.

"I think I've loved you for twenty years." He touched her lips gently with his. "I just didn't know it. Not until tonight, when I thought you were confessing your love for Nick."

She buried her face in his chest. "I can't believe I did that. Don't remind me."

"Are you kidding? I'm going to remind you every day of our lives together. You made me see how much I love you." He pulled away and put his finger under her chin to lift her face. "You are going to marry me, aren't you? I should warn you I don't intend to let you out of my sight until the wedding. I don't want you getting me and Nick mixed up again."

"I can tell you apart," she said.

"You didn't tonight."

"I didn't get close to you, or I would have."

She leaned against him. "Do you really want a baby or were you just making the offer?"

"I don't just make offers," he said, and kissed the top of her head. "I can't think of any better way to celebrate our love than with a child."

"I'm not pregnant now," she told him. "I wasn't ovulating when we made love before."

"Then we'd better get working on it, shouldn't we?"

She laughed and snuggled deeper into his arms. "Where will we live? I'm not sure I'd like New York, but I'd be willing to try it."

"I've already got it figured out. There are studios in Chicago the show can be taped in, and I can commute. I'm thinking of cutting back, anyway. Maybe Nick would like a partner.''

"Are you sure?" she asked. "I don't want you to be giving it all up for me."

"I've been thinking about it for a while," he said. "And you never answered my question. Hurry up because I have another one."

"Yes, I will marry you," she said, slipping from his arms to take his hand in hers. "Now what's your next question—isn't it time for bed? You can come upstairs if you'd like."

"Nice as that idea is, that wasn't my question," he said. He stopped, turning her to face him. "What were you going to do with that rolling pin?"

She threw her head back and laughed. "Well, the use my book suggested for it was very different from what I wanted to do with it," she said. "It was supposed to provide a sensuous massage."

He looked doubtful. "And what did you want to do with it?"

She just tugged him toward the house. "I don't think you want to know. Now, are you coming upstairs or not?"

Epilogue

Lisa leaned on the fence and watched the colt prance and frolic in the early morning air. It was as if the dewy grass tickled his feet. He couldn't stay still, though he kept running over to Ariel like he was asking her to play. He was so beautiful, so full of life. And he had Ariel's star!

"Morning," Neal said, coming up next to her.

She turned to smile at him, brushing his lips with hers as she went into his arms. "Morning to you, too. I thought you'd sleep later. It was late when you got in last night."

"We filmed an extra show so I don't need to go in for a month. No chance that I'll be in Chicago filming when our big day comes." He touched her rounded belly. "How's Junior doing?"

"Practicing his placekicking, I think," she said. "He likes to get up early."

"I can't wait for my turn to get up with him."

"Another few weeks and I'll let you have the chance."

She turned in his arms as the colt came running to say hello.

A moment later, he was gone, rushing around with energy and excitement. Neal pulled her closer to him so her back rested against his chest.

"So have you picked a name for Ariel's foal yet?"

She nodded and pulled his arms tighter around her. "Starfire," she said. "For the night we really began our love."

*   *   *   *   *

So what actually happened at the wedding? And what have Nick and Colleen been up to on their trip? Check out WHO WILL SHE WED?, the second book in this duo, coming next month from Special Edition! Come catch the bouquet!

RITA
—Award
Winning
Author

MARIE FERRARELLA's

miniseries continues with her
brand-new Silhouette single title

In The Family Way

Dr. Rafe Saldana was Bedford's most popular pediatrician. And though the handsome doctor had a whole lot of love for his tiny patients, his heart wasn't open for business with women. At least, not until single mother Dana Morrow walked into his life. But Dana was about to become the newest member of the Baby of the Month Club. Was the dashing doctor ready to play daddy to her baby-to-be?

Available June 1998.

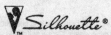

Find this new title by Marie Ferrarella
at your favorite retail outlet.

Take 4 bestselling love stories FREE

Plus get a FREE surprise gift!

Special Limited-time Offer

Mail to Silhouette Reader Service™

3010 Walden Avenue
P.O. Box 1867
Buffalo, N.Y. 14240-1867

YES! Please send me 4 free Silhouette Special Edition® novels and my free surprise gift. Then send me 6 brand-new novels every month, which I will receive months before they appear in bookstores. Bill me at the low price of $3.57 each plus 25¢ delivery and applicable sales tax, if any.* That's the complete price and a savings of over 10% off the cover prices—quite a bargain! I understand that accepting the books and gift places me under no obligation ever to buy any books. I can always return a shipment and cancel at any time. Even if I never buy another book from Silhouette, the 4 free books and the surprise gift are mine to keep forever.

235 SEN CF2T

Name	(PLEASE PRINT)	
Address	Apt. No.	
City	State	Zip

This offer is limited to one order per household and not valid to present Silhouette Special Edition® subscribers. *Terms and prices are subject to change without notice. Sales tax applicable in N.Y.

USPED-696

©1990 Harlequin Enterprises Limited

RETURN TO WHITEHORN

Silhouette's beloved **MONTANA MAVERICKS** returns with brand-new stories from your favorite authors! Welcome back to Whitehorn, Montana—a place where rich tales of passion and adventure are unfolding under the Big Sky. The new generation of Mavericks will leave you breathless!

Coming from Silhouette Special Edition®:

February 98: LETTER TO A LONESOME COWBOY by Jackie Merritt

March 98: WIFE MOST WANTED by Joan Elliott Pickart

May 98: A FATHER'S VOW by Myrna Temte

June 98: A HERO'S HOMECOMING by Laurie Paige

And don't miss these two very special additions to the Montana Mavericks saga:

MONTANA MAVERICKS WEDDINGS
by Diana Palmer, Ann Major and Susan Mallery
Short story collection available April 98

WILD WEST WIFE by Susan Mallery
Harlequin Historicals available July 98

Round up these great new stories
at your favorite retail outlet.

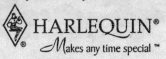

PAULA DETMER RIGGS

Continues the twelve-book series— 36 Hours—in May 1998 with Book Eleven

THE PARENT PLAN

Cassidy and Karen Sloane's marriage was on the rocks—and had been since their little girl spent one lonely, stormy night trapped in a cave. And it would take their daughter's wisdom and love to convince the stubborn rancher and the proud doctor that they had better things to do than clash over their careers, because their most important job was being Mom and Dad—and husband and wife.

For Cassidy and Karen and *all* the residents of Grand Springs, Colorado, the storm-induced blackout was just the beginning of 36 Hours that changed *everything!* You won't want to miss a single book.